The Wolf Road

Richard Lambert

Published in the UK by Everything with Words Limited
3rd Floor, Descartes House, 8 Gate Street,
London WC2A 3HP

www.everythingwithwords.com

Text copyright © Richard Lambert 2020

Printed and bound in Great Britain by
CPI Group (UK) Ltd, Croydon CRO 4YY

A CIP catalogue record for this book is available
from the British Library.

ISBN   978–1–911427–16–2

Praise for *The Wolf Road*

—One of the most stunning books I've read in years. An astonishing exploration of grief and love and courage and wildness. It held me gripped.

Hilary McKay, author of *The Skylarks' War*

— A lyrical debut of grief, loss and growing up.

Fiona Noble, *The Bookseller*, Children's Previews

—A beautiful and suspenseful novel that holds you in its claws from first page to last. Richard Lambert writes with a poet's eye; he has created something magical here.

Jonathan Stroud, author of *Bartimaeus Trilogy*

—A passionately told story of loss, pain, growing up and adventure to haunt any reader's imagination.

Michèle Roberts, author of *Daughters of the House*

—A stunning, special debut about love and loss and how the wildness can save us."

Chelsey Flood, author of
The Night Wanderers and *Infinite Sky*

—This is an insightful novel about bereavement, but also about what growing up might involve in a world that actually needs wolves. To his story-telling skill Richard Lambert brings a poet's vision and precise, spare language. *The Wolf Road* is exciting, necessary reading.

Moniza Alvi (poet)

—Moving and menacing, and written with a cinematic clarity

Andrew Cowan, author of *Common Ground*

—A smart, chilling, page-turner which kept me guessing right up until the end.

Hayley Long, author of *What's up with Jodi Barton?*

—This is a cracking first novel. A sharp, hard, modern story of a young man's losses and loves has been grafted to a larger, far older mythic canvas about the human need for nature and the wild.

Mark Cocker, naturalist, author of *Birds Britannica*

Part One

Endings

The road ran through the summer fields and we raced it like wild things. It was so dusty the back of my throat tickled, and when sunlight struck the windscreen the glass turned misty white. In the verges rushing past, the willowherb had exploded into smokiness and the blackberries looked ripe, as ripe and sweet as the ones Dad liked to pick in the evenings. Mum sang softly along with the radio while Dad whooshed us through the bends of the Somerset lanes.

'Oh, I love this one,' said Mum, dialling up the volume as a new song came on. 'We saw them live once.'

'Were they any good?' I asked, leaning between their seats.

'They were amazing.'

'They were all right,' said Dad, on one of his wind-ups, 'they weren't amazing.'

Mum didn't rise to it, just rolled her eyes at me. I laughed and sat back. It was a Saturday afternoon and we were going into town, Mum and Dad to look at tiles for the kitchen and me to meet up with Mitesh.

Mum's face appeared round the headrest and, in an

undertone that was deliberately loud enough for Dad to hear, she said, 'They *were* amazing,' and winked.

We swept around a bend and Mum's hair swung across her cheek. Beyond her, in the middle of the lane, stood a dog. Dad braked sharply. Mum's face vanished. I was flung forward. We swerved, skidding, and I was slung sideways. Dad shouted in fear. My head struck the window. Another window burst. Branches came in. The car ceiling approached with hundreds of tiny holes in its grey fabric. I was pushed down into my seat with tremendous force, lifted up, turned over, and plunged down again – crunch.

Everything was still.

I lay at the bottom of the car. But now the bottom was the door and above me, coming in through the smashed window, was green hedge. There was a smell of burned rubber and, weirdly, perfume.

Hanging limp in her seat belt above me, like a trapeze artist, was Mum. Her hair clung to her cheek, stuck. Blood dripped from her mouth onto the driver's seat. Onto Dad.

Dad didn't move. He was crumpled against the driver's window, his head bent at an odd angle.

A branch sprang free and whipped the ceiling. When I moved, glass fell on my face. I was covered in white crystals.

'Mum?'

The only sound was blood dripping from Mum's face onto Dad.

'Dad?'

He didn't answer.

The back window was smashed. I released my seat belt and crawled out. Cloud slipped across the sun and I was in cool shadow, then it slipped away. I was on an earth bank. I slithered down. The smell of burned rubber was stronger now, and there was a smell of petrol too, so powerful it filled my mouth and I wanted to scrape it off my tongue.

The dog was in the middle of the road. It was the colour of smoke, or dusk when light has seeped out of the world and it's almost night, except for its eyes which were orangey brown with tiny black pupils. It didn't seem to see me properly although it looked right at me. It looked at me the way a soldier might who is about to go into battle. It stood very still. It had paws the size of a boxer's fists, and long legs. It had a broad chest, a big ruff of fur, and its shoulders were bony. Suddenly it dipped its head as if it was going to attack.

I scrambled up the bank. As I did, from the corner of my eye I saw the animal spring into a long bound. Not towards me, but away. It seemed to flow across the road. It flowed up the opposite bank and into the hedge and all that remained was the empty country lane, scorched by fierce black tyre marks.

It was not until the birdsong began that I realised that the lane had been silent the whole time.

In the birdsong a white minibus zoomed around the corner. It braked and came to a halt. For a moment nothing happened, then its doors were thrown open and men jumped out. All with beer bellies, dressed in cricket whites. Beards and moustaches, all older than Dad, all running round.

*

After the cricketers had prevented me from returning to our car, after the fire engine had arrived, after I had been taken away in the ugly yellow light of a windowless ambulance, after the paramedic kept changing the subject when I asked what was happening to Mum and Dad, after waiting in Accident and Emergency for a doctor, after being X-rayed on a cold slab, after the doctor had refused to answer my questions about Mum and Dad, after I had started shouting at him and his mates, after I had tried to leave, after I had been injected with a dark liquid, I fell asleep.

It was a strange sleep. Not really a sleep, more a blankness.

When I woke it was dark. The bed I was in had thin sheets that were tucked in so tight I could hardly move. I was lying on my side. There were other beds, white shapes floating in the darkness, and I could hear the breaths of other teenagers and children, sleeping. At one end were curtainless windows. The ward must have been high up because the windows framed sky. Just sky. It was night, and the moon was tiny and very far away.

I couldn't believe it – I had slept since afternoon. How could I, when my parents needed me? Whatever the doctor had injected me with must have been strong, so strong I couldn't wake up properly, and the strange blankness lurked. I felt it at the edge of my mind and I knew that at any moment it might return. I had to find Mum and Dad quick. I had to find out where the doctors had put them. I tried to get up but the sheet was too tight and when I rolled over to loosen it, I had such a shock I completely froze.

A woman stood at the end of my bed.

She stood very still and looked at me. Her serious clothes and her grey hair made her seem like a doctor. But she was so motionless I wondered if she might be something else. A sleepwalker, a lost visitor, a crazy person? I decided she must be a doctor. I asked her where Mum and Dad were. Before she could answer, and before I could ask her again, the blankness eased in.

*

When I woke properly it was morning and the ward was full of noise. I was still groggy. A team of cooks were clattering steel hatches on a big, steaming, stainless-steel trolley. In about ten seconds they had brought everyone in the ward their breakfast and rolled out. A pair of nurses were going from bed to bed, wheeling a drugs trolley. They fed tablets in little paper cups to unhappy kids. A cleaner mopped, singing a song in a language I didn't know.

'Where's my mum and dad?' I croaked to the two nurses at the next bed. As they left, I called after them, 'Where's Mum and Dad?'

I kicked off the tucked-in sheets and stood up. For a moment everything in my vision went red and I had to wait for the blindness to go, then I went after the nurses. I was in a hospital gown, open at the back. I didn't remember putting it on. Which meant someone had taken off my clothes while I'd been asleep.

'Please,' said the cleaner in an East-European accent, stepping in front of me. 'You slip on my floor. You go to your bed.'

'I have to find out what happened to my parents. What happened to my parents?'

'I do not know. How could I know? You go to your bed.'

She barred my way with her mop.

I went round her. I rushed towards the ward doors. As I approached they opened and the serious grey-haired woman from the night before hurried towards me, a male doctor in a white coat behind her calling, 'Stop!'

8

'Where's Mum and Dad?'

'Lucas,' she said in a flat, tired voice. 'Lucas.'

'What's happened to Mum and Dad? Where are they?'

'Please,' the male doctor said, arriving out of breath. 'You can't be here.'

'What's happened to my parents? I want to know what's happened to my parents.' I could feel panic, my voice getting tighter, louder. 'Where's Mum and Dad?'

The woman with the grey hair touched my arm and I felt a shock. There was something familiar about her. She was the doctor from the night before but it wasn't that which was familiar – she reminded me of Mum.

Quietly, as if it was difficult for her to utter the words, as if they were rough objects she brought up painfully from the depths of her body, she said, 'They're dead.'

Her eyes were grey with dozens of black flecks in them.

'I'm sorry, Lucas,' she said.

The male doctor said, 'Can I get you some water?'

The woman led me back to the bed. The soles of my feet were cool on the mopped floor. She sat beside me and her tanned hand rested on my forearm. She wore a watch with a red strap, its leather worn. The second hand moved round and it seemed baffling that it kept going like that. How could it, when Mum and Dad had stopped, simply stopped?

'I'll leave you to be alone with your grandmother,' the

9

male doctor said. 'If you need anything, please come and get me.'

It took a while for his words to sink in.

I turned to her.

She wore a grey knitted tank top and a short-sleeved shirt. One collar-tip was under the V-neck and one collar-tip out. Her grey hair was upright, stiff, short. She had olive-coloured skin like Mum's. Her face was broad. She had a small, unhappy mouth. She looked exhausted.

'Do you remember me?' she said.

I'd spoken to her on the phone each Christmas but only met her twice.

Nan.

*

We walked the hallway with a gap between us that widened as we made room for people coming the other way: elderly patients in wheelchairs, visitors striding. I was puzzled that they all seemed ... not happy exactly, but cheerful somehow. A hospital porter pushed a trolley-bed with an old woman inside. She was so frail her head on the pillows didn't make a dent. She stared upwards at the ceiling, tubes taped to her nostrils.

Automatic doors parted and we stepped into warm September air.

'Wait here. I'll get the car.'

I hadn't thought of the future and what would

happen next until that moment. My brain seemed stuck. I couldn't get beyond the absence of Mum and Dad. The fact didn't fit the world. The world didn't fit the fact. The world didn't make any sense. Why were ambulances coming into the courtyard? Why was the day warm? Why were the giant fans on the side of the building rotating? Why were the clouds moving across the blue? It seemed impossible they should all just continue in the same way. None of it fitted with the fact that Mum and Dad were dead.

I couldn't think beyond that.

A small red car drove into the courtyard. As Nan drove towards me I heard again the thunder of our car up the earth bank, the tear of metal, the snap of plastic, the crunch. The reflection of the hospital's concrete and glass flowed up the windscreen and Nan stopped and I remembered how that strange animal had stood in the middle of the road, how its amber-coloured irises and the black pips of its pupils had fixed on me, how it must have stood there during the entire accident because when I crawled out of the car, it was in the same spot.

Nan got out. In the daylight she looked ill, her olive skin almost grey. Squinting against the sun, shielding her eyes, she said, 'Let's get you home.'

I didn't respond; then, suddenly, with the car's lethal bonnet rising beside me, I felt a terror. 'I can't,' I said, pleading with Nan with my eyes.

Nan's face didn't change expression but in a flat voice she said, 'I haven't the energy, Lucas,' and got back in the car.

The hospital fans hummed. The passenger door popped open.

I didn't move. I couldn't.

An ambulance with flashing blue lights pulled up behind Nan's car. The car's door-handle gleamed. The paramedic in the ambulance hooted his horn then waved at me to hurry up.

My chest tight, I stepped forward and pulled open the thick wall of door. As I got in, I was super-aware of the steering wheel, the dashboard dials, the rubber rug in the seat-well. They were almost startling. Nan turned to me as I pulled on the seat belt. She has thick eyebrows like Mum's.

'Okay?' she said in her tired voice, her breath wafting sourness and coffee.

I didn't respond.

'God, what a place,' she said, glancing up at the hospital, then she switched on the ignition, put the car into gear, checked over her shoulder, and as I gripped the side-bar and my stomach clenched, she worked the pedals with round-toed DMs.

Pebble

Nan carried a clear cellophane bag like the ones you take through airport security, in it Mum's purse, notebook and necklace, Dad's wallet and penknife, and their wedding rings, phones, and keys. She took out Dad's keys and went to the front door and before I could tell her it wasn't her house, she unlocked the door and went in.

I had to force myself not to speak out. I followed her inside.

She was already in the kitchen and she hadn't taken off her shoes. I heeled off my trainers in the hallway. I hated the way she dropped Dad's keys on the kitchen table, as if they'd never been in Dad's hand. They landed with a little metal splash. She put down the cellophane bag and came past me to the downstairs loo. I hated the way she used it without asking. On the kitchen table, the tight steel of Dad's key-ring was sticky with blood.

I didn't want to wash off the blood. That seemed wrong. Disrespectful. Trying to pretend what had happened hadn't happened.

It *had* happened.

On the counter was a bowl filled with blackberries

that Dad had picked in the hedge at the side of the field. He was going to make blackberry pie.

The toilet flushed and Nan returned.

She started to fill the kettle.

'You should ask permission to do that,' I said.

She turned to me, her mouth small and tight. 'I've driven two hundred miles and haven't slept. So can I have a cup of tea?'

We stared at each other a few seconds, neither of us giving way, then I walked out, leaving her to bang about in our cupboards.

In the sitting room Mum had left her book open on the arm of a chair. It was about the sea's tides. Mum's presence seemed to be around the book like a physical, invisible force. I thumbed the pages gently. I didn't know what to do now that Mum and Dad were dead. I couldn't just carry on, do normal things as if nothing had happened. A raven flew down into the garden. Dad liked ravens, said they had a good sense of humour. It strode about, cocky. Behind me, Nan said, 'I made you a cup of tea.'

I turned to this odd woman in purple DMs and a man's short-sleeved shirt and a knitted tank top, holding out a mug of tea for me, the hollows of her eyes so pronounced they seemed like moon craters. 'Mum doesn't like people wearing shoes in the house,' I said, and walked past her, going as close to her as I could without knocking her arm and spilling the tea.

Upstairs, the bathroom tap was dripping and I turned it tight. On the sill was a big white pebble Mum had picked up at the beach. When I was younger I used to go with her to the sea but lately I preferred meeting Mitesh and the others in town. But Mum had kept on at me and in the end we'd gone. She collected pebbles and shells at the sea's edge and we lay on the sand and she read her book and we talked, about nothing in particular and nothing that I could remember. I played football, keepy-uppies, and later we went for a swim. The water was freezing. The pebble was white, smooth, nearly perfect except for a puckered crease at one end. I weighed it in my palm.

In my room, I stared out the window. The raven was there, pacing about as if waiting for one of its friends. Beyond the ploughed field and the poplars, in the distance, the pylons were skeletal, their cables faint as cotton threads.

I lay on the bed and put my hand over my eyes and wished that these things would all stop going on, existing, now that Mum and Dad did not.

*

When I woke it was evening and the house was silent. The pylons and their drooping power cables were silhouetted against a bright, diffuse sunset. I thought about the animal in the middle of the road. After the accident the animal

15

was still there. Which meant it hadn't moved while the car had been hurtling towards it. When it looked at me it was like it saw an object. And I had felt the same thing – that I became an object when it looked at me.

On my laptop I searched the internet for breeds of dog. I scrolled through various lists but no picture seemed right. The husky was most similar but the one that had caused the accident was taller and more powerful. I clicked a link and tensed. Because there it was. The animal I had seen on the road.

A wolf.

After a time, a noise roused me from reading. A flapping sound. It was coming from somewhere on the landing. I wondered if a creature had got in. Perhaps that raven. I took Mum's pebble as a weapon and slipped out. The door to my parents' room was ajar. The flapping sound was coming from inside. I edged forward until I was on the threshold, then I pushed the door wide.

Barefoot, hair wet from a shower, her blue blouse untucked, Nan was stripping my parents' bed. She peered at me as if she was half-asleep.

'What are you doing?' I said.

'I have to sleep in a bed,' she said, bundling the sheets into her arms.

I couldn't believe it. She was going to sleep in my parents' bed. Walking right up to her, I said, 'This is *their* room.'

'I've had two hours' sleep. I have to sleep in a bed.'

'Get out!' I hissed, spittle flying from my mouth and landing on her blouse.

Nan's small tight mouth opened in shock, then she reset herself. 'Don't be stupid, Lucas. I need to sleep.' She walked to the laundry basket, dumped in the sheets, then went to the chest of drawers.

There was a roaring inside my head. 'This is *my* house.'

She started opening drawers, delving among Mum's underwear, Dad's T-shirts, shoving their stuff about. I clenched my fists and found I was still holding the pebble. I clutched it hard. When Nan turned she held a clean sheet and I saw her blue blouse was embroidered with flowers. It was Mum's. She was wearing Mum's blouse.

She walked to the bed unfolding the sheet then threw it out so it billowed and I got a scent of recently washed cotton and the nice smell of our fabric softener. The sheet settled. I knew that if I stayed I would scream, shout, hit her, so I rushed out.

*

'I'm not going to live with you.'

'It's not a matter for debate, Lucas.'

'I don't care – I'm not going to live with you.'

'You can't stay here.'

'I can do what I want.'

'The social workers won't allow it.'

'So don't tell them about it.'

'Don't be silly, Lucas. This is reality, not fantasy.'

'*This* is none of your business.'

'For the next year, until you're sixteen, until you've finished school, I have responsibility for you. I'm your legal guardian. So that is precisely what it is – my business. *Ergo*, you are coming to live with me.'

'No I am not.'

Nan and I did a staring match across our breakfast bowls at the kitchen table like a couple of chess players before a crucial move. Nan lifted her mug, slurped her tea, put down her mug and stood. 'Right,' she said.

She walked out.

I smiled, triumphant.

'Going somewhere nice?' I called sarcastically as she put on her jacket in the hallway. 'Like, back home?'

'I've an appointment with your headmaster.'

'You can't do that,' I said, jolting upright and hurrying out to the hall, 'it's nothing to do with –'

'Then I'm seeing your social worker and after that –'

'I haven't got a social worker.'

'Yes you do. She visited when you were in hospital. I told her to go away. After that I'm arranging your mother's and father's death certificates. Do you want to come?'

Hearing the words 'death certificates' felt like a blow to the chest – a slow, thudding punch.

I couldn't reply. All the energy had gone out of me.

18

She stood silently waiting for my response, then she opened the front door to a bright day with all its busy light and birdsong and the distant rush of traffic noise. The door closed, and I was alone in the empty house.

Fiat

Nan did exactly what she said – she dealt with school, the social worker, the death certificates. The cemetery, the undertakers, the priest. The people who were coming to the funeral. The bank, the solicitors, the insurers. Nan was a lawyer and seemed able to do these things easily. Her voice never rose or fell – she dealt with people briskly but with some threat in her voice. I couldn't say how she threatened exactly, it was like you could just tell she would destroy you if you pushed her too far.

She explained how the will named her as my legal guardian and that I would have to live up north in Cumbria with her and start a new school there. She explained how the house belonged to the bank now. She explained that there would be an inquest but that I wouldn't have to attend. She explained that the social worker and doctors wanted me to see a counsellor but that I didn't have to if I didn't want to. I registered each piece of information but I couldn't respond. It was like I couldn't say anything any more, couldn't feel anything any more.

After the funeral service, at the graveside the

undertakers in black suits lowered two pine caskets into the earth on ropes they let out hand over fist, their necks straining inside stiff collars. The priest read his priestly words, and that was it. My parents gone from the world.

After the cemetery, in a hotel bar, people chatted and ate crisps. On the small lawn surrounded by horrible fir trees the bright dead sunlight lay like a fat slug.

*

A week later, a warm September day, we packed the car. Nan's small red Fiat. She planned to drive it along a motorway at seventy miles an hour, metres from haulage lorries and speeding vans and motorbikes.

Mitesh came to help us pack and say goodbye.

'Yo bro,' he said when he arrived, as if he came from the toughest streets of Baltimore and not Somerset. 'Wassup?'

I attempted the fist-bump/handshake he'd taught me. As usual, I failed.

'I'm about to travel two hundred miles in a death-trap and live with a weird old woman up north,' I said. 'What's up with you?'

'Your nan's cool, man. Helping you 'n'all.'

'She's not cool, Mitesh. Anyway, how can she drive this stupid thing all that way?' And to prove my point I gave one of the car's tyres a toe-poke.

21

'Yo! Lucas's nan, wassup?' grinned Mitesh as Nan appeared. She was carrying a taped-up cardboard box.

'You're the friend of Lucas, I take it,' said Nan. 'Well, don't hang about, boys, we've a lot to do.'

We began ferrying out my things. The house seemed to watch, gradually abandoned, as each journey out Nan's red Fiat sank lower and lower, like it was struggling with the task of its journey before it had even begun.

On the last trip out, I found Nan leaning against the car, head bowed.

'Are you all right?' I asked, worried.

'I'm fine,' she said, flashing a frown and going back into the house.

She wasn't fine. She was tired. Or she was ill. Probably she had a weak heart. What if she fainted, or had a heart attack on the motorway? Our car thudded into the earth bank like a fist, and once more Mum hung in her seat belt, hair wrapped round her cheek, Dad's head bent at that weird angle.

'I'm not going,' I said to Mitesh.

'Oh,' he said, surprised. 'Why not?'

'She's going to crash.'

Mitesh took a breath as if he was going to say something, bit his lip, then said gently, 'Give her a chance, man.'

'But Mitesh, this is my home. I've lived here all my life. This is where my friends are. Why can't she live

22

here? Besides, she's weird. Mum hated her. She *hated* her. Whenever she spoke to her on the phone it took her about a day to get over it.'

The look on Mitesh's face shifted into discomfort while I gave this little speech, his mouth twisting as if he was trying to work out how to say something difficult.

'Is that a fact?' said Nan behind me.

Mitesh and I locked eyes and heat rushed to my face. She'd heard me. But why should I be sorry for what I said? It was true. Mum *did* hate Nan. I turned to face her.

Her eyes were hard like quartz.

'I'm not going.'

In a voice barely above a whisper, she said, 'You damn well are, boy.'

A silence followed in which birds chortled and Mitesh scraped his shoe across grit on the road before saying, 'If I might interrupt at this juncture.'

I'd never heard him speak like that before. Usually he tried to sound like he was from Detroit or somewhere. He was squinting one-eyed at the sky. Nan followed his gaze. I did too. I wondered what he was looking at. We stood silently, the three of us examining white clouds as they sailed past so very high above us.

'Lucas's nan,' said Mitesh, fixing her and me with a serious look, like he was a teacher about to make a big speech. 'Perhaps Lucas is disinclined to travel by *car*?'

'Disinclined?' said Nan, puzzled.

'To travel by *car*,' Mitesh said, emphasising this last word with a widening of his eyes and a nod at the small red Fiat, low on the ground, heavy with boxes. 'After the *car accident*.'

Nan's head jolted backwards a fraction as if she had been physically struck by this information and I watched the new thought spread across her face. Then she looked at me and seemed to see me afresh. Finally, she stared towards the distant pylons and power cables. Mitesh and I exchanged a glance.

'Will you get the train instead?' Nan said at last.

Surprised she'd given an inch, I decided to meet her halfway. 'All right.'

'Then I'll pick you up from Kendal station this evening.'

'Yo! Nice one, Lucas's nan.' Mitesh turned to me. 'Lucas, I'm gonna split, man.'

Again I attempted the fist-bump/handshake and again I failed. We hugged instead. Mitesh slapped my back so hard it hurt, then, both of us blinking shining eyes, we nodded goodbye and Mitesh swaggered off to walk the mean streets of Somerset.

*

Trains took me north. From Tiverton Parkway to Bristol Temple Meads, Bristol to Birmingham, Birmingham to

Preston. At Preston, I didn't listen to the announcement about a change of platform and missed my connecting train.

I texted Nan to tell her I would be late.

The last train was slower.

Dusk.

Night.

Outside I could see darkness, sometimes sprinkles of lights but mainly the blurred reflections of the carriage: a mother with two kids, a man drinking a can of beer. I cupped my hand against cold glass.

I knew outside were hills, I could sense their blotting shapes in the darkness, towering over the little train. And even more than their size, their cold.

*

Nan met me at Kendal station. I was going to apologise for missing my train but she ruined it by saying, 'You've kept me waiting an hour and a half.'

She turned on her heel and strode away.

I followed her to the Fiat, the northern chill working its way through my thin jacket.

She stood at the driver's door, her face slack and tired, waiting for me to get in. But I couldn't.

'You sleeping here, are you?' she snapped, then climbed in and slammed the door.

I didn't move. The car windows began to cloud.

Numbness crept into my fingers. My lungs burned with the cold air.

I couldn't stay here all night.

I opened the door and got in.

*

Once, Dad drew a car engine on a piece of paper to show me how it worked. The drawing showed how the engine has chambers in it, how the chambers have pistons in them, how the pistons fire up and down when the petrol explodes and pushes them, how the pistons turn the crank shaft, which turns the wheels. You open the bonnet of a car, you marvel at that volume of cast metal. Then you imagine that object hurled backwards through the dashboard into the front seats at sixty miles an hour.

*

The road from Kendal swooped up and down. I gripped the side-bar with one hand and the seat edge with the other, keeping my eyes on the road because I had to prevent Nan from crashing the car and killing us both. She drove almost hunched over the steering wheel.

It was about a quarter of an hour into the drive that it happened. Her head nodded.

'Nan!'

She sprang upright. I opened my window to keep her awake.

'Close that, please, Lucas.'

'You were falling asleep.'

'Close the window. It's freezing.'

I closed the window. An expanse of water opened at my side. The road swept away and we entered a long valley between white-topped mountains.

'Is that snow?' I said, surprised to see it in September.

'It appears to be, doesn't it?' she said in a sarcastic voice.

I fired her a look of contempt.

She returned it.

'Keep your eyes on the road!' I said.

We drove down the valley in silence.

Nan's head began to nod.

'Nan!' I shouted.

She jumped in her seat. The car wobbled violently from side to side.

'Look out!'

She steadied the car, slowed, slowed further, then bumped onto the verge and stopped. She covered her mouth with her hand then switched off the ignition. The headlamps continued to light the bright grass. All around were dark fields. A gust of wind buffeted the car. She didn't move.

'Nan?'

She didn't respond. It was like she'd been turned to stone.

'Are you ill? You're ill, aren't you?'

I reached out. I was going to shake her by the shoulder but at my touch she quivered, then she began to cry. She shuddered like a little kid who's hurt herself on the playground. I didn't want her to cry. I didn't know how to make her stop crying.

I said, 'The battery will go if you leave the lights on.'

Eventually, she stopped. We sat silently, buffeted by that big wind. She switched off the lights.

'Have you got a tissue?' she said, her voice hoarse.

'No.'

She wiped her nose with the back of her hand like a little kid. She took in a deep, shuddering breath as if she was readying herself for a big task, then sat up and turned on the ignition, switched on the lights, put the car into gear and, without looking at me, bumped onto the tarmac.

*

We turned off the main road. A lane ran gently uphill between stone walls towards dark woods at the foot of the mountains. Above the woods, I could see a deep fold in the mountain ridge where white water rushed.

We entered the woods and the headlamps lit a gold and yellow tree-tunnel. Then, suddenly, there it was, on the right – her cottage.

28

Cottage

The tyres made an odd buzzing sound as we bumped through the gateway. Headlamps swept over a gravel turning circle with a raised nub of turf at the centre, then they crossed the cottage's walls and I got the impression of grey stone and black slate before they lit a fence. We hurtled towards it. Nan braked hard and the car stopped inches away from hitting the wooden slats. The engine, then headlamps, died.

I stepped into chilled thin air and deep darkness. All I could hear was the wind rushing softly in the leaves, the crunch of Nan's feet on the gravel, then a muffled root-through in her bag for keys. The breeze stopped but I could still hear a rushing sound. The white water on the mountain? There was a snap of a branch in the woods.

'Nan?'

She was still rummaging. Hurrying over, I took the bag. 'Is this it?' I held up a door key. I felt her annoyance at me finding it, but she took it. The key tapped against the lock.

'Do you get animals in the woods?'

The key turned softly then a blaze of light illuminated a red door and she stepped inside.

With a quick glance to the darkness, I followed.

Straight ahead were the stairs and on the immediate left, past a bin of walking sticks, a dark room. To the right was a short hallway that led to an open door. Nan put her bag on a table under the stairs and firmly shut another door on the right as she went through the open door at the back, switching on the light to what I saw was the kitchen.

'Do you want some food?' she said.

I followed, stopping by a fold-up formica table.

'Plates are in there.'

She nodded at a cupboard while taking out a loaf. I took out some chipped, faded crockery.

She opened, poured and stirred beans, watched bread toast under the hissing grill.

'Can you put the heating on?' I said.

'No.'

We ate. I could hear her jaw click when she bit. Not her teeth, her actual jaw.

Afterwards, she took me upstairs to what was to be my room.

From the huge chest of drawers she took a towel and some bed linen as faded as the plates from which we'd eaten our beans on toast.

'This was your mother's room.'

She flung a sheet so it billowed over the bed.

'Go on,' she urged, so I went round the other side and tucked it in like Mum had taught me.

We made the bed in silence and when we'd finished, she stood for a moment, dazed with tiredness. She was so exhausted I felt sorry for her.

'Thank you,' I said.

She didn't seem to hear, and went out.

I stood where I was, listening. I heard the boiler fire up as hot water ran in the bathroom, then the bump of the bathroom door and, a little later, her bedroom door.

The cottage was quiet. It was also freezing. I was still wearing my jacket, and my breath made faint clouds.

Shape

I woke boiling hot. My throat was sore and I was sweating. I still had my clothes on. I dug in my pocket for my phone – not yet four.

Wind whispered drily on stone walls.

For a while I lay without thinking. I could make out the chest of drawers, a deeper block within the darkness. The blanket was pale. It smelled different from my duvet – musty. The sheets were softer than at home but not in a nice way, more as if they were about to disintegrate with age.

Beyond the cottage, in the distance, was the faint sound of water. Endlessly, a deep, cold whisper.

The house and its things listened to me as much as I to them.

A car on the main road drew closer, passed at speed, then faded into the distance, leaving behind the house, the running water on the mountain, and … something else.

There was something else out there.

I stiffened. Then, with a kind of anger, I threw back the covers and went to the window. Darkness.

I crossed the room and opened the door onto silence. After listening for a few moments, I went onto the landing.

A faint tapping sound came from one of the downstairs rooms. I walked round the landing and descended the stairs slowly. The circle of warped glass high up in the front door showed a buckled moon. It gave some light to the hallway, showing spear-like walking sticks and umbrellas. The open door to the sitting room was dark. I turned towards the kitchen. That was where the tapping sound was coming from. I entered slowly. Not tapping. Dripping. Mum in her seat belt, hanging. I turned the tap tight.

Silence.

Another car approached out of the distance. It seemed to take an age for it to arrive at the bottom of the lane. It sped past, and after it had gone, the cottage, the mountain and the stream seemed more present.

And suddenly I knew – it was still there, whatever I'd felt upstairs.

I went to the back door, unlocked it, and opened it. An empty garden. I stepped out. The concrete was freezing under my bare feet.

Frost had claimed the grass. The trees stood dark and still. I shivered.

Then something came out of the darkness.

I leaped inside, banged shut the door, locked it, thudded through the cottage and grabbed a walking stick.

I retreated to the sitting room, and an armchair. I put my knees up, wrapped a throw round me, and stayed like that, listening to the silence.

*

I don't know what it was. I turned away before I could see. I didn't *want* to see. But I had the impression of something that shouldn't have been there.

*

'Do you want a cup of tea?'

Nan swished back the curtains of the sitting room and faced me in the gloomy dawn light.

She was wearing a pink towel-fabric dressing gown and white socks. Her shins were stubble-dark.

She went out and I got up, stiff with cold. The cudgel-like stick clattered to the floor. I walked to the window.

The lawn was oval in shape, cupped by the woods. Where the fingers of the woods reached round as if to touch at the end there was a wire fence, then a field that sloped gently up to the foot of the mountain.

The cottage did not face the mountain squarely, but at an angle, so it looked partly down the valley. The mountain rose high and almost vertical, its lower flank covered in brown bracken. Above that were areas of dark heather, then the grass was smooth and undulating with stretches of scree and, at the top, a jagged stony ridge that ran right along the valley. The smoothness of the grass and the jagged spine made it seem like a body. In places, granite-grey rock stood up in packed blocks. To my left, if I craned my head, I could see the long spine of the ridge turn inwards to make a fold. That was probably where the white water came down that I had glimpsed the previous night.

At the end of the garden, on a fence post, stood a raven, glossy and big, with a beak that curved like a dragon's tooth. It flopped up into the sky and flew across the empty field.

*

In the light of the kitchen, Nan looked strange as she shuffled about. Her grey hair stood on end like a cartoon character who's just been electrocuted. Her face was puffy. Her small mouth drooped. Her mouth was a lot like Mum's, she had full lips, but in Nan the folds in her cheeks made two vertical lines that ran from the corners of her mouth to her chin.

The grill hissed.

She put a packet of butter on the table then went to the sink and stood gazing out the window, lost in thought, her head cocked on one side like Mum.

Righting her head and facing me, she said, 'I've arranged for us to go to school this morning.'

I started. If I had to go anywhere it was only to bed.

'I don't feel well enough.'

'What's wrong with you?'

'I feel nauseous.'

'Eat something then.'

She brought two slices of toast and leaned them against the pack of butter. She clacked plates and knives onto the table.

'I have to sort my things out first.'

'Sort them out when we get back.'

She took one of the slices, buttered it.

'We meet the headmaster at noon.'

I wanted to tell her I wasn't going to do it, and I raised my face to do just that but she had tilted her head and got dreamy again, like Mum. It was sort of like Mum's ghost was in her.

*

'Are we going to have this argument every time we get in the car, Lucas?'

I was standing by the cottage door, eyeing the Fiat. Nan stood on the driver's side with her keys. Her lips were bright with lipstick, her hair tidier, and she was wearing a smart woollen jacket. Thankfully, she wore thick stockings that covered her stubbly shins.

'Yes,' I said.

'Oh, speaks, does he?'

The front door was locked and I didn't have a house

key so there wasn't anywhere I could have gone, unless up the mountain. Which I didn't want to do.

'Come along, we've got an appointment, and I won't be late because of you.'

'But I *have* to be there. So you need me.'

'Precisely.' She opened the car door. 'So get in.'

I frowned at her muddy logic as she lowered herself into the car and threw open the passenger door.

I got in.

She made slow, big turns of the wheel then moved off in too-high revs which didn't fill me with confidence. Something in my pocket annoyed me and I found a white pebble. Mum's. We buzz-rattled over a cattle grid and whined in second gear down from the cave of the woods into the morning.

School

'Are you going to take that in with you?' Nan said, directing her eyes to the fat white pebble.

I put it in my pocket, gave her a stare.

'Sulky sulky,' she said, parking.

She got out. After a second I got out too.

The school stood at the bottom of a slope, down from the main road. It appeared to be made of various boxes fitted together, all panels and glass. The entrance was entirely glass so you could see into the wide reception space which had a set-back balcony above. In the classroom I could see into, a lesson was going on. I put my hand in my pocket to feel the pebble's cold weight. I gripped it until I could feel the bones of my fist.

*

'We've put you in 11F, Miss Andrews' class. She's assigned a boy to show you round for the first few days.'

The headmaster, Mr Bond, was bald. He occasionally covered his skull with a big palm when he spoke, smoothing back non-existent hair. It wasn't natural the way he did that. Not the way that Nan cocking her head on her side was natural. His big-handed covering of his scalp, as he rocked back in his chair, he did on purpose, but I couldn't work out what the purpose was.

'Will Lucas be able to do his GCSEs this year?' Nan asked.

'That will be up to Lucas, in part,' Mr Bond smiled, glancing towards me. He had been doing this throughout and I got the sense that in spite of his smiles and words he was examining me like I was one of those insects we had to take apart in science. I lowered my eyes. Under the desk was a faint stain.

Mr Bond was speaking again but I couldn't hear him now, instead I could hear a steady beat, something like a drip.

'It's up to Lucas, hmmm?' Mr Bond was saying.

I raised my head. He was studying me again. I had the urge to tell him to get lost.

'Hmm, Lucas?' Mr Bond repeated.

Then suddenly it felt like all my anger drained out of me. 'I want to work,' I said, returning my gaze to the carpet. 'I just want to do my work.' I was aware of the stain, hovering at the edge of my vision. 'I'll work hard,' I said in a flat voice.

'When can he start?' Nan asked.

'Monday.'

'Well, Mr Bond, thank you.'

'My pleasure, Ms Lansdale.'

She stood. Then he stood. They shook hands, and it was like I was a big-name footballer being signed to a new club. Or like I was being handed over to a devilish power.

When I stood, the dripping sound sped up, and I realised it was my pulse, beating in my ear.

Walking the empty corridor, Nan said, 'What did you think of him?'

I shrugged.

'I thought he was so far up his own arse he was going to come out the other end,' she said.

I stopped mid-stride, shocked.

'Come on, let's not hang about, Lucas.'

Monday

Everything was different now. The chill light, the smell of wood smoke in the sitting room, a scent of faded perfume in my room; and on Monday the new school uniform. We got it from a shop in Kendal at the weekend. When I got ready that morning the only things the same were my underwear and shoes.

Before I left, I put the white pebble in my pocket.

I would have to do things alone now.

*

Malcolm. He had a handkerchief that he was always pulling from his pocket and blowing his nose into. On that first day, when he pointed something out, he did it with his handkerchief scrunched in his fist. And every time I saw him after that he had a cold.

'The library,' he said in a voice so bunged-up it came out as *De lie-burr-ee*. 'And here we are back at the playground.'

We stopped on the tarmacked rectangle between classrooms whose hard surfaces echoed back several hundred voices and the scuffs and shouts from about eight games of tennis football. A real football made a splashy sound when it struck the high fence of the five-a-side football pitch. This stood on the playground's fourth side.

'That's the Cage.'

Boys moved about inside, white shirts untucked, shoving each other, yelling – 'Pass!' – 'Here!' – 'Tackle!'

Thunder rumbled along the valley and when I turned, a black fighter-plane slid over the tree tops. It passed so low I could make out the chin and mouth of the helmeted pilot in the cockpit. It disappeared over fir trees.

'What the hell is that?'

I had to shout because the jet's roar grew after it had gone until it filled the whole sky. No one else in the playground seemed to pay it much attention.

'Pilots training for Iraq,' Malcolm said when the roar had died, peering glumly.

'Nah,' said a voice, and I turned to find a tall, black-haired boy standing close to me. So close I had to take a step back. My surprise seemed to amuse him because he gave a faint smile. 'I reckon the military's hunting the new kid.'

His black hair was gelled and his eyebrows were extremely dark and he took another step so I wanted to retreat again and had to fight not to. His smile became a smirk. Then he did something surprising. He put his hand out to offer a handshake. I wasn't sure if he was ripping it out of me or not, but I took his palm.

'What's his name, then, Malky?' he said.

'Lucas,' I said.

'Where's he from?'

'Somerset,' I said, nettled by how he kept addressing Malcolm, and again he seemed pleased by my annoyance because now he laughed.

'What you doing here, mate?' he said directly to me.

If I had been Mitesh I would have said something stupid like, 'My dad's joined a circus in Kendal,' but because he'd caught me off-guard I said, 'I've come to live with my nan.'

'Why? Your parents split up or something?'

I was so surprised by this question I didn't know how to answer. It was like he had an ability to make a beeline for the stuff I didn't want to talk about. I smacked my lips while I tried to think of something to say, probably appearing like a goldfish.

''kin 'ell, Malky, this one don't know what happened to his own parents.'

Now I wanted him to get lost.

'Doesn't he speak?' the boy said, smiling to Malcolm, and before Malcolm could answer he snorted a laugh and walked away, giving me a wink and jabbing a forefinger towards me. 'See you later, Somerset, watch out for the hunters!'

I stared after him as he strolled towards the Cage. His hair had faint twists that stuck out over his ears where the gel hadn't worked properly. I thought about taking out my pebble and hurling it at his head.

'Don't mess with Steve Scott,' Malcolm whispered. 'He'll put you in hospital.'

I shot Malcolm a glance.

'Seriously,' he said.

Before I could find out any more about Steve Scott putting people in hospital, two boys arrived who, judging by their size, were a few years below us.

'Malky!' one announced with wide, innocent eyes. 'We've been searching for you everywhere. We're meant to be at war.'

Malcolm checked his watch. He frowned as if in a torment of indecision, then said, 'Do you play any role-playing games?'

'No.'

He nodded sorrowfully. Then he started making funny faces, like he wanted to use the toilet.

'You go if you need, Malky.'

'I'm the game master, you see. You can come too if you like.'

I thought about it then shook my head. The three went away in a huddle, the two younger ones glancing over their shoulders, listening to whatever it was Malcolm was telling them about me.

*

The first time I saw Debs, I thought she was a self-important cow. She was slouched at the issue desk in the library, chewing a stick of gum with an open mouth, a book called *The Bell Jar* under her arm. I was waiting to get a library card and the librarian was trying to find something under the counter. While she searched, Debs leaned on the counter with her hip, and rolled her eyes. She was gazing past me as if I wasn't there but standing so close to me I would have had to turn away not to look at her.

Pale brown hair to her shoulders. Straight and fine. She had one puncture mark in her nose for a piercing, and two in her ear lobe. Her eyes were blue. Not sky blue, pale blue, almost grey.

'What you staring at?' she said.

Now it was her mouth that took my attention, the chewing sound coming from it. *Smackety-smackety-smack*, gone up a gear in irritation.

'I'm waiting to get a library card,' I said.

'You'll have a long wait here.'

The crouched librarian shot her a peeved glance, still rummaging.

'I'm in Year 11,' I said. 'What year are you in?'

She continued to chew her gum. Her breath smelled of spearmint and cigarettes.

45

'You fancy me or something?' she said finally.

'No,' I said, blushing slightly. 'I'm new. I've come for my library card and I'm making conversation.' I turned away, giving her the shoulder.

'Here it is,' the librarian said, standing to hand Debs a slim book. The cover showed the drawing of a wolf. The book was called *Lupercal*.

Debs didn't move for a moment. 'See you, then,' she said uncertainly. But I was occupied by the wolf on the cover, its head low between its shoulders, staring out at me, ravenous.

*

Miss Andrews was my form teacher but I also had her for English. This was in our form room, which had full bookshelves and bright pictures on the walls that her students had made. She made an effort, you could tell. I took a seat near the back, at the side, by the plants. Luckily she didn't pick on me to answer questions about the book she was teaching, *The Call of the Wild*, although her glance picked me out a few times to check I was paying attention. I was trying to but I hadn't been able to take in very much. Not just in her class, all my classes. When she spoke, I could hear the words but I couldn't make sense of them. I tried to break them down by thinking about individual words and what they meant, but by the time I'd worked out one word, she was several sentences on. I didn't use to have this trouble. I wondered if it was to do with the accident. If I had brain damage.

Steve Scott was in my English class. He didn't say much unless he was asked to, when he gave sarcastic answers that made everyone laugh except Miss Andrews. But she didn't seem to mind his answers, either; she would quip something back and move on.

Outside were the mountains, green and gold. Cloud shadow flowed across them.

'Lucas Pettifer, just because you haven't read the book doesn't mean you can sit there daydreaming.'

I felt my cheeks flush.

'But Miss,' Steve shot back, 'the book's so boring we're *all* daydreaming. It's just the new kid hasn't learnt how to hide his feelings like the rest of us.'

Everyone laughed.

'No, Steven, I would never mistake your expression for interest. Now, someone, has Buck changed since he left California, d'you think?'

Steve Scott fired me his sarcastic half-smile, then went back to offering it to Miss Andrews. I got the impression he was goading her. I couldn't make him out. Was he being nasty when he quipped like this, or just funny? Maybe when he'd been like that with me on the playground, it was just his way of trying to be friends.

After the class, Miss Andrews asked me to stay behind. I trudged up.

'How has your day gone?'

I shrugged. She wore white summer sandals. Her ankles were bronzed and smooth.

'Here,' she said, handing me a form. 'Your grandmother will need to sign off your homework until she's set up online.'

She knew about Nan being my guardian, then. Which meant she knew about my parents. I hated the idea of all the teachers knowing about my parents. I took the sheet. At my last school, they had the same system, and it brought it home that Nan was responsible for things like this now.

'You'll have a lot to do to catch up. Do you like reading?'

I shrugged.

There was a hole at the end of the sandals and you could just see a bit of painted toenail – bright green.

'If there's anything you want to ask me about, if there's any difficulties here, come to see me. Okay?'

She had a rainbow-coloured band on her wrist. I wondered how old she was. I couldn't tell from her face, partly because she was a teacher and I can't tell that sort of thing easily about teachers, and partly because she was waiting for me to say something, which made it difficult to think.

'All right, then,' she smiled, in a way that meant

this is the end of the conversation. She gathered books and papers and put them in her voluminous briefcase that had wide jaws that probably ate homework for breakfast.

I folded the form she'd given me and put it in my bag.

Carcass

I got off the bus in the village and walked back to Nan's cottage. I walked on the road and, when a car approached, on the verge. I felt the whoosh of air from each vehicle and pretended I wasn't frightened at getting hit by a metal meteorite travelling at sixty miles an hour about half a yard from my knees.

I had to go through the woods and felt the trees' quiet in the late afternoon. It was like they were listening to me. Listening out for something, anyway.

Nan's car wasn't in the yard. I used the house key she'd given me and tried to do my homework at the kitchen table but I couldn't concentrate on *The Call of the Wild*. The main character seemed to be the dog Buck, who had been stolen from a nice house in California and taken to Canada and put in a team of huskies, pulling a sled across snow-fields. But I couldn't keep my focus for more than a minute. There wasn't internet and I had no signal on my phone so I couldn't do the geography research. I gave up and went to the kitchen window. A song thrush stood on the path. It had a snail-shell in its beak and it was bashing the shell against the concrete. It cracked the shell and pecked at the snail. Then it flew away, leaving a mess.

I wondered how long Nan would be. If she'd fall asleep at the wheel and crash and die.

Under the stairs was a table with a globe on it. Beside it a telephone. When I switched on the globe it glowed, sea-blue and wheat-yellow. I flicked the light off, on. Off, on. If I phoned she'd only think I was being weird. I turned off the globe and went to the bin by the front door and took out the cudgel-like walking stick. It had a bulb of wood on the end as big as a lemon. I swung it back and forth, pretending I was hitting whatever it was I'd seen out in the darkness. Then I opened the door Nan kept shut.

Inside was a big dark dining table, smelling of polish. By the window stood a bureau, the desk part lowered, papers cascaded across it. On the dining table at the end by the bureau were lots of A4 binder files. The cattle grid growled and Nan's small car whizzed into the yard and fizzed to a halt in the gravel. I hurried out.

'Were you in my study?' she asked when she came in.

'No.'

She put the kettle on.

'I don't want you to go in there.'

'I didn't.'

'It's private.'

'I need internet.'

'I haven't got internet.'

'I need it for my homework.'

'Well, I haven't got it.'

There was a long silence while the kettle boiled. She poured herself a mug of tea. 'Do you want one?'

'I don't drink tea,' I said, gathering my books and heading for the door.

When I was at home, I used to tell Mum about school. I paused in the doorway. 'School was all right,' I said.

Steam rose from her mug. She twisted round to me.

'Did you learn anything?'

'Story about a dog.'

'A dog?'

'Yeah.'

'Did you enjoy it, this story?'

I shrugged.

There was a quiet and she faced front. I remembered how easy it had been to tell Mum what had happened; she used to laugh at what I told her.

Upstairs, I stared out the window at the big trees, their leaves going yellow, gold, rust, orange, all the colours between living and dead. I tried to do my homework. I took out the form that Nan was meant to sign. I tried to do my homework again.

*

I got up early the next morning to read *The Call of the Wild* but I couldn't do it. I tried reading the introduction. It said it was about a dog that really wanted to be a wolf but I couldn't concentrate. It was like my brain was broken.

Nan called from downstairs for me to hurry up for school.

I took out the form she was meant to sign.

I bent over the sheet, took up my pen and signed Nan's name.

*

At school, everyone had their own groups. I didn't know which one to join, or how to join. I didn't want to speak to anyone, anyway. They all kept wanting to know why I'd moved. So I hung out with Malky and watched him play his role-playing game with his fantasy friends. They wanted me to have a character but I wouldn't. Other times I went to the library where I stared out the windows at the gold mountains and the fighter-jets screaming down the valley. A few times I noticed Debs in there, chewing gum, pretty, reading. She was always on her own. She clocked me once, and scowled.

*

On Friday I heard about the wolf.

We used to have dinner at the red-topped kitchen

table and afterwards Nan would go through to watch the local news. It was deathly dull but that night I didn't want to face my textbooks again so I sat with her.

And it was there on TV that I heard about the wolf.

The screen showed a valley. 'The mountains of the Lake District,' a news-voice said. The camera panned across the mountains then cut to a reporter standing in a field, earnestly holding a microphone.

'A region renowned for its peace and tranquillity. But something has disturbed this tranquillity, and danger has come to this peaceful corner of England. Because something has been killing the flocks that pasture here.' The camera showed a bunch of black sheep nibbling grass. 'So far, three sheep have been killed. The killer is an animal. And, says one farmer, this predator is a wolf.'

I felt so shocked by the word my entire body tightened.

The TV picture cut to a windswept man with glasses and an intense stare. He wore farmer uniform – waxed jacket and checked shirt.

'You believe these animals were killed by a wolf?' the reporter said, sticking the microphone under the man's nose.

'They had their intestines ripped out. Lungs and heart. Nothing left but a carcass. Nothing but a wolf did that.'

'And what do you say to those who believe it's a dog that has gone wild?'

The man paused momentarily, his tone dropped a fraction, then he said: 'Were a wolf.'

'Sheridan's a bloody idiot,' said Nan.

'D'you know him?' I said.

'Everyone knows him. Gets an idea in his head, can't get it out.'

'Is this near here, then?'

'Man's a fool.'

'I saw something in the woods on the night we arrived.'

She glanced at me. After a second, she said, 'Don't be silly.'

It was dusk and the woods were dark. The fell rose solid and vast from the valley, equally dark.

*

On a Friday night at home I would have been doing something. Going to the cinema, or round to a friend's. So I phoned Mitesh. I couldn't get a signal so I had to use the landline and stood by the table under the stairs, spinning the globe while his ringtone faintly sounded.

'Yo!' he answered.

'Hey.'

'Who's that?'

'Luke.'

'Lucas! Wassup?'

'Not much.'

'Bro, you're so funny. So – what's it like there?'

The globe glowed bright. 'There's mountains,' I said. 'And lakes.'

There was the faint roar of laughter. 'Man, you're the funniest.' His voice sounded like he was walking outside and he didn't say anything for a few moments.

'How's things?' I said.

'Bro,' he said, as if divulging secrets. 'Joey's a hipster! Tattooine!' He hooted so loud I had to hold the phone away from my ear. I span the globe again, watched Finland disappear. 'Can't believe his mum let him get a tattoo!' He stopped moving suddenly. 'Sorry,' he said, his voice dropping a tone. 'Didn't mean to bring up …'

'Bring up what?'

'You know … parents. You all right?' His voice went high at the end, awkward.

'Yeah,' I said as Russia skimmed by.

'Good,' he said, quickly, moving again. 'So, we're going to see this band tonight.'

'Yeah? Who?'

'The Vanguard.'

'Never heard of them.'

'I'm nearly there.'

'Oh!' I said, getting that he was in a hurry. 'Okay. See you, then, Mitesh.'

''kay, bro?'

'Sure. 'kay. 'kay.'

'I'll phone at the weekend. 'kay?'

Before I could say that it *was* the weekend, he'd gone.

The globe had stopped at the Pacific Ocean. I turned it off.

Nan was in her armchair, reading.

'How's your friend?'

I sat in the armchair opposite. Her book was about a strike; it showed angry faces in black and white on the cover.

I stared at the unlit fire. This is what my life was like now. *Was* this what my life was like now? I thought about going out on my own, then about the woods. They were already dark.

'What's that book about?' I tried.

She looked at me over her reading glasses.

'How the British state went to war against the people.'

'I'm going for a walk,' I said, standing up.

She turned a page.

'Take a torch with you,' she said. 'The woods are dark.'

'I know,' I said, taking the torch that hung by the walking sticks, and went out.

Shelter

When I hurried out from the woods I could see the lights of the village so I tramped along the verge of the main road towards them. Headlamps flew at me, dangerous as killer dogs.

The only open shop was a 7-11. The two on shift were talking about a guy named Danny who'd been charged with GBH. After patrolling the aisles for five minutes, I explored the rest of the village. It was small and there was nothing to do. Right now Mitesh and the others would be in some hot room listening to The Vanguard. I shivered, fingers numb. Down a side street I found a park.

It was walled. On its far edge was a dark pavilion, about the most interesting thing I'd seen so far.

It was good going into the darkness after the brightness of traffic and streetlamps. It was like I was invisible and could pretend I didn't exist. That none of what had happened, had happened. Mum, Dad, the crash. Moving here. School.

There was someone by the pavilion.

I slowed.

The figure watched me approach. Slowly I began to circle back the way I'd come.

'Somerset!' he called.

I stopped.

He strolled over and when he got close the sarcastic half-smile was right in place. It was dark, but his sarcasm was so strong I knew who it was.

'All right, mate?' said Steve Scott.

I nodded.

'Don't say a lot, do you?'

'What you doing here?' I said.

'I live here. Where d'you live?'

I waved a hand vaguely.

He laughed. 'I'm waiting for my brother.' He put an arm round my shoulder and began to walk. Unless I was going to throw his arm off and make a big deal of it, I had to go with him. He steered me towards the pavilion. When we got close, I saw there were two others there.

He let me go as we reached what was not, I saw now, a pavilion but a park shelter. Steve stepped onto the bench and sat on the backrest beside a thinner, smaller boy. The second boy, chunky as a professional rugby player, was leaned forward on the bench like he had a stomach ache.

'This is Zed.'

The chunky, bent-over boy lifted his head. He wore

a tracksuit top and had his chin tucked into it. He was huge. His head seemed box-shaped. This was partly due to his close-shave haircut.

'And this is Alex.'

'Aw'right,' said Alex from the backrest in a reedy voice.

'How you finding it here?' said Steve, taking out tobacco and papers.

'All right. What's there to do?'

'Nothing. It's a living death.'

Alex whinnied a laugh at this.

'What's Somerset like?' Steve said.

'Not as cold as this.'

Steve chuckled, fiddling over his roll-up. Alex didn't take his eyes off me.

'Why'd you live with your nan, then?' Steve said, his features flaring in the light of a match, his gelled hair gleaming.

I didn't know how to answer.

He shook the match dead. 'Where's your parents?'

'When's your brother turning up?' I said.

Steve sucked on his roll-up. He exhaled. 'You're boring me, Somerset.'

I felt my skin prickle. I was only here because he'd asked me over. I shoved my hands in my pockets, felt the white pebble. I squeezed it in my fist. A car turned off the main road and growled towards the shelter.

Steve said, 'Here he is now. We'll give you the grand tour.'

The car stopped, its door opened and the interior light came on, silhouetting a man. The door clunked shut and he vanished. He reappeared a few seconds later round the corner of the shelter.

'Steve?' he called softly.

'Danny.'

'Idiot, make me come and get you.'

'Talking to our guest.'

The man glanced at me, then without saying anything, he headed for his car.

Steve jumped off the bench. Alex leapt nervously. Zed rose. And rose some more. He was giant.

'Come on, Lucas,' Steve called.

I decided there was nothing else to do on a Friday night in the wasteland of Cumbria, so I followed. Their bodies were silhouetted as the passenger door opened and the interior light came on. Watching Zed get in was like watching a rhino try to squeeze into a phone box. Alex zipped in after him like a whippet.

Steve waited for me.

'Come on, mate.'

The engine snarled, revved to a bark.

Scattered jewels of glass. Dad's bent neck.

'Is he coming or what?' whined Alex from the back seat. 'I'm freezing me tits off.'

Steve leaned into the car. 'Shut up!'

Alex yelped and Steve straightened, smiling. 'Sorry. He's a retard. Well?'

I was still staring at the car.

I looked at Steve. He was watching me curiously.

I shook my head.

Steve shrugged then got in. The door shut and the car exploded into motion, its circular rear lights glowing like dragon's eyes, its rear tyres squealing in a fishtailing skid out onto the road.

Its engine sounded for minutes afterwards down the valley, souped-up, ripping the silence.

Ewe

I didn't know that darkness could get so close. Reach up to your face and touch you. Press against your temples. Cover your mouth. Suffocate.

The woods were silent.

The torch showed them like the inside of a tunnel.

I walked, pretending I wasn't scared.

*

On Saturday I woke to the scrape of claws.

I slid from bed, went over to the curtain, and peeked.

Nan was raking leaves. I opened the curtains properly and she lifted her head. We stared at each other. Then she went back to raking.

I had cereal then went out. The top of the mountain was hidden by grey drifting cloud. Nan was putting leaves in small piles.

Our garden at home was nice. Mum liked to garden.

'Do you want a hand?' I said.

'You can get the wheelbarrow.' She nodded at the shed.

Inside, the shed was chaos. The gloom hid a lawnmower,

tins of paint, stacks of newspapers, a log pile and, propped against a worktop, a rusty bicycle. Tipped up against a wall was the wheelbarrow. I tilted it down and bashed it through the clutter.

We worked for a while without speaking, Nan raking and me scooping the wet leaves into the wheelbarrow and rolling them to the compost heap. Suddenly Nan straightened, put a palm to her hip, and arched her spine. I felt the edge of fear. After a few moments she returned to raking. She seemed even older now.

'Should you be doing that?' I said.

'Why not?'

'Because of your age.'

She laughed and went on raking. I was surprised at her laughter. She looked a little like Mum when she did that. I turned away.

The mountain's colours seemed to be brooding on darker versions of themselves: the bracken deep brown, the grass a greyish green, the granite black. Above the trees I could see a touch of white water, and it made a cold, constant thunder. I could see a track, too. Presumably that led up from the lane.

'Where does that go?'

Nan peered. At first she didn't see where I meant.

'The fells,' she said finally. 'And you can get to the Benedict farm that way.'

She went back to raking.

'What do you think of that news story about the wolf, then?' I said.

'I told you, it's nonsense.'

'What about that farmer, though?'

'There aren't any wolves,' she said, looking at me as if I was an idiot. 'There haven't been wolves for hundreds of years.'

'But what if there were?'

'You're a dreamer, just like your mother.'

To hide the flush on my cheeks, I crouched and spent a long time picking up individual leaves.

The rake twanged and I lifted my head to find Nan doubled over.

'Nan?'

She didn't move.

'Nan?' I said, coming to her, and when she didn't answer I touched her shoulder.

She bashed my arm away. 'I'm fine!'

After a moment she straightened, winced, and pressed her stomach. Then she walked to the house.

I watched her pour herself a glass of water at the kitchen window then she moved out of sight. A sleek, mouse-brown bird flew to the cottage, vanished under the eaves, reappeared and flew away. I couldn't see Nan. The bird returned and disappeared into a hole in the mortar where it must have had a nest. I went to check on Nan.

'Nan!' I called, coming in the back door.

The cottage was silent.

I hurried through the house and found her in an armchair in the sitting room, eyes shut, head lolling. One wrinkled hand curled palm-up in her lap.

She was dead, I knew, but then her chest rose and fell, and her mouth made a little click as she inhaled, the noise Mum used to make when she slept.

When you die you lose all the noises of your body. You lose everything. Even things you take for granted like sleeping.

I went back outside and made my way round to the front.

The lane trickled with run-off. The trees dripped. I crossed the cattle grid and followed the lane to where it began to rise uphill. The air was very still. The only sounds were water gurgling in a ditch and the far roar of the stream.

Soon the lane became a grass-cambered track. After a few minutes, I paused. I had already climbed quite high. Directly below lay the woods, inside them the dark slate tiles of the cottage. Beyond the trees were the main road, the village to one side and the lake to the other. I was high enough to see onto the lowest parts of the mountains on the far side of the valley. I turned and went on, nearing some sheep standing close to the track, black and shaggy, mud and dung hanging from their coats.

Bolder than normal sheep. They watched me suspiciously as I passed.

The path ended at a stone wall with a wooden ladder fixed to it. The stream was louder now, more like a waterfall. To my left, about a mile distant, stood a house – that was probably the Benedict farm. It was reached by a steep road from the valley but I couldn't see how to get to it from here.

Beyond the wall a stony path led up into the cloud.

I climbed the ladder and came down another ladder on the other side and crossed the wet grass to the stream. It tumbled off a ledge into a black pool. Bare thin trees stood at the pool edge. From the pool the stream continued downhill in a rush.

After watching the water drop for a few minutes, I returned to the path. The air grew colder as I climbed. I crossed the cloud-line, the light dimmed, and when I turned, I couldn't see further than about twenty yards.

It began to snow. The flakes patted my jacket. Ahead stood several black sheep. As I approached they all retreated to a safe distance except one who was lying down. It was odd, how it lay. Snow settled on it.

When I was about a yard away, I saw that its coat was more of a dark brown than black and that it had a deep red mark on its neck where the farmer must have dyed it to mark that it was his. I wondered if it was asleep. Or sick. I checked around for a stick to poke it but couldn't see anything so I took out my white pebble and tossed it gently.

The pebble landed on the sheep and rolled off but the animal didn't move. Its mouth was slack. Its eyes were yellow. For a few seconds I stared, then I stepped forward and snatched up my pebble. The red on its neck wasn't dye – it was blood. The sheep was dead.

Snow-crystals collected on its shaggy coat.

'Oi!'

I whirled.

Coming fast through the snow, long hair swinging, strode a man. I turned to run, tripped on the sheep, and fell. My palm slid on its wet coat as I scrambled to my feet.

'What you done to her?'

I ran.

'Get back here!'

I ran into the mist. After a minute, I checked over my shoulder. He wasn't following. I stopped. The air was like ice. I cupped my hands to blow on my fingers, which was when I saw the blood – one hand was covered in sheep blood. A red snow-crystal slid along a finger, melted, and dripped.

I crouched and wiped my hand on the grass.

In the mist, close by, a form slid. I didn't move, not even when it changed direction and came towards me. Then it emerged: a black sheepdog with a white eye-patch, coming fast. I couldn't move, could only watch, then I understood I had to act or I would die. I stood and raised my arm to hurl the pebble at the dog. The dog halted. I jerked my arm back as if to throw and it sprang away. Then it bounced towards me and barked.

I retreated but it moved round me, still barking, cutting off my retreat, forcing me to change direction. It kept coming so I kept moving. I was heading down the mountain.

The man emerged from the mist. He paused as if to take in the scene, strode towards me and before I could throw my pebble at him, he reached me and grabbed my wrist so tight it was like I'd been scalded.

'Polka!' he barked.

The dog fell silent.

The man had the face of a corpse. His glasses were dotted with water.

'What you do to my sheep?'

'Let me go!'

'Don't be daft, lad,' he said, but released me.

I ran for it.

I was jerked round by my collar and his thumb stuck in my windpipe. The dog barked crazily.

'Stop it!'

I stopped wrestling. The dog stopped barking. The snow pattered. The man studied me. Then, as if deciding I wasn't worth it, he pushed me away.

I coughed, rubbed where his thumb had been in my throat.

'I'll get you done for assault,' I said.

'Away!' he whispered, so sternly I took a step away but when his dog shot into the cloud I realised that he was talking to the animal.

'You'd better get off the fells,' he said. 'Unless you want what happened to that sheep to happen to you.'

'I didn't touch your bloody sheep.'

I thought he was going to punch me but he swung away and stalked after his dog.

'Nutter!' I shouted.

He was lost to cloud. I rubbed my throat then started downhill. He shouted something but when I turned, I couldn't see him. His voice came again through the mist: 'There's a wolf up here, you understand?'

I told him to go and be friendly with his sheep, only I didn't use those exact words.

*

When I emerged from the cloud-line, the air felt mild, and when I looked back at the cloud cutting off the mountain it was as if everything that had happened there was a dream.

In the cottage, Nan was making up a fire, scrunching newspaper at the grate. She threw a glance over her shoulder, saw me wet and muddy, and resumed her work.

She had such a dismissive expression on her face I didn't even ask her if she was feeling any better, just went upstairs to change.

Mum's old room. A faded perfume. The worn rug. Mum had been young when she'd been here. That was after Nan and her husband, my grandfather, divorced.

'I'm going out,' I said, coming downstairs fast, putting on my school shoes and banging out the front door.

Debs

The village was busy with tourists in bright jackets and fancy boots. Outside the bicycle shop the bicycle-shop guy was leaned over a mountain bike, adjusting something. I had stopped to watch, wishing I'd been able to bring my bike up north, when I saw Steve Scott and his whiny sidekick Alex.

Beside me, a bus lurched to the pavement and its door opened with a gasp.

Alex spotted me and said something to Steve, who lifted his head, and I was about to give him a nod of recognition when he got that amused look on his face and I felt a rush of dread, so instead I stepped onto the bus. As the doors closed I watched them hurry towards me, Steve in front, weaving to avoid the tourists. When the bus moved off they broke into a run and as Steve reached the bus he slapped a side-window. He had an animal expression on his face, baring his teeth with the effort of running, but the driver did not stop.

*

We drove along the valley. Motion brought it all back, the grey wolf in the middle of the road, the bang. I clutched the bar of the seat in front of me, shut my eyes. When I opened them, a car was sweeping round the corner towards us. I went rigid. The car zipped past. I tried to concentrate on the conversation of two old women. They were talking about a sheep killed on the hills. 'One of the tourists' dogs, I shouldn't wonder,' said one.

In Kendal, we pulled up near the train station. I walked up the ramp to the platform and sat on a bench. The sky was huge and you could see across the rolling hills a long way. The gentle view helped, and I began to calm down. A few people were waiting for the train. The first one was for Carlisle. The other destinations sounded just fine too: Lancaster, Oxenholme, Manchester. I imagined escaping to one of those places. Away from here, and all the junk of car journeys and bus journeys and school and a wolf. Then I wondered what I'd do when I got there, and decided not much, so I got off the bench and headed into town.

Kendal had a few cobbled streets, a river, closed-down shops. Some boys I recognised from my year were gathered in a small knot outside the arcade. I felt their eyes on me as I walked past. The place felt as bad as school and I was glad to get off the street and into the library. There, at least, it was peaceful. I sat in the reference area, put my head back, and stared at the old-fashioned glass roof.

When I was young Mum used to take me to the library in town. It had a large wooden ship with cushioned benches round the sides. She loved reading. Dad loved being outdoors. Sometimes on a Saturday he'd take me to visit one of the places he was working. While checking plants, he'd stop to point things out to me: a toppled phoenix oak with new shoots sprouting, a beech tree with heart rot, hollowed out by fungus. When you thought about it, Mum and Dad had it worse than me. Because they had lost more – they had lost their lives, whereas I had only lost them.

I wondered if you can feel, after you die, the loss of your own life. If you feel anything at all. Or if you don't exist in any way at all.

I sat up.

A student was bent over his files; a shabby guy was reading a newspaper. Both absorbed. I browsed the shelves, reaching the wildlife section, where I took down books on woods. Pictures of great trees. That's what Dad worked on. I felt a wave of emotion, like I was going to cry. It passed and I saw the word on the spine of another book – *wolves*. I thought of that animal in the middle of the road and part of me wanted to leave the library right then, to get as far away as possible. But part of me wanted to face it, to kill it and so, my heart pattering, I reached out and put my finger on top of the book and pulled it down. The cover showed a grey and white wolf. The spine creaked as I opened it. A wolf-pack in deep snow. A wolf swimming a lake. A wolf devouring prey.

What does the wolf want?

I closed the book with a snap and took it to the issue desk.

'Card, please,' the librarian said.

I stared.

'I need your library card, please.'

'I don't have one.'

She opened her hands in a helpless gesture.

Someone said, 'You seem to have a problem with libraries,' and I turned to find Debs behind me. Only now she wore her nose stud, earrings, plus crookedly applied eyeliner. She also wore a black shoelace necklace, a long raincoat over a black T-shirt, and black, ripped jeans. She seemed somewhere between a goth, a punk, and a homeless person. Her breath smelled of spearmint and cigarettes and her jaw was working *smackety-smack* at chewing gum.

She took the wolf book from me and handed it with her card to the librarian.

'You can't take it out for him,' the woman said.

'I'm not. I'm really into' – she read the cover – 'wolves.'

The woman pursed her mouth sourly, seemed on the point of arguing, then issued the book.

'Thank you *so* much,' said Debs, wobbling her head sweet-sarcastic before marching out.

I followed.

The book struck me in the chest and I had to grab it to stop it from falling. Debs marched on without breaking her stride.

I didn't know whether to go after her or not and in the end I just called, 'Thanks!' but my voice sounded too loud and the only response it got from Debs was a vertical hand giving me the finger over her shoulder.

She was definitely weird.

I wandered the streets for a while until I came to a fast-food place where I thought I'd read my new book and where, alone at a table, reading her book and her headphones in, sat Debs.

For a few seconds I thought about leaving because she hadn't seen me yet, then I thought, *why should I?* While I queued for a soft drink I watched her; she was immersed in her reading, and in the end I decided that she *had* helped me even if she was up herself.

'Hey,' I said, approaching her table with my drink.

She lifted her eyes and stared sullenly at me from under her fringe.

'Why'd you get that book out for me?' I asked.

Her eyes didn't leave mine.

I repeated the question.

Her eyes dipped to her book.

I tore the wrapper off my straw, speared the plastic

top of my drink, sat down opposite and opened my new book.

'What do you think you're doing?' she said, sitting up and taking out her headphone buds.

'Same as you. What's ... Sylvia Plath like?'

'Did I say you could join me?'

'Why'd you get this out for me?'

She opened her mouth extra wide, showing a grey wriggle of chewing gum, then chewed with a revoltingly open mouth. She kept eye contact, too, like she was daring me to call her on it.

'Why?' I insisted, ignoring her mouth-chew.

'Because I don't like one person telling another person what they can do, like that librarian did. You can go now.'

I smiled sweetly, which seemed to annoy her, because she put her earphones back in, turned up the volume, and returned to Sylvia Plath.

'My name's Luke,' I said.

She flicked a page.

'What's yours?'

She didn't lift her eyes from her book.

'Is Sylvia Plath any good, then?'

She didn't respond. I slurped my drink then I put it down, leaned forward, and pulled out her earphone cords.

It was like she'd suffered an electric shock. Her eyes blazed, her face seemed to get thinner. Then her gaze fell on my drink and she snatched it up. She held it like she was going to hurl it at me.

I shielded myself with the wolf book. 'You throw that and this book gets it. And it's on your library card so you'll have the fine.'

She weighed the cup as if she was weighing her decision. Her mouth was a tight line and her eyes might have combusted there was that much spark in them. Suddenly she shrugged, put down my drink, slumped back and returned to reading Sylvia Plath.

'What's she write about?' I said.

'Nothing you'd understand.'

'Go on, tell me.'

'Pain. And suffering.'

'That what you into, then?'

'What are you into, Luke?'

'Remember my name, then?'

'What do you want?'

I glanced around the fast-food place then back at her. 'What's your name?'

She didn't answer. I took a sip of my drink.

'Debs,' she said. Then, after a pause, she said, 'So why'd you start a new school?'

'My parents died and I've come to live with my nan.'

She didn't say anything for a moment, studying me carefully. Then she said, 'What's your nan like?'

'She's a bit antisocial.'

'That where you get it from, is it?' she said.

'You can talk.'

She ignored this. 'Why'd you want that book on wolves, anyway?'

I slurped my drink. 'There's a wolf killing sheep on the mountains.'

This surprised her for some reason. 'Everyone says it's a mad dog,' she said warily.

'It's a wolf.'

She seemed to think about that for a while. The atmosphere had changed a bit. It felt slightly more relaxed. She went back to reading, and I opened my book. After a while, I said, 'What were you listening to?'

'The Young Savages.'

'Can I have a listen?'

'No.'

'Go on.'

She handed over a headphone bud, which I placed in my ear. Violent screeching. I handed it back. She studied me, then snorted with what seemed contempt.

'Well,' she said, standing. 'I have to go.'

She held out her hand, arm straight. We shook. It felt very formal like we were explorers from some previous century meeting in a foreign land.

'Bye, Debs,' I said.

'Bye, Luke,' she said, half as if she was bored by me, half as if she was puzzled.

Glass

By the time I reached the village it was dusk. Cars whooshed by, headlamps dazzling. I trudged back on the verge and headed up the lane. A few spears of gold light shone down the valley but the woods were dark. I was determined to keep an even pace and not be freaked-out by them but when I entered their deep quiet, the stillness pressed on me like a weight. *Keep an even pace*, I told myself, *keep an even pace.*

Dad had felt safe in a wood but I was scared. The plastic cover of the big hardback scuffed loudly against my leg. I reached the gate to the cottage and stepped across the cattle grid.

Nan's car wasn't on the turning circle.

'Hello!' I called, coming in.

The cottage was silent.

I switched on the central heating and started clearing last night's fire. As I picked out the charcoal I pictured Nan's face, hunched over the steering wheel, head nodding. I shut my eyes tight and when I opened them, the grate's soft ash felt the most desolate thing in the world. I went to the hallway to phone Nan. I'd tell her to drive back carefully, and started dialling. Then I heard something.

I stood motionless.

I put down the phone. I entered the kitchen. I tightened the tap, just in case it was that which had made the sound.

Pat.

For a while I listened but heard nothing. I sneaked out of the kitchen, along the hallway. When I reached the bin by the front door, I eased out the cudgel.

Pat.

I froze.

It was coming from the study.

I went up the hallway, hardly breathing, cudgel ready.

For perhaps half a minute I stood near the door, listening. Then I stepped forward and opened the door. It swung wide and I stepped inside. A weak ray of sunlight fell on the wall. A blue butterfly flew across the room and butted against the glass. *Pat.* For several seconds I watched it bump, then I leaned the cudgel against the wall and went over. The butterfly clung for a moment on the glass, opening and closing its wings. I tried to cup it in my hands but it fluttered up and landed again so I undid the latch and pushed the frame and it vanished into the cold dusk. The papers on the bureau rustled in the thin breeze. Leaves shuffled on the turning circle. I shut the window. There was a thick envelope on top of

Nan's papers. In the last gold light I read the handwritten name on the front.

Rachel.

Mum's name.

The flap was open and inside were lots of papers.

A purr sounded from the cattle grid, lights swept across the room.

I hurried out. Nan appeared and began putting the shopping away. She didn't say anything. She walked right past me and turned off the heating. She finished putting things away, lifted a pack of mince, stabbed it with a long knife so it popped loudly. Then she turned to face me.

I was meant to say something, it felt like. I didn't know what.

She turned away, took out a huge frying pan, clattered it onto the ring, shook the lump of mince in with a heavy thump. Then she started bashing at the solid chunk of meat which was beginning to sizzle in the pan.

'I told you not to go in my study.'

I wondered why she never spoke about Mum.

I wanted to ask her but I couldn't. I went upstairs.

Bus

Early morning. The house was still and dark. Outside, the trees were dark too, like they were waiting for light to get a move on. I dressed quick. Cold feet on the thin rug. Bedside lamp on, squinting against the bulb. In the bathroom I brushed my teeth, splashed my face. Didn't put the hot water on; the boiler was next to Nan's room and made too much noise, plus Nan said we had to save money. Which seemed odd to me; I thought lawyers had plenty of money. Nan was already up, reading a boring document, her green mug steaming on the table. She eyed me over her reading glasses. I got out a bowl. The cereal was already on the table with a quarter of a pint of milk. I began to pour.

'Don't use it all.'

I finished the milk.

I could feel her stare. I crunched. She went back to reading, scribbling with a pencil in the margin. Sipping tea.

I thought about the maths homework I was meant to have done.

'I made you some sandwiches.'

I stopped mid-crunch.

It was the first time she'd made me sandwiches.

'Thanks,' I mumbled through cornflakes and sleepiness.

She didn't respond, got up and boiled the kettle.

I finished my cereal, put bread under the grill.

She put a mug of tea beside my bowl.

'I don't drink tea,' I said, searching the cupboard.

'What are you trying to find?'

'Nothing,' I said, still rooting. 'Did you get any more jam?'

'No,' she said. 'How did you sleep?'

I shrugged. I didn't want to tell her about the dream that had woken me. I didn't remember it, but I could remember the sense of dread.

I smelled burning and clattered out the grill-tray with blackened toast.

'Here,' she said. She scraped off the worst and handed me a de-burned slice.

When I'd had breakfast and was ready, I paused at the front door. I wasn't sure whether to say goodbye or not. I could see her standing just inside the kitchen, like she was listening for me.

'Bye!' I called.

'Goodbye,' she said stiffly.

The wooded lane was as dark as a tunnel but with the sun coming up it didn't feel as bad as it had on Saturday, and I could push my fear back. It didn't go away entirely, just stayed at a distance, at the edges of my mind until I was on the slope to the main road.

There were two bus stops in the village, one in the middle and one at the edge. I always waited at the edge, where I could be alone and prepare myself. By the time it reached this stop, the bus would have picked up kids from all along the valley before the journey of the last few miles. It would be almost full. I heard it before I saw it, groaning into the village like a complaining old person. And then it came, lit up in the pale dawn, eerie shapes moving behind fogged windows. The breaths of nearly a hundred kids.

The indicator blinked, the bus slowed. It stopped with a creak of brakes. The pneumatic doors hissed open and I stepped into animal chaos.

Standing room only. People talked about football, music, what they did at the weekend, sealed away in headphones, in noisy or muttered conversations. I had to push past. I had to keep my fear down. The bus lurched off. I tottered and gripped the steel bar at the top of a seat. My body heated up. I unzipped my jacket. I shut my eyes.

Someone touched my hand and I let go of the seat-bar.

'Jesus, you're nervous today.'

Debs.

No piercings in or make-up.

'So,' she said, 'Good weekend? Read any good books about wolves?'

'Um, yeah. How about you?'

'Read Ted Hughes. Had an argument with my dad. Hey, what do wolves eat?'

'Um … Mice. '

'Mice?'

'As well as bigger things, obviously. Why?'

'My dad says a wolf is on the fells killing the flocks.'

'Oi, Eggs Benedict!' someone shouted. 'Got a new boyfriend?'

Debs hoisted a hand and gave the finger to a baying chorus of laughs.

I checked up the aisle to see who had shouted – Steve Scott, his hair gelled blacker than black water, his skin pale as dough.

'Hey, Lucas, mate!' He was sprawled like a king on the high back seat, flanked by Alex and the giant Zed. 'Come and join us. Budge up.' He gave Alex a shove and patted the seat beside him.

I glanced at Debs. She had her eyes on me to see what I would do.

The bus swung round a bend, I missed my grip on the seat-bar, the bus strained uphill and I was thrown towards the back. I scanned faces, began to feel dizzy.

'Come on, mate!' said King Steve. For a moment

it was just him and me on the bus, everyone else clouded out.

Out of the crowd, red-nosed Malky grew clear. Our eyes locked and, almost imperceptibly, he shook his head.

The bus lurched as the driver changed gears and I nearly fell into the gap between Alex and Steve.

'A'wright, mate, how's it going?'

I could feel Steve's elbow in my ribs. Not deliberate, I reckoned, it was just a tight fit.

'You ill? You seem a bit ill?'

'I'm fine.'

'Does he look sick to you, Alex?'

Alex's face swung close to mine, stinking of crisps. It was the first time I'd seen him properly by daylight, and he had acne, no chin, and a narrow face. He looked a bit ferret-like.

'Bit of a twat's what he seems to me,' Alex said.

'Oi!' Steve's fist shot out and he thumped Alex on the arm. 'What happened to you on Saturday? Saw you in the village. Didn't want to say hello?'

'I was going into town.'

'Oh yeah? Do anything good?'

'Um … had a look around.'

'Boring, isn't it? I told you this place was a living death.'

We clattered along, branches banging and twigs scraping against the roof and windows. A girl made a

87

porthole with her sleeve and I saw the lake, right beside us. My stomach turned over and I faced away. Zed, huge, his chin hid in his zip-up top, swivelled his eyes to mine. His face had no expression. It was impossible to know what he thought. I locked my eyes on the floor. It was stuck with black spots of ancient chewing gum.

'I reckon you get travel sick,' said Steve Scott.

I glanced at him, startled.

'I can tell things about people.' I believed him. 'See him, for instance.' He pointed at Malky, who was fishing in his coat pocket for his handkerchief. 'He's happy with a quiet life. He wants to be left in peace. Plus, he's a dreamer like you.'

That's what Nan had said – that I spent my whole life daydreaming.

'And her.' Now he pointed at Debs. 'She's got no friends and she hates herself for it.'

He turned to me so his face was only a few inches from mine. I was trying not to show my fear. 'Don't worry, mate,' he said, 'I won't tell anyone what you're scared of.' Now I wanted to pee. 'So, why'd you live with your nan, then?'

The bus groaned as we started up a steep hill. I wanted to close my eyes. I wanted to get off. I wanted to breathe fresh air.

'Are your parents divorcing or something?'

I could feel it inside me, like the fact was at the bottom

of a depth of water, rising up. And suddenly I wanted to say it. To tell him.

'They're dead.'

'How they die?' asked Steve without missing a beat, as if it was the easiest thing in the world for parents to die – which it is.

'Car accident,' I said.

He turned away and gazed out the window for a while, not saying anything. I stared ahead. Stared like a zombie, thinking nothing.

'That's rubbish, mate,' said Steve, turning to face me again, without any sarcasm or amusement, which I was so grateful for I started to tremble like I was going to cry. 'That's really rubbish.'

I nodded. It was. It was.

Firs

The day passed in a brain-haze. I couldn't hear what the teachers said. It was like my thoughts were too loud. Only, I didn't have any thoughts. No, it was more like my brain was a piece of software on a computer continually loading. I spent most of the day drawing circles on my books and filling them in. Except in Miss Andrews' class. I couldn't even draw circles there. My eyes kept wandering to the classroom walls. The bright pictures had come down and there was just this red card running around the middle of the room awaiting new pictures.

One good, amazing thing – not a single teacher asked me about my missing homework.

*

At lunch Steve Scott came and found me and asked if I wanted to play football in the Cage. So I did. I didn't have to speak to anyone.

Steve was ruthless in the tackle. Frenzied, almost. Some people hung back when he had the ball and wouldn't tackle him. And when they did it was like small explosions. One stocky kid limped away, shin-kicked, and

I noticed him throwing sullen glances at Steve for the rest of the game. We played well. Alex was on the other side, and once when I got the ball, running up the wing, he swiped my ankle so I fell headlong. Steve erupted into laughter. When I got to my feet Alex was still glaring like the trip was repayment for something. But I didn't know for what.

The bell went for the end of lunch.

'Mate, good game, hey?' said Steve, grinning, arm round my shoulder, heading for the Cage door.

'Yeah.'

The stocky kid who Steve had kicked was putting on his sweatshirt and picking up his bag.

'You'd have been sent off in a proper match,' the stocky kid said.

'Don't be a bad loser, mate,' said Steve.

Something seemed to settle in the stocky kid's face and he stepped across to us. 'You shouldn't be on a football pitch,' he said, 'you should be in a –'

I didn't get to hear where Steve Scott should be because Steve punched the stocky kid in the stomach. The stocky kid doubled over. There was a shocked silence. Steve walked on, his arm sliding round my shoulder again.

'So me and Danny are going out Thursday night, fancy coming?'

We walked across the playground. The boy had been hit hard enough to be injured, badly. People were funnelling for afternoon lessons. I checked over my shoulder. A few of the boy's mates were gathered round him. Alex and Zed were walking along in our wake.

I ducked my head from under the arm.

'Gotta go,' I said, 'or I'll be late.'

'See ya, mate,' Steve called after me, and it sounded sarcastic as hell.

*

After school, I went to the computer room. It was almost empty so I took a seat by the windows. Down the hallway, doors banged as kids rushed out of their classrooms for home. I went online and read what Mitesh and everyone had been doing since I'd left. Nothing unusual: school, hanging out. But now their lives seemed like strangers' lives that had nothing to do with me.

I searched online for wolves.

Palms banged corridor doors.

Wolves choose their prey with great care, I read. No one knows what causes their decision.

I lifted my head. Outside, a kid was walking the trail that crossed the field at the back, heading for a line of fir trees. A car crackled across the playground and careered round the corner.

When the wolf chooses its kill, something strange happens – the prey senses it's been chosen. If the animal bolts, that's when the wolf attacks. If the prey holds its nerve and remains where it is, sometimes the wolf backs off.

The lone kid had gone. The trail led to a darker patch in the fir trees, an opening. The low chugging hum and swish of a buffing machine approached along the corridor.

If the prey bolts, most of the time the wolf will catch it in seconds. If the wolf has to chase for more than a few minutes, it will usually give up. But sometimes, on rare occasions, the wolf will pursue its prey for hours. Very occasionally, for days. One scientist used a radio collar to track a wolf for more than one hundred miles while it pursued a caribou. Through forests. Across rivers.

Someone left and I looked up to find the computer room empty. The gap in the fir trees had taken on the shape of a mouth. And that group of fir trees seemed, in that strange dull light that comes mid-afternoon when the sun has fallen behind the mountains, an elongated face.

I wondered how long the wolf-dog had waited on the road for us – for me and Mum and Dad. A few minutes? Half an hour? Longer? Then I thought of that sheep on the fells, that sudden wound across its throat. The far beat of footsteps, then the bang of the corridor doors, the boom of heels. *Thump, thump, thump.*

And I thought of the wolf.

Thump thump thump.

The footsteps reached the computer room. A raven flew from the fir trees. The footsteps passed. In the darkness of the fir trees, something moved.

As carefully as I could, I gathered my things, and left.

*

By the time the bus reached the village, the sun had slid behind the mountains. I hesitated at the foot of the lane. The wind blew over the fields, a dog howled long and longingly. I started up the wooded lane.

A raven in the empty field bounced about, crowing with laughter.

I kept my pace steady.

I went under the trees, my stomach tight, my breath shallow.

As I approached the cattle grid, something thumped softly behind me onto the tarmac. I didn't hear anything else, I was running, my soles slapping the lane. I leapt the cattle grid, a swish of my clothes and schoolbag, then the crunch of gravel as I sprinted across the turning circle. I fumbled for my door key.

I slammed the door behind me so hard the door-knocker cracked against the door.

Saucepans rattled gently. There was a smell of beef and rice.

'You're late,' Nan called.

I ran upstairs.

From Nan's room, I saw the autumn leaves whirl around the turning circle.

Nothing else was there.

When my mind had settled and my heart had stopped racing, I went downstairs. The kitchen windows ran with condensation. In the cutlery drawer I found a knife – a six-inch silver blade with a black plastic handle. I slid it up my sleeve, went upstairs and hid it under my pillow.

After dinner, on the local news there was another story about sheep killed on the fells.

Chair

The stars in the frozen sky. The mountain, deep in frost's fur.

Something crunched. The sound frosty grass might make under a foot.

All I could hear was the vast silence of the empty sky and the white water on the mountain –

Crunch.

I gripped the plastic handle of the knife and slipped from my bed. I crawled across the cold rug. I lifted my head between curtain and sill.

Everything was still and bright. The garden was empty. I scanned the woods, the field, the fell.

A draught ran up my back and I went back to bed, but not before I had taken the chair and leaned it against the door.

*

The rest of that second week: grim, dark. Break-times I joined Malky for his fantasy game. I avoided Steve Scott and his idiot mates. No sign of Debs, except one morning I heard Steve shout above the bus crowd, 'Oi,

Eggs Benedict, your dad lost it lately?' and everyone laughed.

Evenings I sat with Nan, who either read her big book on the miners' strike or worked in her study. I thought about the envelope with my mum's name on it. That week Nan was home before me each afternoon so it meant I couldn't go in her study, unless I sneaked down in the night, and I didn't want to be caught doing that.

On the rare days that the skies were clear, I could see more snow on the peaks. I kept watch from the window, the light chill, the knife close, the chair propped under the handle.

Bike

At the end of that second week, on Saturday, I was woken by Nan knocking on my door then coming in, clattering the chair to the floor.

'What's this for?' she said.

'Wuh – ?'

She righted the chair, whipped open the curtains.

'It's gone nine. You're not lazing about all day. Get up.'

'Uh – '

'I'm not joking,' she said, banging out.

*

Spider webs shone in the misty sun. They were everywhere, hung up between plants, on the fence, across windows. Autumn's the time of the spiders. Fat sacs huddled in the middle of big targets, waiting for grub. It was the dew made their webs shine. The lawn silver with it. I went to the shed. I had a plan for the bus.

It was dark in there, the window fogged with dirt. I stepped over cardboard boxes to my goal – the bicycle.

Deep basket. Bulky mudguards and gear guard. Rust-dotted handlebars. The seat split and stuffing poking through. Flat tyres. I heaved it into my arms, got it out, stood it upside-down on its saddle and handlebars. I fetched a bucket of soapy water, cloths and an old toothbrush, and cleaned it. Finally I oiled it. When I cranked the pedals the back wheel span and the spokes breathed coolly on my cheek.

'It was your mother's.'

Nan stood at the kitchen door, watching me.

I remembered learning to ride – Mum's palm on the small of my back, that gentle push, coasting off, wobbling. Later, the three of us used to cycle together.

'So, have you got it working, then?'

'Tyres are flat.'

Nan folded her arms like she was settling down for some entertainment.

'I don't want an audience,' I said.

'What? I'm enjoying this.'

'I need a pump and a repair kit.'

Reluctantly, Nan went into the shed. She was gone a long time but returned with a long, dirty white tube and a small tin box.

I couldn't see how the pump worked, and she had to pull a length of cord from the end before I understood.

'This is ancient!'

Nan snorted.

After a while, she gave up watching and went back inside.

Finally it was done, punctures fixed, seat raised, brake cables tightened. A blue bicycle.

I rapped on the sitting-room glass and gave Nan a smile of triumph. She opened the window and, holding the window lever, considered the bike. Then she looked at me and said, 'Have you done your homework yet?'

She knew how to ruin a moment.

'I need the internet for it.'

'I haven't got internet.'

'Well, I need the internet to do it, Nan.'

She studied me. 'I'll get it, then.'

She shut the window with a bump.

*

Nan said she was going into town to deliver items to the food bank and asked if I wanted to go with her. I said no. 'Suit yourself,' she said. Once she had rattled over the cattle grid, I went into the study to seek out the envelope with Mum's name on it.

It struck me that Mum was all that Nan and I had in common. If it wasn't for Mum, I'd have nothing to do with Nan and she would have nothing to do with me.

Morning shadow dimmed the study. The dark oval dining table was stacked with more papers than usual. The envelope wasn't on top of the bureau where it had been. I shifted work papers. Dear Mr This, Dear Ms That. Big binder files. A laptop. Her green mug. No envelope.

I opened the bureau drawers.

More papers. Some tied with string. But the bottom drawer held other kinds of documents. A file marked 'Medical' that I decided not to open. Letters from the bank. Bank statements. Nan seemed to work for almost nothing. But no fat envelope bearing the name Rachel.

There was one drawer, though, that was locked.

I searched for the key in the little trays at the top of the bureau but found only paperclips, drawing pins and staples.

I went up to Nan's room. It was neat. All she had out was her heavy book on the miners' strike, which lay on the bedside cabinet, a hairbrush on a chest of drawers, and her pink dressing gown, which hung on a bed-post. The bedsheets were tucked tight. I opened the drawer of the bedside cabinet. Silver packets of pills, tubs of tablets. In the wardrobe smart jackets, her bags, a few pairs of shoes, and drawers with her underwear, T-shirts and jeans. But no envelope.

And no key.

The Dilapidated Hut

When I freewheeled the blue bike down the hill to school, the crowds were gathering. Probably for the latest kill. As I passed one group, I swear a girl made the comment, 'There goes Death Boy.' I scooted in under the Perspex racks, locked my bike with a brand-new D-lock, and headed for the main building.

Steve appeared from nowhere. Put an arm round my shoulder.

'Ignore her,' he said. 'People say cruel things.'

He didn't have the sarcastic half-smile but the arm-round-the-shoulder felt sarcastic. Beneath his gel-black hair, in his white-white face, his eyes were giving nothing away. Alex was with him, ferrety. Zed too, looking stupid in his school jumper because he was the size of a nightclub bouncer. Perhaps he *was* a nightclub bouncer at the weekends.

Steve stopped so the crowd had to flow round us. 'Were you there when they died?'

His eyes had the faintest of flickers.

'It must have been tough,' he went on, and I didn't know if he meant that kindly or not.

I shrugged.

'So you did, then – you saw them dead.'

'Gotta go,' I said, and marched.

It was only two weeks to half term. If I could keep going till then, I'd have some respite. From Steve and his stupid mates who went round together like an animal pack or a tribe from some faraway country named Stazakstan or something. That would be right – Steve, Zed and Alex, the Stazaks of Stazakstan.

As I flowed with the crowd I thought how I'd be free from them and from everyone else too. The whole carnivorous, murdering zoo.

*

The field between school and the line of fir trees that had spooked me was high-grassed, uncut, and it had a dilapidated hut in the middle of it. I'd taken to going there to avoid the Stazaks – and, one morning break, coming round the corner I found the usual stack of wet pallets but, leaned against them, smoking a cigarette and chewing gum, I also found Debs.

She was startled to see me but recovered herself and nodded a greeting.

I nodded back.

'You can join me if you want,' she said.

I nearly told her I didn't need her permission to be there but decided it was probably unwise to antagonise her. On the top pallet beside her lay a book by someone called Emily Brontë.

'That any good?'

She didn't answer, just sucked on her cigarette.

'Did you know a wolf can hear you from up to five miles away and smell you from a mile away?' I said.

'Yeah?'

'Yeah.'

After a bit, I started thinking the silence might go on forever. I prodded the Emily Brontë book and said, 'Did you finish that Sylvia Plath book, then?'

In response she took another long drag. She kept her cigarette before her face and when she smoked only her wrist moved, with a sharp, attention-grabbing and dismissive flick that went to and from her lips. Now she flicked her cigarette away from her pursed lips and blew out a long breath of smoke, and I blew out a great sigh.

'How come you're into wolves, then?' she said.

I looked at the fir trees.

'I saw one near where I used to live,' I replied.

'I didn't think there were any wolves in Britain.'

'There aren't.'

'What was it like?'

The question surprised me. 'Like a dog but different.'

'Different how?'

'Dunno.'

She snorted dismissively.

'A dog is lazy,' I said. 'A wolf is serious.'

She nodded thoughtfully. 'What did it do, this wolf?'

'Walked into a hedge.'

I picked up her book. On the flyleaf, in green ink with a smiley face at the end, was her name – Deborah Benedict. That name was familiar.

She snatched the book from me.

She wasn't leaning on the pallets any more but stood facing me squarely.

'Don't touch my stuff!'

'Okay,' I said. 'Where do you live?'

'What?'

'Are you in the farmhouse above the village?'

'Are you a stalker or something?'

'No. My nan's house is further along the valley, and your name's Benedict, that means we're neigh –'

'Go away!'

'But we're neighbours. Eve Lansdale's my nan.'

'I didn't ask you to come bothering me. Go away.'

'This is *my* spot. I come here every break.'

'Listen, you weirdo, go away!'

Her face was angry and she looked stupid.

'You know that Sylvia Plath?' I said.

She chewed and smoked, smoked and chewed, but I kept staring and eventually she said, 'What about her?'

'If you met her, would you be such an idiot as you are now?'

Her cheeks flushed and I walked away.

'Sylvia Plath is *dead*, you moron,' she called after me.

I wheeled.

'I don't want to hang out with you any more,' I called.

'That a joke, is it?'

'No. *You're* a joke.'

She flicked her cigarette at me and a few tender little orange sparks hissed into the wet grass.

I marched on, giving her the finger over my shoulder, Eggs Benedict style.

*

After that, I kept running into Debs: in the library, in the hallways. Once I was staring straight ahead at a long table in the canteen when she walked up the aisle opposite seeking a spare seat. Our eyes locked for a millisecond. She blushed faintly and glanced away.

The rest of the week went by. Then the next started – the last before half term. A routine developed: a sullen breakfast in the mountain-shadowed kitchen with Nan, then my cycle to school where I spent break-times listening to Malky sniff and trumpet about orcs, giants, goblins, and elves.

I didn't take in any of my lessons. I had trouble with words, understanding them, putting them on the page. I was still forging Nan's signature on the homework sheet. Miss Andrews hadn't said anything about it yet. And none of the other teachers seemed to have noticed. It was like they were all only vaguely aware of me. Like I was tolerated, or I wasn't really there, like a ghost.

I wondered if I was dead, if I'd died in the car accident and *was* a ghost, only I didn't know it yet.

One evening Nan came into the sitting room where I was browsing her books and asked me to help her make the fire, so I slid back the Emily Brontë novel I'd been looking at and went to help.

She kneeled on the hearth, sighing deeply with the effort. She was good at building a fire. She showed me how the balled newspaper went on first, then the best way to place kindling before the larger pieces of wood went on.

'Why don't you ever use the heating?' I asked.

'I will do when I get my banker's bonus.'

'But you're not a banker, are you?'

She looked incredulous, then handed me the box of matches.

'Oh, that a joke, is it?' I said, lighting the fire. 'Anyway, I thought lawyers earn loads.'

'I'm not that kind of lawyer.'

The flames took hold.

'Did Mum do this when she was here?' I asked, facing her.

For a moment she seemed lost then she stared at the fire.

'Until she went to university.' The flame roared softly through the paper.

'Didn't she come back when term ended, then?'

'Hardly at all. Then she stopped altogether.'

'Why?'

She was still staring at the fire. I opened my mouth to ask about the envelope in the bureau but she got off her knees and, groaning, stood. 'I'm getting old.'

'Why don't you talk about her?'

She went out without answering and left me with the small, crackling fire.

Death Boy

I nearly made it to half term without anything going wrong.

It was the last Friday. English was after lunch, and the red card that ran in a belt around the room now contained pictures of huskies and wolves. Like us, Miss Andrews' other years must have been doing *The Call of the Wild*. The kids had drawn dogs pulling sleds across snow and fighting one another, and wolves howling at the moon. I felt them. All around, their devouring teeth. I wanted the lesson to end. When it finally did, I made a dash for the door.

'Lucas, can I speak to you, please?'

I tried to get out but there was a knot of kids at the door.

'Lucas Pettifer!'

I trudged up to her desk.

'You've missed a lot of homework,' she said. 'Why is that?'

'I don't feel well?'

'You were well enough to come to school.'

'No, I don't feel well now. I have to go.'

The edge of her desk had a teardrop scratched deep into it.

'How do you feel your first month has gone?'

I clamped my jaw tight. Felt the wolf-pack on the blood-red wall.

'Would you like to see the school counsellor?'

'Why?' My voice sounded too loud.

'About school. About being in a new place.' Then her voice changed, grew kinder. 'Your parents.'

The multi-coloured band on her wrist had a frayed end.

'Your homework record suggests things aren't right. And you're often distracted. How are things at home?'

'Home's in Somerset.'

'How are things in your grandmother's house?'

'Fine.'

'Your grandmother has been signing off that you've been doing your homework. But you haven't.'

'I'll catch up over half term. All right?' I risked meeting her gaze.

'I have to speak to her about how you're doing.'

'But Miss, I just arrived. Like you said, it takes time to settle in a new place.' I hated my whiny tone but I kept my eyes fixed on her.

She seemed to be thinking about what I had said, coming to a decision.

'Please, Miss.'

She pressed her lips together, nodded once, tightly. 'You have half term to catch up, and if you haven't, I'll speak to her.'

*

I joined the flow out of school but almost immediately stopped. Where the road came down the slope to greet the Perspex bike shelters stood two of the Stazaks: Steve with his sarcastic smile, and Alex.

'Death Boy!' shouted Alex.

'Oi,' snarled Steve, thumping Alex's arm.

I went into the bike shelter.

'That yours?' smirked Alex as I wheeled out my bike.

Steve blocked my path.

A black car braked beside us. The window buzzed down and there sat Steve's brother, Danny. His eyes stayed on me, appraising. Glanced away.

I tried to ease my bike round Steve but Alex got in the way so I tried to go the other way but he stepped across. Steve tugged his sweatshirt, which ballooned, and the pair spluttered with laughter.

'Sorry, mate.'

I pushed my bike up the slope.

'No need to be like that, mate!'

Alex shouted the worst word he could, and they laughed getting into the car.

As I pedalled uphill, I noticed Debs queuing for the

bus and she gave me a nod like she approved of how I'd dealt with Steve and Alex.

Danny's black car passed, revving so hard I nearly fell off my bike. I heard their laughter through the open window.

'See you after half term, Death Boy!' Alex called, then they were gone.

Half Term

In half term I read about the wolf. I listened to the cold stream sighing on the mountain. I searched for the envelope bearing the name *Rachel*. I even tried picking the bureau lock. It didn't work. And then it was the final day of the holiday and I had dread in my stomach. That last Sunday in October felt so final. But for the first time in weeks the mountains weren't cut off by smoky cloud. It was a beautiful, clear, bright day. I decided to visit Debs.

With my rolled-up exercise book in my inside pocket, I crossed the cattle grid. I headed up the track and soon I was high enough to see the Benedict farm – a large stone house with outbuildings. A thin path of beaten grass led towards it, about a mile away. Wind shook the grass. Below, I could see the village and, on the hills on the far side of the valley, little tarns shining in the sun.

I walked for half an hour then crashed down through stiff dead bracken. A sheepdog came out the front door and trotted across the muddy yard to an army-green Land Rover, followed by a man. The dog jumped in the back and the Land Rover drove off. I walked over to the house and banged on the door.

While I waited, I checked the nearest window. On the windowsill stood a saucer with a bar of pink soap veined with dirt, and a jug of flowers. The door opened.

A woman resembling Debs stood there. She had the same fine brown hair, the same oval face, the same button nose. She flashed me a frown I was also familiar with.

'Debs in?' I said.

'Who are you?' she said, smiling broadly, a smile I was completely unfamiliar with from knowing Debs.

'Luke.'

She went to the foot of the stairs, leaving the door wide open. She wore jeans, a thick jumper, and thick woollen socks. 'Debs!' she called, then to my surprise said to me, 'Come in,' so I did, wiping my feet and following her into a chaotic kitchen of unopened post, cereal packets, and snoozing cats. The smell of fried bacon. A giant oven on top of which another cat lounged. Radio playing Sunday-morning pop.

'She'll be down in a mo.'

I sat at the table and pushed up tight against the hot radiator. Nan never had the heating on for more than a few minutes.

'Are you in Debs' class?'

'No.' She seemed surprised. I tried to think of how we knew each other. 'She lent me a book.'

Debs' mum also seemed surprised at this.

'Where d'you live?' she said.

'Over there,' I said, pointing.

She frowned. 'D'you know Eve Lansdale, then?'

'She's my nan.'

She stared, even more surprised. She had probably heard all about Mum and Dad. I read the back of the cereal packet.

She went into the hall. 'Deborah!' she called to silence. 'Luke's here.'

The silence grew longer.

'Anyway, I'm out,' she said, taking her coat off a hook and heading for the front door. 'Enjoy your morning.'

The front door shut.

I waited. My heart thumped harder. The radiator radiated heat. A tub of butter, breadcrumbs, mugs of tea. It was a lot like home. I pictured Mum and Dad on a Sunday. We used to go out on a Sunday afternoon.

A car engine started, accelerated out of the yard, dwindled down the track.

Feet thumped on the ceiling, then down the stairs, then a silence broken by – Debs.

She wore ripped jeans, black T-shirt and her shoelace necklace, grey woolly socks pulled up her shins, and her hair was pushed back by a butterfly hair-slide.

'All right!' I said, standing up, knocking the table and spilling tea everywhere, including on me.

A cat jumped off the stove.

'Can I borrow your internet?' I said. 'I can't miss

any more assignments and I have to research the Gold Rush.'

I was holding my exercise book high up, the way people in the movies hold the bible in court.

Her glance went down and up me.

'You look like you've wet yourself,' she said.

I glanced down. 'It's tea.'

'Aren't you going to clean it off, then?'

'Nah, it'll dry.'

In the silence, the cat stretched.

'So can I use your internet?'

She gave the longest exhalation in the history of humanity. 'Wait here.'

I did just that while she thumped up the stairs and the cat trotted after her. She returned with her laptop and led me into the sitting room where a wood burner was throbbing with heat. Putting the laptop on the sofa, she opened the wood burner, put in a log shaped like a slice of pie, and clanked it shut. Flames licked behind glass.

'Call me when you're done,' she said, and stomped out.

After a minute, violent guitar music started from upstairs – The Young Savages. After a quarter of an hour of trying to read a page about the Yukon Gold Rush, I gave up. From the foot of the stairs, I shouted. She didn't answer so I went up, sourcing the atonal, unpleasant sound to a door bearing her name. I knocked.

Debs flung the door wide, glaring.

'Can you turn the music down?' I said. 'I can't concentrate.'

'Whose house is this?' she shouted over flaring guitars.

'Er … yours.'

'So why should I turn it down?'

'I can't concentrate. I can't concentrate on anything.'

She pressed her lips tight like she was deciding what to say next.

'Can you help me?' I said.

'What are you trying to do?'

'My homework?'

'I *mean*, what's it about?'

'I've got to write something about the historical … context or something of *The Call of the Wild*, which is the Gold Rush in the Yukon. Which is in north-west Canada at the end of the nineteenth century.' I tapped the corner of my forehead with a forefinger. 'Nothing goes in.'

Her face was blank.

'I'm not thick or anything.'

She flung the door in my face, the music shut off, then the door opened and she rushed past me in what felt something like fury.

'Thanks,' I said, going downstairs after her.

She sat beside me on the sofa, legs curled up, not saying anything, sometimes reading the laptop over my shoulder, sometimes reading her book (Emily Brontë).

For some reason, the words began to go into my brain. Not easily, but they transferred. It was like my brain had started to work again, like an old clock mechanism operating through sludge. I wrote sentence by disjointed sentence in my exercise book until, forty minutes later, it was done.

'Thanks,' I said.

Debs didn't respond. She was still sitting on the sofa, legs tucked under her, peering over my shoulder. Her arm rested against mine.

She put a palm out. 'Give it, then.'

She took the laptop and put it on the coffee table then crouched at the wood burner. I could see a knuckle of her spine where her T-shirt rode up. The metal door of the wood burner clanked shut.

'Did you tell anyone at school about my parents?' I said.

She looked over her shoulder at me.

'Why?'

'Some people started calling me Death Boy.'

Her face contorted. 'Scum!' Her focus drifted before returning to me. 'Who else did you tell about them?'

'Steve Scott.'

She snorted. 'Well, there you go, then.'

She turned to glare at the amber flames.

For a while we watched them.

'The wolf was in the road,' I said. 'It caused the accident.'

She twisted round again.

'My dad tried to avoid it and we crashed.'

Her face changed. The glare faded from her eyes and they seemed to grow more liquid.

'We went … upside down. I saw … Mum and Dad, you know?' My voice felt thin. I could hear the flames consuming dry wood. 'Then some people came.'

She pressed the sole of her foot with a thumb. The silence felt like it had gone on too long. I said, 'How come you're on your own at school all the time?'

She pulled her knees up to her chest then laid her cheek on her kneecap and her expression went far away. As if she was half-asleep, she said, 'I've got nothing in common with them.'

Silence, a long silence, broken by an engine coming up the hill.

'That's my dad.' She got to her feet and threw herself into an armchair, elbows on chair-arms, steepling her fingers. 'You'll love him,' she said sarcastically.

Soon we heard the back door. Almost immediately the sitting-room door quivered open and a black sheepdog flowed round the corner of the armchair. It had a white patch on its eye. After that her dad came in – the nutter farmer with glasses, eyes swimming behind thick lenses, red-nosed from the cold.

'You!' he said. His glance went to Debs. 'Is he a friend of yours?'

She crossed her arms defensively. 'Yeah. So what?'

I wasn't sure she actually meant I *was* her friend, I think she said it more to annoy him but still, it felt pretty good to hear her say it.

'Might have guessed,' he said, sniffing and taking off his tarpaulin-dull coat. He bent to undo his boots. 'Friend of the wolves, he is.'

'I'm no friend of wolves.'

He straightened slowly.

The silence went on for a few seconds while he did the Benedict super-glare that must run in the family, then he moved. He had sharp, almost aggressive movements and he fizzed out of the room.

'He's staying for lunch!' shouted Debs as he went.

She got up and shut the door, sat down again.

The door flung wide.

'If he's staying then you pair can help.'

Debs twisted her mouth and lifted her eyes heavenward.

'It's a hard life, isn't it?' her dad said. 'Get the vegetables, would you, unless that'll spoil the royal Sunday.'

Venting a deep sigh, Debs struggled from her chair and we went into the mud-strewn back porch.

'Here,' she said, handing me potatoes, carrots, parsnips, onions, and a cauliflower.

In the kitchen, her dad was bent over the sink, scrubbing his face. He dried his face with kitchen towels that he crumpled into balls and hurled into a swing-bin so hard he might have been trying to knock down skittles.

Debs joined him and they moved about, clearing spaces, getting out utensils, washing up. The oven was heating the kitchen so fiercely the window onto the yard steamed.

'Kill any wolves this morning, then, Dad?'

'Oh, yeah, a wolf or two.'

'He thinks there's a wolf on the fells,' she explained to me.

'Oh, there's one there all right.'

'Everyone thinks you're mad, Dad.'

'Since when did you care what people think? Anyway, *he* believes me.' Her dad pointed his vegetable knife at me.

'He's got a name, you know,' said Debs.

Her dad was still staring at me. He did weird stillness better than anyone.

'It's Luke,' I said.

'Oh, he believes me, all right,' her dad said, and turned back to chop vegetables.

With her forefinger, Debs made madman circles at her temple.

A car engine came up the hill and an estate bumped onto the yard.

'Thank God, some sanity,' said Debs.

A minute later, her mum came in.

'Hey, love. Oh, you've started.'

'Luke's staying for lunch. Dad's been freaking him out about wolves.'

'Sheridan,' Debs' mum scolded.

Sheridan Benedict. The farmer from the telly, the one Nan said was weird. I hadn't connected that person on TV with the nutter on the fell. I should have done. It was obvious now. My brain definitely didn't work properly.

'Good meeting?' said Sheridan Benedict to his wife.

'Yes. Your gran was there, Luke. She's going to the local MP.'

'What about?'

'Closure of the village chemists.' To her husband she said, 'Eve Lansdale's his gran.'

'Is she now?' he said. 'Roast's in. Cup of tea, love?'

'Please. I'll do Yorkshire pudding. Is there any more ice cream?'

'Not sure.' He was different with her. A bit gentler.

'Could you check? As we've got a guest.' She gave me a smile.

He poured her a mug of tea.

'Come and give me a hand with this ice cream, wolf boy. I want to show you something.'

'His name's Luke,' said Debs.

I threw a glance at Debs, who made a face as if to

122

say she couldn't do anything about him, then I followed Sheridan Benedict outside.

I tried to keep as much distance between him and me as possible.

We entered a gloomy outbuilding with a concrete floor. I stayed by the door. In the corner stood a white freezer the length of a coffin. It popped gummy seals to exhale a frozen breath and he bent right in, head lost in frost, chucking boxes and bags about. On the wall in the grainy light hung a giant map of the Lakes – the mountains spread like the open fingers of hands, the long lakes between. And stuck in the map, coloured pins. Red and blue. Dotted here and there.

'The red are the kills, the blue sightings.'

Sheridan Benedict stood holding in both hands a tub of vanilla ice cream. 'That's what I wanted to show you. I'm going to hunt that wolf down and shoot it. And I won't stop until I've killed it.'

*

Debs and I watched a stupid US serial-killer show while the roast cooked. Later, her dad came down. He'd changed out of his farming clothes, shaved, and appeared almost normal. He read the paper. Then her mum called Debs in to set the kitchen table and Sheridan Benedict and me sat amid bloody crime scenes until I couldn't stand his weird silence any more and scarpered to join Debs.

Lunch

It was the best meal I'd had in months – roast beef, veg, and a dish-shaped Yorkshire pudding filled with gravy. Debs was vegetarian.

There was quiet while we ate. After a while, Sheridan Benedict said, 'Auction next week.'

'Buy anything?' asked Debs.

'Tupp, mebbe.'

Quiet. Crockery clack.

'How's that book you're reading?' asked Debs' mum.

'All right,' said Debs.

More quiet. It didn't feel bad or good, just quiet.

'How's school, Luke?' said Debs' mum suddenly. 'Settling in?'

'Yeah.'

'Takes time,' said Sheridan Benedict. The first decent thing he'd said to me. 'Teachers are fools. Most of the pupils are fools.'

'Ta, Dad,' said Debs.

'Don't take things to heart any of them do. If I took things to heart here with these two running the place,'

Sheridan Benedict went on, bobbing his knife at me, 'I'd not have survived.'

'I don't know how *we* survive with *you*, more like,' laughed Debs' mum.

Sheridan Benedict chuckled. 'What's your gran like to live with?'

'All right,' I shrugged. 'She's a bit hard work.'

Sheridan Benedict laughed. 'Too right, wolf boy.' He banged the balls of his fists on the table in rumbling applause.

'God, you're like it's the last century,' said Debs.

'The *middle* of the last century,' said her mum.

'Well, that bloody woman.'

'Sheridan!' said Debs' mum. 'That's Luke's grandmother you're talking about.'

'Well ...' he grumbled.

'They argue,' explained Debs.

'What about?' I asked.

'Politics mostly.'

Debs' mum was giving the Benedict glare to her husband.

'Apologies, wolf boy,' he said. 'Didn't mean to offend.'

'His name's Luke!'

''s all right,' I said.

He winked at me.

Debs' mum rolled her eyes at Debs, and Debs laughed.

'You know wolves?' I said, not quite sure what I was about to say. 'They don't have one leader, they have a male *and* female as head of the pack.'

It felt like everyone's eyes were on me.

'Really?' said Debs' mum.

'Yeah,' I said, feeling a bit odd because it was like they were waiting for me to say more. So I said, 'And when the pups are born, the rest of the pack, all of them, the females *and* the males, care for the pups.'

Debs murmured warmly.

'You sure about that?' said Sheridan.

'Yes. They have a rise in this hormone that makes them care for the pups. Even the males.'

'See,' said Debs, as if this solved everything. 'It's only human beings have got it wrong.'

'Well,' said her dad, as if he was surprised by this information but couldn't keep from saying something.

'Tell us more about wolves,' said Debs' mum.

I searched my mind for interesting facts while the cats snoozed on the oven, the sheepdog Polka blinked sleepily on his rug, chin on his paws, and the tinny, turned-low radio sent out happy Sunday-afternoon songs. I was about to tell them how a wolf that leaves its pack to start its own family will travel vast distances to find a new territory, when on the radio came a song I knew. The song that had been playing on the radio right at the moment of the car accident. All my feelings drained out.

'Are you all right?' said Debs' mum.

'So tell us something about wolves,' said Debs enthusiastically.

I couldn't speak and after a horrible silence of them waiting for me to say something, their conversation moved on.

Then it was like being far away, watching everything far below going on without me.

*

After lunch, when I was ready to go, Debs said, 'See you at school, then.'

'Yeah,' I said. 'Thanks for your help.'

Hands in back pockets, she shrugged one shoulder and curled a lip like it meant nothing to her.

'You'll have to come again, Luke,' said Debs' mum.

I nodded.

'You sure you don't want a lift?' said Sheridan Benedict. 'It'll be dark soon.'

'It's not far.'

'Go by the road. You don't want to be on the fells at night. That wolf has had two of my ewes.'

'For God's sake, Dad,' said Debs, turning on her heel and disappearing upstairs.

'I tell you, you don't want to be up there after nightfall.'

I said goodbye and hurried out.

Low cloud threatened but I figured I had a good hour before it got dark. I glanced back to check Sheridan Benedict was out of sight, then I headed for the mountain.

Fell

I was surprised how dark the day had got. The cloud wasn't any lower but it was definitely darker. Yet it was too early for dusk. I couldn't work it out.

Panting up through the bracken, I grew hot and was glad of the cold breeze. In the valley, a chainsaw buzzed and a dog barked and it began to grow dark.

In the distance, below and ahead of me, I could see the light from Nan's cottage flickering through the trees. Above me, the mountain and sky were nearly joined in darkness but I could just make out the long black line of the ridge-top. The chainsaw stopped buzzing.

I checked the time. It was too early for night. Then I remembered – it was the last Sunday in October, which meant the clocks had changed.

Slowly, I felt myself rooted to the spot.

I reckoned I had thirty minutes before it was pitch black. I scrambled upwards.

Soon I reached the line where the bracken ended but now I couldn't find the path I'd taken that morning, although the grass wasn't high so it would be easy to make my way even without a track. My feet tilting, I put out a hand to balance myself against the mountain and raced along its side. I made good time but gradually the incline grew steeper and I had to go more carefully and at one point I slipped and hugged the ground to stop myself from sliding down the mountain. I was terrified of going off some invisible drop. My heart beat against the fell's side. Faintly I heard the dog bark. A little above me the ground drew back as if it levelled out so I climbed up and, as I suspected, found a gentler slope, almost a ledge. I marched, stumbling at times in the draining light. Then I stopped hard.

I didn't move. It didn't move either and in the gloom we faced each other then it lowered its head and ripped something between its teeth. It was as if it was warning me what it was going to do to me. It sounded like it was tearing the earth, tearing the mountain itself. Then I knew what it was tearing.

It was tearing grass.

It was a sheep.

'Baaa!' I shouted, lunging at the ewe, which sprang away.

It cantered uphill and I hurried on, grumbling about Sheridan Benedict's stupid sheep.

Twenty yards ahead I found its pals. All the sheep grew still as I approached. It was like they had been turned to stone. The wind dropped and now I could hear the frenzy of the dog in the valley. Its savagery. Its chain

130

rattled then its bark transformed into a fearful begging. The mountain's presence grew stronger. And something else now. A creeping sensation up my back, like when you know someone is watching you. The dog stopped its din and in the silence that followed I felt an overwhelming sense that something bad was going to happen.

And then it did.

The shape appeared in front of me.

The ewes scattered, the beat of their hooves thundering through the turf.

The shape approached. But slowly.

I started downhill. Almost immediately my heel gouged turf, my back slammed the ground, and I skidded. Perhaps fifteen yards. When I stopped, I saw the shape coming after me.

I got to my feet and immediately my feet went out from under me and again I skidded down the slope. Only this time I did not stop. I slid onto scree. Little stones cracked about me. Below, thirty yards away, was an edge; beyond it, nothing.

Nothing.

My back burned with the skid as I put my arms out to stop. I spreadeagled myself, bare palms against the scree. I slewed to a halt.

Stones clinked. Dust wafted with a hiss. A little stone flicked my sleeve, bounced into the air. I didn't hear it land.

I dared to move my head. Ten yards below was the drop. Above, the scree spread in a wide expanse and at the edge of it, the shape crouched. There was no way for it to get to me unless it wanted to risk the loose ground.

I checked below again. Nan's cottage was close. I tried to keep my focus on a way down and saw, several yards diagonally below, a thin stretch of grass, right before the mountain veered off into nothing.

I spoke to myself. *Be calm.*

Moving with my arms and legs spread wide, nothing between me and the drop but treacherous loose stones, I worked my way towards the thin platform of grass.

After an age, I reached it. The turf felt good beneath my feet. I tightrope-walked along it, the strip widened, then I ran. I came to a wider slope that led all the way down to the woods and now I hurtled, gravity pulling me until I began to overbalance and, my legs unable to keep up with my body, my arms windmilled and I went over.

I somersaulted, took off from a bump, then sailed through the air for what seemed an age but was probably less than a second before dozens of fingers poked me and I cried out. For a moment I hung there while the world span around me, then I disentangled myself from what I discovered was a hawthorn bush and stood to find I was beside a dry-stone wall. Head spinning, I clambered over it and clattered through the woods.

My breaths were so gaspy and my heart walloping so loud I couldn't hear if the shape was behind me. Several times I bumped into trees and once I lost my balance and sat down hard and had to roll onto my hands and knees to stand up. When I did, my head was reeling. I wove a crazy path towards Nan's cottage, then I stepped into emptiness.

I landed on the lane, my knees jarred and my jaw clapped shut.

The cottage was thirty yards away. I ran for the light like a dizzy robot. Somehow I didn't fall over. Something thudded onto the tarmac behind me. Claws clicked in a skittering run and I sprinted. Reaching the cattle grid, I leapt. I raced over the turning circle and slammed into the door.

'Nan!' I shouted, cracking the door-knocker.

The creature landed on gravel behind me. It must have leapt the cattle grid.

The door opened and I fell in.

'Oh!' said Nan, standing above me.

'Shut the door!' I screamed.

'Why? What is –?'

I kicked the door shut so hard the knocker bounced and cracked.

'What on earth do you think you're playing at?'

'It's out there!'

I crawled into the sitting room, stood.

The turning circle was empty. And the woods?

My sweat cooled. My breaths grew steadier. I shivered.

Nothing. But I had seen it. Hadn't I seen it?

And it had followed me, hadn't it? I had heard it, hadn't I?

Nan turned on the light and the window became a mirror. I gasped and whipped shut the curtains. I stayed with my face in the wood-smoke-scented curtain, my snot running into it.

Nan's hand on my shoulder made me jump. She tried to pull me round. I wouldn't turn. She pulled harder.

I faced her. My eyes fell to the wooden floorboards, their knots, their black pits where nails had been burned in.

'I'll run you a bath.'

She went upstairs. I heard water jet into the tub. I put my head in my hands.

I stayed like that a long time then I felt something soft against my chin and opened my eyes to find a white towel at my chest. I felt Nan's bony, thin hand on the crown of my head. And then all at once, something flowed through me and I began to sob.

I sobbed until my stomach ached.

'Go on, Lucas. Or you'll catch your death.'

I didn't move and she stayed stroking my head. Finally I took the towel and went upstairs.

134

The hot water tumbled into the hot bath and steam gathered in rolling clouds in the electric light.

I undressed and waited for the bath to fill.

I wondered if it still waited, that shape, that thing, that animal.

Prayer

When I went to bed that night, I couldn't dispel the wolf. It lurked outside in the cold, under the sailing cloud, the creaking trees, by the rushing stream.

I took out the knife. The blade was pale in the dark. I held the handle tight, the cold metal pressed flat against my chest.

Then the wolf came into the garden.

I could have gone to the window and put my head between the curtains and I would have seen it. It would have lifted its head and put its amber eyes on mine. But I didn't go to the window. I held the knife. I gripped it hard. I clenched all the muscles in my body. I squeezed my eyes tight. I mouthed a prayer – *Stay away, stay away, stay away*. My lips and tongue patted drily against each other.

Then I heard it.

Below my room, somewhere at the back of the house.

A long scrape, like the sound of a claw moving down a door.

It was trying to get in.

Cage

November. Frosts. Bare trees. The day barely getting light. The world's mood matching mine.

Cycling to school one morning, the sky blue except over the mountains where cloud hung rose-pink, I saw a long V of birds flying at speed towards the rising sun. When they passed overhead, they honked faintly – geese. Everything was abandoning this place. In the bare trees you could see birds' nests, black bowls of wet twigs, empty. The only things moving on the sleeping mountains seemed the rushing white water. And that was true, because the farmers had taken their flocks off the fells – eight ewes had been killed. News of livestock killings was on most nights. Farmers demanded action. Not just Sheridan Benedict, others. I saw them one night on the TV shouldering long black scabbards Nan told me contained rifles and I remembered what Sheridan had said – that he wouldn't stop until he'd killed the wolf.

Sometimes I felt it, watching me from the fir trees at school, or cycling home in the darkness, moving at my side, flickering among the trees.

I would meet Debs by the dilapidated hut. We would

lean on the pallets, she would smoke and talk, I would listen. She liked to talk about all kinds of things: people in her year, teachers, her parents, Nan, music, books, films. And sometimes she was quiet. We would lean there, facing the fir trees' darkness. And she would read her book.

Then one day, rounding the corner and expecting to find her, instead I found Steve Scott, Alex, and Zed. Plus others. The whole Stazak tribe. They were standing in a big circle.

'Death Boy!' Alex yelped.

The circle opened and closed about me. Steve Scott didn't say anything, hair twists sticking out over his ears where his gel hadn't worked properly, the rest perfect.

Zed juddered a cough and everyone laughed. He was holding a particularly stinky roll-up.

'Give it here, Zed,' said Alex.

Zed passed the roll-up to another boy.

'Hey,' Alex said, pushing Zed. 'I was next.'

Zed, glassy-eyed, grinned.

'He's off his skull!' said Steve.

'Give it,' said Alex to the boy with the roll-up, but he didn't so Alex turned and shoved Zed crossly. Slowly, Zed turned. Slowly, a massive forearm closed anaconda-like around Alex's neck and slowly Alex was lowered until he was bent double.

'Famous by dinner-time,' said Steve, taking out his phone and filming them.

They all laughed, even Zed, who I had never seen laugh.

Suddenly, like a trap, Alex was released. He sprang straight, acned face flushed darker red; then he saw the phone-camera. He blinked fast, fighting back tears. His eyes flashed round the circle, frightened, lit on me and immediately he stepped forward, swiped an arm round my throat in a hug that became a headlock, and I had to bend double so he didn't break my neck. His other hand came up and grabbed his wrist, tightening the grip.

'How'd you like that, Death Boy?' he whined.

I couldn't breathe. I could see his chunky black shoes, scuffed at the edge, one lace-end longer than the other, lying on the mud. His jacket had billowed like a lifebelt at his waist. I punched him between his legs.

He whinnied like a horse and released me.

I dropped to a crouch. There was an odd silence. I didn't want to move. My neck felt weird.

Slowly, I turned my head from side to side. Rubbed my neck. Shaky, I straightened.

They were all watching me.

'Death Boy nearly died,' said Alex, still clutching his groin, but no one laughed.

'You all right, mate?' said Steve.

I marched away.

'Oi!' called Steve. 'Mate!'

I heard him swish through the long grass after me.

He caught me up.

An arm draped across my shoulder.

I wheeled. 'Stay away from me.'

'Mate,' he said, holding up both palms. 'He didn't mean it. He's a tool.'

I ignored him.

He caught me up again as I reached one of the covered walkways. I pushed through doors into a busy corridor.

'Mate,' said Steve, plucking at my sleeve.

I stopped and faced him. He was smiling, not sarcastic this time. My neck ached.

'They like you. You should come and join us afters. We'll go round my brother's.'

'No.'

'I know what it's like,' he said.

I stared blankly at him.

'I know what it's like when people leave you.'

He was talking about my parents. Was he talking about my parents?

'My dad left us. Me brother and me. It's the same.'

Blood fizzed in my head and I couldn't see anything around me. *The same? It's the same?* I stepped forward and put both arms up and flexed them straight as I put my palms on his chest. He didn't so much stagger back across the hallway as trot like he was on rewind. He hit the far wall with a thump so loud two girls up the corridor stopped talking and looked.

'I couldn't give a toss about your stupid dad, you moron.'

His face – the first time I'd ever seen this expression on him – seemed wide open with shock. The shock was replaced almost instantly by a wild fear I couldn't understand, because he was bigger than me and used to fighting. Then a blankness entered his face the way dusk enters a mountain.

'You shouldn't have done that,' he said.

I waved a dismissive hand and walked off.

'You shouldn't have done that,' he called after me, and what frightened me was not what he said, but that he said it soft.

*

I would cycle home in the dull, wet light, glancing across my shoulder when I felt the gaze of the wolf. In the twilight, I would wander from room to room, checking the woods and mountain from the windows. I would watch the raven circle, flop down to the field. Listen to its late-afternoon kerfuffle. I would phone Nan at her office, remind her of the dangers of the road home.

At school, I kept my head down. I stayed in the library, hung round the entrance hall. I didn't go near the dilapidated hut or the playground.

One night, I woke in the middle of a ferocious storm. The cottage quivered under fists of wind. I felt the cold running through gaps in the window-frame, round the door, through the floorboards. The trees creaked. A branch snapped.

The wolf entered the house.

Light came on under my door. I sprang up, ran to it, flung it wide.

'Nan!'

Nan stood in her nightdress, frowning sleepily at me from the bathroom doorway.

'Sorry to wake you,' she said.

She went into the bathroom.

I shivered.

The toilet flushed, the landing light went out. The wolf receded into the darkness of the cottage, into the storm, into sleep.

*

At break-time the morning after the storm, I searched for Debs. Instead I found Malky, dressed in a long black coat that looked like a giant sleeping bag, who suggested I try the Grassy Knoll.

'Where's that?'

Sniffing, he gave directions. I walked through the school and out, then uphill past the bus stops to the main road. On the other side of the road a stile mounted a stone wall and beyond that a muddy path led upward through the trees, which I followed until it opened onto a grassy slope that led to a wide, crooked oak where, on a giant root, hunched in her combat jacket, sat Debs.

She was reading.

'That any good?' I asked, walking up.

She didn't answer. She must have finished Emily Brontë – this one was called *Good Morning, Midnight*. She was chewing gum and smoking.

I sniffed.

She handed me a wrinkled, snotty tissue.

'Er … no thanks,' I said.

Breath rose white, mixed with cigarette smoke.

'What's it about?'

She flicked the book out for me to read the blurb. I couldn't take in the words so just said, 'Oh.' She fired me a glance and went back to reading. I sat on one of the roots.

Rotating her head slowly, she gave me a stare. 'If you're going to disturb me, go away.'

I pulled my knees up. Neither of us spoke. The last few bronze leaves rustled high up in the breeze. It was too cold to be sitting outside. She turned a dry page.

The shadow-shape. It was in me sometimes.

She must have felt something was up because she said, 'You all right?'

I couldn't speak.

A spider moved along my leg, its black sac shining in the sun, its tiny legs flickering.

'Look at that!' I said.

It abseiled down to the grass.

I didn't say anything.

She didn't say anything.

'I'm worried about myself,' I said.

She put down her book. I heard the page, soft.

I smelt her near – spearmint and smoke.

Soft, softer than her page, she said, 'What is it, mate?' The softest that she'd spoken.

'The wolf came last night.'

'Ah.'

'It came into the cottage.'

She put the ball of her fist into the tender part of my back between spine and shoulder and thumped softly three times like she was knocking on a door. Then she butted my shoulder with her forehead.

Across the air the bell rang.

'Gonna be late,' she said.

'Yeah.'

'Again.'

'Yeah.'

'Come on, then.'

We walked down the muddy slope to the stile.

*

Miss Andrews said as I came in, 'Why are you late?'

I sat in the spare seat. Super-strength silence.

'Why, Lucas?'

'I was discussing *Good Morning, Midnight.*'

There was a momentary widening of her eyes then she said, 'Well, if you could discuss Jean Rhys in your own time, I'd appreciate it. So, anyone, why doesn't Thornton let Hal and the others take Buck across the frozen river?'

'Because the ice is going to melt and Buck'll drown,' someone said.

'Because they're stupid,' someone else said.

'Why are they stupid?' Miss Andrews asked.

'Ask Lucas,' said Steve Scott in a low voice. 'He knows about doing stupid things in dangerous situations.'

'Leave your disputes outside, please, Steven. And answer the question. Why does the author think they're stupid?'

'Oh, Miss, it's just banter,' said Steve.

'Banter, my arse.'

'Miss, you're not allowed to say "arse".'

'So when you're recovered from the emotional trauma, sue me, would you? And answer the question – Why are they stupid?'

Arrogant silence.

Malky said, through a stuffed nose, 'It's because they're too civilised and don't understand nature. He's saying nature is dangerous and if you don't understand it, you'll die.'

'And how do you understand nature?'

145

Because Malky had a bunged-up nose, it sounded like he said, *Pie bee-pummin piled*. Everyone laughed.

'*Wild*, I think you mean, Malcolm.'

'That's what I said, Miss. *De caw of de piled.*'

Everyone roared. Except Steve. Except me.

*

Wolves live in packs. They hunt in packs; they move in packs. And they stay in packs, too, until one is thrown out or leaves. The pack is organised, like any group: school, a family. Each animal in the pack has a different role. These roles form a hierarchy, with the leaders at the top. The leaders might not be the biggest and strongest in the pack, but they are the ones who make the decisions for the group. They are supported by a bodyguard, who is usually bigger than the leader, and who often does the leader's fighting. Then there is the one who goes out and scouts, who stays alert for danger – the look-out. And finally there is the one at the bottom, usually the smallest, often the one who the others pick on, who they take out their frustrations on, who is the butt of their jokes. Unless he chooses to fight or leave, he will remain in this position, at the bottom of the ladder. Fight. Or leave.

*

One week later, at lunch, unable to find anywhere to be (couples at the Grassy Knoll, a gang of smokers

146

behind the dilapidated hut, a meeting about public library closures in the library), I circuited the noisy playground.

Steve Scott was playing football in the Cage.

The thing about moving on your own is you become an easy target for the pack. I had strayed off the playground to where a crowd of sparrows were singing happily in the hedgerow. They shut up when I approached but didn't fly away, making flicky watchful movements of their heads. Waiting for me to push off so they could get back to their singing.

A hand grasped my arm.

'No need to take fright, mate.'

I wanted to pull away but didn't want to show I was scared. Plus my other hand was free if I needed to fight. 'Want a game?' said Steve, nodding at the footballers in the Cage.

'Nah.'

He loosened his grip.

'Come on, mate. Sorry about the other day. Lost my temper, yeah?'

I walked away but he rushed to my side and when I walked faster he kept up. To stop bumping against him I had to veer slightly away so that he was steering me.

We were heading towards the Cage. The others had stopped playing and were watching. There was Alex, Zed, and others. We reached the Cage door. When it opened, it creaked. Behind me the sparrows had started chortling. Hilarious.

Five-a-side, plus me.

Kick-off.

I was out on the wing. The game was silent and serious. Then, with the first pass to me, Steve steamed in. He threw me against the fence. He actually shoved me with his hands, it wasn't even a tackle. I fell down the fence, the ball trapped against my chest. Then he kicked me. I put my hands and knees up to protect my front but he stamped on one hand. My shins got the heaviest blows, pulled up for protection. Someone else joined in – Alex. Solitary laughter. Heaving breaths. 'Go on,' Steve said, softly. Other than that, the dull thuds. When I said stop, it came out in a chesty judder, there were so many blows going through my body. They left off. They all played on in silence, the odd call – 'Pass!' – 'Goal!' – while I tried to stand. It took me a minute or so before I could, then I made my way along the Cage fence. I was shaking. My hand throbbed. I couldn't use it and I had to use my other hand to open the door.

'See ya, mate!' called Steve. 'Cheers for the game!'

I shuffled across the playground. I stayed in the toilet until the bell, then I walked to the bike racks. It hurt to cycle and when I got back to the cottage I went to bed. Nan came back. I told her I was ill. She said she'd call me when tea was ready. I said I didn't want any.

Knife

Woken from a deep sleep, my body aching, I heard a dog bark in the distance.

I rolled over and a spasm of pain spangled my ribs. Keep still. Don't move. The dog's bark cut off.

Silence.

A silence so true I could hear for miles – the frost crystallise on grass, ice seize the slate tiles, the sub-zero stiffen the trees.

Minutes passed. Then came a soft creak, like frost being trod on.

I held my breath.

Something tried the back door. A soft thump followed.

I held the knife.

For minutes I heard only silence.

The wolf withdrew its presence slowly. It had not gone away altogether but only somewhere else.

I sat up with a gasp. I knew where it had gone. Inside.

I banged out of bed, thumped across the rug, opened the door wide.

The yawning darkness of the landing.

I took a breath to call Nan's name – held it. There was no noise except, perhaps, the faint sound of the mountain stream.

Then I felt the wolf. It was here. I held out the knife and went, step by step, around the landing. Stopped.

Nan's room.

The shining white door.

I watched my white fingers reach out, fasten on the handle, and lower it.

I opened the door.

I listened, heard nothing, not even breathing, and stepped into the room, knife ready.

In the dark I could just make out Nan, motionless, flat on her back.

I approached.

I leaned forward.

I could hear nothing. No breath.

I put my hand out, over her mouth, to feel if there was any breath at all.

Her eyes opened.

'Whu –'

I froze.

'Get out!' A blast of foul breath. 'Get out!'

The bedside lamp came on. Her eyes narrowed against the light then landed on the knife. She screamed.

I stared at the knife.

'Get out!'

I didn't move.

'Get out!'

'Nan, –'

'Get out!' she screamed.

I ran out.

In my room I put the knife on top of the chest of drawers.

She came onto the landing, went downstairs. I heard her in the kitchen; then from the bottom of the stairs she called: 'Lucas.'

I went to the doorway. A floorboard creaked.

'Lucas.'

She stood at the bottom. Her hair was a mess. Her face was puffy.

'Where's the knife, Lucas?'

'I was trying to protect you.'

'Will you bring the knife?'

'I was trying to protect you.'

'Will you bring the knife, please, Lucas?'

I fetched it and came down holding it in my fist. She kept her eyes fixed on mine as I descended. She held out her hand. I stopped on the last stair. I stepped onto the floor and placed the knife in her hand.

She looked at me a long time then said, 'Put your jacket on.'

'Are we going out?'

'No, it's cold.'

I took it from the hook. She took hers. Then she switched on the heating. I knew it was serious then.

We went into the kitchen. I didn't see, but heard, the cutlery drawer open and shut and when she turned, she didn't have the knife any more.

She boiled the kettle and poured two mugs of tea. The fridge grunted as she opened it for milk. She got a spoon and stirred, waiting for it to brew a bit. I didn't have the heart to tell her again that I don't drink tea.

I knew that something awful had happened only I didn't know what.

She dropped tea bags into the bin and put the mugs down and sat. I sat opposite.

'One client I had was a woman with a scar.'

She traced a line from her eyebrow to her cheek then curved it to her chin.

'A man did it. With a glass.'

I had no idea why she was telling me this.

'Some men get rages, Lucas.'

My heart did double time.

'There are people I need to telephone.'

'Nan.'

'What?'

'I wasn't …' I murmured.

'You weren't what?'

I pushed the chair back and stood. 'I'll go.'

I went upstairs. I shoved things into my schoolbag. I didn't even see what things. I didn't even know what she meant, properly. Only that I'd done something terrible.

A waft of sour breath and bath soap, and I turned.

'Why did you come in my room with a knife?'

'I was trying to save you,' I said, and my voice got thick suddenly.

'From what?'

I couldn't see through the mist of tears, so I shoved more stuff in my schoolbag.

'From what?'

I balled my fists and ducked my head under them. I felt her close behind me, then her palm on my back.

'Sit down,' she said softly.

I sat on the edge of the bed and she sat beside me.

'I bring death,' I said.

'No you don't. Tell me what happened.'

An image came into my head – a thin, small dog, leaping against a wall in a prison yard, trying to get out. It could not get out but it kept throwing itself against the wall. Again and again.

'What were you trying to save me from?'

'I thought I heard something.'

'What?'

'I thought I heard something in the house.'

'What do you mean?'

'I thought … you were dead and, and, the, the … was

153

in there, with you.' I stared at my knees. I felt, suddenly, exhausted.

'The what? What was in there with me?'

I didn't want to answer.

'We need to do something about this,' she said, slowly, as if thinking out loud.

I looked at her, expecting her to say she was going to send me away now. Instead she said, 'I haven't addressed this properly.'

I stared uncomprehending but she didn't elaborate. On the bedside table was Mum's pebble. Beyond it, the curtain. And beyond that …

'We can talk about this in the morning.'

'About what?'

'You need some help, Lucas.'

I felt the beginnings of a headache throb.

'School have been in touch,' she said.

'What do you mean?'

'Miss Andrews phoned about how you've been at school.'

'I've been fine.'

'Not concentrating. Not doing homework. I have a meeting with Miss Andrews and the headmaster next week.'

Amazingly, then, she laughed.

'I wouldn't worry about it. He's a bit of a prat, isn't he?'

I sort-of laughed. A cough more than a laugh.

She stood abruptly and suddenly I felt the loss of her beside me and wanted her to sit back down and hug me. Like Mum or Dad would have done.

'If you can sleep some more tonight, that would be good. You have school in the morning.'

She went to the door. 'Do you want your light on or off?'

I lay down.

She stayed in the doorway.

'Are you going back to bed?' I said.

'Not for a bit, no.'

'Can you turn the light off but leave the door open?'

For a while I could hear her moving around downstairs, then the fire in the sitting room being made up. I went and switched off the landing light then came back to bed. From downstairs a faint glow came through the open door. I could hear wood crackle and blister. Outside, I felt the wolf in the trees watching and waiting. Watching and waiting.

Watching and waiting.

Howl

Morning. The world sealed in ice. The gutters wearing beards of ice. I let out a little moan when I tried to sit up. Their kicks had gone right through me. I swear to God when I opened the curtain the grass had animal tracks through it.

I tried not to move too much at breakfast. Nan had done a fry-up but I hardly touched it.

I pushed a tomato round my plate.

'Lucas?'

'Mm?'

'How are you?'

The mouse-brown bird, sleek, with an eye-mask like Zorro, flew down from his home in the cottage wall. Some birds stay around. They don't take off for the winter.

'What's that bird?' I said.

She went to the window but it flew off before she saw it.

'Not sure,' she said.

Dad would know.

'It's all right,' I said, suddenly bold, suddenly full of happy. I smiled, which seemed to startle her. 'School doesn't matter anyway, there are some things more important than exams.'

She didn't seem to know what to say. I pushed my knife and fork together and winced as I stood.

'Are you sure you're all right?'

'Yeah.'

'You seem like you're – '

A roar like a cooker's gas-flame but a hundred times louder filled the air. I let out a cry of fear.

'What is it?' I yelled.

'The British state practising for murder,' said Nan, and I understood – it was the usual troubling thunder of a fighter-jet.

I went upstairs, got ready for school. Everything hurt. When I washed I found my skin was black in some places, purple in others. Part of me wanted to go to the kitchen and take the knife but after what had happened, I knew I couldn't. But I took the white pebble.

I ached too much to cycle so I decided to brave the bus. To hell with Steve and Alex and Zed, the whole damned Stazak tribe. I wouldn't run away from those idiots.

The white pebble in my pocket banged against my hip as I left the house. My ears burned with the cold.

I trod the cattle grid and walked through the woods.

The frost was melting. Dripping. On the flat felt roofs of some shops in the village, it smoked up into the air. The trees against the gold ball of the sun were frazzled

157

black silhouettes. Empty birds' nests were blackened bones. The bus complained its way through its gears, finally arrived. The doors hissed, and I entered.

*

The Stazaks hogged the back row, high up like judges. I slid along a double seat and squeaked a porthole in the fogged glass and watched the white world slide by.

'Oi.'

The lake appeared. Ice at the edge, water black. I didn't care if we'd take a spill or not. We'd all go: me, the Stazaks and the rest.

'Oi!'

The other side of the bus, trees clattered on the windows. Wiped windows revealed black limbs, wet hills.

Something hit my head. A male explosion of laughter. I didn't know what had happened. Warm liquid trickled under my collar, down my back. A soft-pack of juice lay on the floor, gurgling dark fluid down the gangway.

'Oi, Death Boy.'

Slowly, I turned to face them. I had to do it slow because my torso hurt to move.

'He moves like a queer,' Alex shouted.

'You gay, Death Boy?' Steve called.

I stared at them, sat like corpses. And I grinned at the

thought of them dead. They seemed a bit shocked by something. I faced front.

They kept on shouting for a bit. About how I would get my legs broken next time. And for a moment, I had a strange feeling. Like I wasn't there any longer. Like I was removed from myself. And I didn't feel frightened any more and I looked around and saw it.

It was a flash of black. Sometimes condensation hid it and sometimes the trees hid it but it ran there. It didn't run like a dog, or like a horse, it flowed like water. Speed and weight and bulk. Sometimes it fell behind but when the bus slowed for steep hills it reappeared.

A wolf can run at forty miles an hour. Easy to keep up with a bus.

Coldly, quietly, from the back, and it carried over everyone's heads, Steve said, 'You know what I reckon – I reckon it was his fault they died.'

'Yeah, I reckon you're right,' Alex whined. 'How'd they die?'

'In a car accident,' called Steve, equally loud. It was like they were on a stage talking to an audience. 'He made them crash.'

A burst of laughter from the back.

I turned.

I wasn't looking at Alex or Zed or any of the others. I was looking at Steve Scott.

'He's a murderer,' Steve said, looking right at me.

I stood. I walked up the gangway. I found I had the white pebble in my hand and I knew what to do with it. I threw it.

Glass smashed. I ran down the gangway. Steve raised both legs and I threw a punch over his feet before he kicked me. Blood jumped. I punched and punched and punched. Screams. I was pulled off by my clothes, my arms, my hair…

The bus lurched to a halt. The engine died. The roar of a hundred lunatics.

And then I knew exactly what to do. For the first time in my life I was sure of what to do.

I howled.

I howled the howl of pain and blood and death.

Part Two

Ian

Inside was bright electric light. Outside was dark. He hadn't closed the curtain which meant you could see Kendal's sky, lit by the orange glow of streetlamps. I could hear rush-hour cars on the wet road. Kids' voices. Just before Christmas but no sign of that here. Empty shelves. A vase with dried flowers. Three low comfy chairs. Empty space between the chairs for our feet: Nan's DMs, my school shoes, and a pair of brand-new, blue skate shoes frothing white laces. The skate shoes belonged to Ian. He introduced himself that way, not as Mr but 'Ian'. I hate it when people in authority introduce themselves by their first name like they want to be your friend.

'Are you sure you don't want to take your jacket off, Lucas?'

I pretended I hadn't heard.

Nan had taken off her coat and hung it on the coat-stand by the door. It was uncomfortably warm and I wished now that I'd taken my jacket off. He'd asked me first when we came in so if I took it off now I'd look a right fool.

Ian wore jeans, a high V-neck jumper and a bright

red checked shirt. Plus those stupid skate shoes. He had grey curly hair. His smile was a lie. So was his deliberately warm voice – a liar's voice.

He was explaining what happened in this room, how counselling was meant to help me, but I wasn't listening. I was thinking about Mum and Dad and how it didn't matter what happened to me, that for them it was worse, because they were dead.

'Do you understand what I mean, Lucas?' Ian was asking in that liar-warm voice.

The radiator glugged.

'Lucas?' said Nan, a note of strain in her voice.

I nodded at Ian's question.

'So, Lucas, perhaps you could tell me what led you to come here?'

I glanced at Nan.

She was waiting for me to speak.

'I have to be here or Mr Bond will expel me and you people will put me in foster care.'

Cars swished by, water trickled in the radiator, I began to sweat.

'Lucas has been having a hard time since…' The silence went on forever.

'Since …?'

'His parents died.'

He must have known that. He was just a liar, pretending he didn't know.

'Was that your daughter or your son who died?' Ian said to Nan, and I wanted to tell him to mind his own business.

'My daughter,' said Nan.

'Did they die at the same time?' Ian asked in his soft liar-voice.

'Yes,' said Nan. 'In a car accident.'

'Nan!' I said.

Nan glanced at me.

'It's none of his business. Anyway, it wasn't an accident.'

'What do you mean?' she said.

I wanted to tell her about the wolf. But I didn't.

There was a long quiet.

'Lucas, that's a huge thing to happen,' said Ian with a frown of concern. He was so disgustingly false I wanted to punch him so I stared at the rain-dots on the window. New ones landed. 'You've suffered a big loss.'

The radiator sounded like it had indigestion and was trying to get a big meal through its stomach.

'How has that been, Lucas?'

I met his eyes and wished him dead.

'It has taken some adjustment,' said Nan. 'A new school. A new place ... Everything's changed.' Her voice sounded funny, like she had a cold.

'And you, Eve?' It was weird hearing her first name. 'How has it been for you?'

'For me?' She sounded surprised.

165

'It must have been difficult for you – it must *be* difficult – having to become the main carer for Lucas. While you're dealing with your own grief for your daughter.'

'This is not about me, *Ian*,' she said, annoyed.

Ian didn't seem worried by Nan's irritation and gazed placidly at her.

'This is about Lucas,' Nan went on. 'About the problems he's having. About … He's not doing his schoolwork. He's getting into trouble. I can't – I want you to do something about it.'

'What do you do, Eve?'

'Do …? Lucas goes to school, I go to work, we …'

'What do you do for a job?'

'I'm a solicitor – I thought this was about my grandson.'

'It is. Lucas will be coming to see me on his own after this, if he wants to come to see me, that is –'

'Oh, he will.'

'– so I want to take this opportunity to hear about how things are for you. But you're right, Eve, we should hear from Lucas.' He faced me. 'Lucas, is there anything you would like to say? Or that you want to ask me?'

'No.'

The bubble of air struggled to make its way through the radiator. While I listened to the radiator's pressure build, I began to feel very warm. Now I really wished I'd taken my jacket off.

166

'Can you open the window?' I said.

'It gets cold in here. Especially in winter. And it's raining.'

'No it's not.'

He twisted to the window, then he faced me.

'You're right,' he said. 'Why don't you take off your jacket?'

'I'm all right. *Thanks.*'

The radiator strained.

'Do you mind if I ask you a question, Lucas?'

I stared him some hate.

He seemed to be waiting for me to answer so I shrugged.

The radiator took a breather like it had just stopped after a long run.

'If you could have one thing tomorrow that could change, Lucas,' said Ian, super-soft like he was reading me a bedtime story. 'If you could wake up tomorrow and one thing would be different, what would that be?'

My parents would be alive.

I dug my fingers into the arms of the comfy chair.

'Lucas?' he said.

I heard the saliva click in my throat, and when I opened my mouth to speak, it made a stupid smacking noise.

He was gazing at me.

'I'd open the freaking window, *Ian,*' I said, only I didn't say freaking. Then I stood. I didn't think about standing up, it just happened. I had a dizzy spell and when it passed I rushed for the door, hitting the chair with my knee on the way. The door had a wickedly powerful closer so it slammed, which was a pity, because it meant I couldn't slam it myself.

*

There are hills about Kendal, and I felt the wolf in them, that it had crept off the mountains and followed me here and now stood watching me from their blackness. It wanted something. To kill me? Finish off the family after Mum and Dad? I put my hand to my head and rubbed my temples. I had to keep it back.

I decided that whatever I did next, I would never tell anyone in authority about the wolf. Because they would think I was mad. Perhaps I *was* mad. Headlamps of cars on either side of the river dazzled. A few school kids were heading home, one whirling his bag by the strap round his head, his mates laughing.

'Lucas?' said Nan.

I expected her to say something harsh, angry. But she didn't. She said, 'Why did you do that?'

We listened to the cars rushing and to the black river.

'What do you want to do?' she said when I didn't answer.

'Go back to the cottage.'

'No, I mean when you finish school.'

Mum had worked in a school. Dad had worked for an environment charity. You could ask Dad questions about things – like the names of trees and wildflowers and birds, and his specialist subject, how to protect woods. Not many people know about these things. I wondered who I was going to ask about these things now.

'Lucas.'

The water and traffic flowed.

'*Lucas.*'

'What?'

'You have to get your grades.'

Her hand came out and she held the rail. Old, mottled skin. Bones.

'Some things are just bigger than algebraic equations,' I said.

'But they matter, too, Lucas.'

'How can they matter compared to someone living or dying? That's what matters.'

'I know, but …'

'But what?'

'I wish you could understand. You have your whole life.'

'What does that even mean?'

'What are you going to do when you leave school?'

'Work for the environment like Dad.'

'So you need an education.'

'So?'

She sighed. Mum and Dad watched, disappointed in me for walking out on Ian, for causing Nan all this trouble.

'You can't be expelled. You need to get your exams. It's six months. Less. That's all. All you have to do is see this *Ian* man.'

She said his name with such derision that I laughed.

'Will you give it a try?'

I tipped my head back in exasperation to the orange glow of the streetlights.

'Well?'

*

Ian had a buff folder trapped under one arm and a brown two-tone coffee mug gripped in his other hand and he stood in the doorway between the waiting room and office. He managed not to appear surprised to see us.

'Lucas,' he said. 'You came back.'

I was getting tired of him spelling everything out.

'Can we talk?' said Nan, smiling hard at him. Her eyes gleamed. I wondered if it was the cold and wind causing her eyes to shine, or something else.

'We're only scheduled for the introductory session and I've got another client in ...' He looked around helplessly for a clock.

'Oh, *Ian*,' said Nan, stepping forward and touching his elbow. 'We'll only be a *few* minutes, won't we, Lucas?' She gave me a pointed glance.

170

'Um, yeah,' I said.

'You see, Ian, we've smoothed it out. Haven't we, Lucas?'

'Yeah.'

Nan was still smiling into his face, hand on his elbow. I tried to appear interested.

'Well ...' said Ian, coming to a decision, 'I can give you ten minutes until the next client.'

I followed them upstairs, Nan asking him lots of personal questions that he wasn't responding to. On the landing he turned and held his buff folder against his stomach and explained that he couldn't give any personal information about himself to his clients, it wasn't professional.

'But of course, how silly of me,' said Nan. 'It's exactly the same in my job.'

In the counselling room, Ian put down his buff folder. Nan took off her coat.

So did I.

'So, Lucas,' said Ian when we were sat down, 'do you want to talk through how things have been for you lately in these sessions with me?'

I nodded.

'Tell me, why did you walk out before?'

I shrugged.

'Lucas, this is only going to work if you want it to. Do you want to come here, to see me, and talk about things?'

'Yes, he does.'

He didn't take his eyes off me.

I felt my mouth go dry and when I opened it, it made that funny smacking sound again. 'Er, yeah,' I said.

'You see, he does,' said Nan. 'So he'll see you next week at the same time.' She was already leaning forward to stand.

'Wait a minute, Eve.'

Nan paused.

'I don't believe you, Lucas.'

He was gazing placidly at me.

'What I think, Lucas, is that you've only come back because your grandmother persuaded you to.'

'Ian, he's agreed to come –'

Ian put his hand up to stop her. 'If you want to come here to talk about things, Lucas, I'm happy to be here for you. You've had a big loss. I believe I can help you. But there's no point if you don't want to.'

'He's going to attend. That's all you need to know.'

Ian seemed to be waiting for me to respond.

'Could you tell me the complaints process here, please,' said Nan.

'In a moment, Eve,' said Ian, without taking his eyes off me. 'First I'd like to hear from Lucas.'

I examined the carpet-tile joins.

The quiet went on for perhaps half a minute.

Eventually Ian said, 'Why don't we leave it there and

172

you think about it over Christmas? If you want to come back when we start again in the new year, you would be very welcome. But if you're not going to engage in the process, we shouldn't continue.'

There was a silence. I could feel Nan straining to keep quiet.

'How does that sound?' Ian said.

'Yeah, okay,' I said.

Nan was about to say something but Ian picked up his buff folder, took a pen and wrote in his notebook, and she waited, then he tore the sheet off and handed it to her.

'That's the link for the complaints procedure,' he said.

We went over to the coat-stand, I took my jacket and Nan her coat, and we left.

Celery

Mr Bond had suspended me for the last ten days of term for attacking Steve Scott on the bus. He had also called Children and Young People's Services who had sent a social worker to see me. Nan must have been really worried after the bus incident because when the social worker asked how she was coping with me, she hesitated. That scared me. At the end of the interview the social worker said *neither* of us seemed to coping, and that he'd help us by arranging a psychologist for me. I told him I didn't want one. The social worker said I had to see a psychologist or they'd consider putting me with foster parents. And so, because of all that, I didn't mention the wolf to Nan. She would think I was mad. And if the social workers found out, then they'd think I was mad too and put me straight in care and probably a mental hospital. But the local TV believed in the wolf. So did the local paper. And the farmers whose flocks had been attacked. It was up there on the mountains, wild, free, killing things.

*

On Saturday, Nan called from the front door, 'Someone to see you!'

I came down to find Malky zipped into his black tube of a winter coat. His face was white except for his nose, which was bright red.

'Thought I'd see what you're up to,' he said, sounding like he had a cold.

'Not up to much,' I said.

We stood facing each other in the December chill.

'D'you want to come in?' I said.

He shrugged, then stepped inside. Nan was in the sitting room so I took him upstairs. He glanced around my room. 'Don't you have any posters?'

'I do at home.'

He nodded as if he hadn't considered I had a home somewhere else. 'So,' he said, 'what happened after your, um … attacking Steve Scott?'

I told him about being suspended until the new year and having to see Ian, and Malky told me about Steve and *his* suspension for hitting me, then about how he (Malky) was in the third week of an epic role-playing game.

After we'd swapped news, I suggested computer games but he wasn't keen so I dug out Mum's board games from the bottom drawer of the chest. We decided on Connect 4 and dropped plastic disks into the frame.

After we'd been playing a while, I decided to risk telling him about the wolf, and about how it had been following me alongside the bus when I attacked Steve Scott.

'What did it look like?' asked Malky.

'Like a wolf.'

'Oh,' said Malky, disappointed. 'Nothing like a warg, then?'

'It's not *Lord of the Rings*, Malky.'

'What *is* it like, then?'

'A leopard.'

'What, it's got spots?'

'No, it moved like a leopard. It was grey, or black.'

'Did you tell this Ian man about it?'

'No – "Hello, Ian, I see wolves"? He'd think I'm mad.'

'That's what he does, isn't it, talk to mad people?'

'S'pose.' I dropped a disk into the frame.

'What's he like?'

'About seventy and wears skate shoes.'

We dropped yellow and red disks into the frame.

'Do you think I'm mad, then, Malky?'

He studied me. 'A bit,' he said, dropping a disk. 'Row!'

He cheered, pulled a lever and all the disks cascaded out in a pleasing plastic crash.

We chuckled.

After lunch, Malky said, 'Right, I'm going.' He got into his sleeping-bag coat and rustled out. He had an appointment at the games shop in Kendal to sit with four other game players and talk about orcs, warriors, and elven princesses.

Nan spent most of the weekend in her study working on her legal papers. When she wasn't doing that she was in her armchair by the fire with her history of the miners' strike. She'd nearly finished it. Outside were wild blue skies. Bare trees swung madly in the wind.

That night, after I had gone to bed, the wind grew stronger. The trees groaned. The TV aerial creaked like a rusty hinge. And something scratched at the wall outside.

I went to the window.

I couldn't see it.

But there! It scratched.

I hurried to the chest of drawers and began to push it in front of the bedroom door. It was hard work. There was a knock at my door.

'Lucas?'

My heart flippety-flipped against my pyjama top.

'Are you all right?'

'Yeah.'

'It sounds like you're moving furniture around in there.'

'I dropped something behind the drawers.'

Nan didn't respond.

'Good night,' I said.

I heard her go across the landing.

I got into bed. I listened to the wind, the creaking TV aerial, the groaning trees.

*

By the next morning, the wind had died and I surveyed the garden wreckage – broken branches and a piece of felt from the shed roof.

Nan didn't go to her office that morning. She worked in her study but left the door open. I sat in the kitchen, trying to do mathematics, science, geography, English. I couldn't concentrate.

At noon, she started to make a soup but discovered she had no celery so gave me some money and sent me to buy some.

'My bike's got a puncture,' I said, which was true.

'Your legs still work, don't they?'

'So do yours.'

'One: you're fitter than me. Two: I'm at work.'

'No you're not, you're making soup.'

'And three: I need some celery for it.'

'Can't we have soup without celery?'

'No, it's celery soup.'

So I put on my shoes.

*

Bare branches. Sunlight low down showing their dusty green limbs. The trunks wrapped in ivy. The cattle grid filled with brown leaves. The floor of the woods spread with brown leaves. Little squares of colour and light, easy for the wolf to hide in.

Nan watched me from her study.

'Yeah yeah yeah,' I muttered under my breath.

I took the cattle grid rung by rung.

I walked down the lane on the earthy central camber, tense, awaiting the thud onto the tarmac, the click of claws, the snarl and teeth-rip.

On the mountainside the chimney of the Benedict farm smoked, and I pictured Debs in school, chewing gum arrogantly, smoking defiantly. The soft sound of her hair being swept from the back of her neck. The sound of her blink. I stopped to wait for traffic to pass. A car whooshed. I crossed over. Walked the verge. The village was empty. I entered the 7-11.

The giant white fridges buzzed and sighed. I searched out a plastic pack of celery on the fake grass matting of the fruit-and-veg shelves, and there I caught sight of myself in their mirrors. I was as white as Malky and my hair had got long and a bit wild. My eyes were starey. I took the celery and headed for the counter.

A frail old man was ahead of me and bought a lottery ticket. His hands trembled and he had trouble counting his coins. The girl – bored – collected the coins and fetched his scratch card. He scraped away the surface with a coin. The door buzzer sounded. The old man shuffled away.

I paid for the celery then turned to go.

'Hello, mate,' grinned Steve Scott. He stood with his brother Danny, blocking my exit, and he had that stupid sarcastic smile on his face. He also had a blue bruise round one eye from where I'd hit him. It made him look like a pirate with an eye-patch.

Danny Scott stepped forward and I lifted my forearm to fend him off but he knocked it aside and bunched my collar in a cig-stenchy fist. His other hand swept into my vision sideways and he punched me in the back of my head and I felt all the things at the front of my face try to exit – teeth, cheekbones, the snot in my nose. We did a stagger for less than a second like dancers (he smelled of armpit) then we hit a Christmas display of chocolate bars and he lost his balance and let go.

The buzzer sounded as I ran out. I nearly knocked over the old man and sprinted across the road. A horn jeered, a car swerved. Steve shouted – I'm not sure what – then Danny: 'We'll wait!'

I ran for the cottage. Not along the verge but across the fields, white but for the puddles that had been frozen into cases of black glass.

Manchester

On Friday, the last day of term, I asked Nan if she would drive me to Kendal when she went to work. I couldn't stand being in the house any more. I didn't even care about going in the car.

On the way, she asked if I'd decided about seeing Ian after Christmas.

I didn't answer.

We passed school, packed with animals.

In town, I wandered aimlessly past shops displaying Christmas gifts under glitter and fake snow. Shop workers passed. Business people. Pensioners. It was so cold my earlobes and fingertips stung so I went in the library. I was flicking through a book on trees when a woman began shouting at the top of her voice. Everyone stared while a greasy-haired man tried to gentle her down with his palms. It didn't do any good, she went on shouting. It was as if her shout was a thing of its own, as if it had taken control of her. Her mouth was a hole, her eyes unseeing. So I left.

It felt weird on the main street now, as if the woman's madness had got into everything. I thought about walking out along the river and finding Ian and telling him I'd see him. And perhaps I would have done except, right at that moment, I saw whiny Alex.

At the same moment as I saw him, he saw me.

I entered the nearest building – the shopping arcade. I strode. The doors walloped behind me. I sprinted into a stairwell then into the low-ceilinged dark of the multi-storey, echoing with tyre squeals. Down ramps, Alex sole-slamming after me. Under the opening car-park barrier and across three honking carriageways. And when I looked back, he wasn't there.

Sweat cooling, I stood with my hands on my knees. I was in the riverside park. And then I saw Alex, ugly, skinny, hunting. He was on the road. Turn and he'd see me.

I didn't breathe.

He moved behind a row of houses. I ran in the opposite direction, reached the railway station. I jogged up the slope to the platform.

The next train out was in a few minutes.

*

Manchester. A cold as deep as England. Taxis black as ravens. The station entrance high and the city all around. Crowds moving. People pouring up the long slope. More people together than I'd seen in months. I walked to the parapet. In the dark, the city seemed dim and gloomy, like a dream.

As I descended the slope, no one paid me attention, not the people in suits, not the shoppers, not the homeless man with a red Big Issue bib. I was invisible. Diesel engines roared as I waited at traffic lights. The traffic stopped and people flowed.

Christmas lights. A man selling fluorescent bracelets. A funfair in a small park. A smell of roasting chestnuts mixed with kebab. My parents appeared from a department store and joined the crowd, faces turned to each other. It was them, I was certain: Mum's cocked head, Dad's leaning-back, relaxed walk. Mum and Dad.

They turned down a side street.

For a moment I did nothing, then I sprinted, terrified they would be gone by the time I reached the corner.

They were still there. His relaxed, slow stride like he was thinking something. The way she opened a door along the empty pavement, the way Dad, hands in pockets, went in after her – it was definitely them. I hurried up the street.

The place they had gone was a Chinese restaurant and my parents sat at a table, the waitress handing them menus. They sat in profile, heads bowed, reading. I opened the glass door.

Cosy warm. They sat across the empty restaurant's red tablecloths, obscured partly by a pillar.

A faint chiming music played from somewhere. Then I heard the muffled tread of my steps on the deep carpet as I crossed the restaurant.

'Table for how many, sir?' the pretty waitress said.

I pointed towards Mum and Dad. The waitress wouldn't get out of my way so I walked round her.

The pillar obscured their faces, then I moved beyond the pillar and I was right by their table.

Mum lifted her face from the menu.

She was different. Her whole face. I don't know why I'd seen a resemblance.

I turned to Dad.

'Are you all right?' he said.

His voice wasn't Dad's. It was someone else's voice. And he didn't look anything like Dad.

'Something the matter, love?' the woman said.

There was a horrible moment of them gazing at me and me gazing at them. The speakers played flutes.

*

I sat in a burger bar until it closed. It had started to rain so I stood in a doorway and watched it. It was wind-driven, spat from drainpipes, bounced on paving slabs. Bus glass steamed. A crowd of Father Christmases ran screaming across the road, drenched to the skin.

In the building's deep shadow, time undid itself and I became invisible again. I was nothing.

184

I wondered how you could tell if you were mad. If there was a test for it.

Seeing dead people. Being followed by wolves.

I turned on my phone. I had five missed calls, plus texts and voice messages. I decided I had better go back to the station but when I reached it, I had already missed the last train.

*

In a late-night cafe I cupped a mug of scalding tea I didn't drink. Men with hoarse voices bought chips. The crew of cooks bashed pans and deep-fat sieves and the old woman who took orders had a face so thick-skinned and such clear, sad eyes I thought there was someone else inside her begging to get out. But when she came round to wipe tables and I quizzed her eyes with mine, she just flicked her gaze away sourly.

I left when the cafe shut. The rain had stopped and the ground had frozen. Crystals of ice tinkled and cracked under my feet. It was so cold a throbbing ache rose in my spine. The cold seemed to swell, reach a crescendo. It was so cold, I thought if I touched anything, like a car wing mirror, it would snap off.

The station re-opened at six am.

The train pulled out in the dark and I fell asleep. I only woke when the ticket collector shook my shoulder.

A rosy light raked bare fields that had collected snow in their furrows.

When I got to Kendal it was mid-morning. The fells were white. From the bus I saw birds standing on lake ice.

I walked back from the village.

Nothing had changed.

I was emptied out. All I could hear were my steps on the hard ground, the roar of cars, the faint water hurdling off the mountain. The call of a raven, repeating his terrible jokes. The wolf was silent.

*

Nan sat in her study, a woollen shawl wrapped round her shoulders. She watched me walk stiffly from the cattle grid. Her face was unreadable. The cottage was cold. She rustled into the hallway and I expected her to be angry but there was something pleading in her eyes, then her expression went hard and she studied me as if I was a stranger. She went to the phone. I kicked off my trainers.

'Could I speak to Constable Strang, please.'

A flash of terror went through me. She was going to send me into care. She faced me, hand on hip, kneading her stomach. 'Hello, Constable Strang? This is Eve Lansdale regarding my grandson … Yes, that's right … Lucas is here … Yes. He walked in the door just now … He's fine … He is well, I tell you. Thank you for your, and your colleagues' time. I am very grateful but he is quite well. This matter is closed. Goodbye.'

Without giving Constable Strang a chance to respond, she put down the phone and returned to her study.

'This house is freezing!' I shouted, and switched on the central heating. I opened a tin of baked beans and toasted some bread on the grill. Then I went to bed.

*

'Where are you?' I said to the empty garden. 'I'll get you,' I said to the woods. 'I'll *have* you,' I said to the mountain. 'You picked on the wrong one when you picked on me.'

'Who are you talking to?'

I whirled.

Nan stood in the sitting room, reading glasses in one hand, hefty book in the other.

'No one.'

'Lucas,' she said ominously.

I curled my fists. Time for the *talk*.

'Are you becoming unmanageable?'

I wanted to storm out but she did that before I could. She thumped upstairs and the door of her bedroom shut as if she wanted to reach it before she burst into tears.

*

I dreamed I had a wolf pup only she was on a long wire that went round her neck and I held the other end. And she hated being on the wire and pulled to get it off. And she was a heavy pull on my arms and the wire round her neck cut into her flesh. I felt it rubbing into her, vibrating through the wire into my hands and up my arms. There was blood. And I wanted to let her go but I held on.

Visitor

I waited till Nan had gone to work before getting up. She'd left her green mug on the kitchen table. Oily brown patches floated on the surface of the tea. I put some toast on the grill and watched the mouse-coloured bird with the Zorro mask I didn't know the name of zip in and out of a hedge. Finally it flew off for good, replaced by a gang of sparrows. Dad said sparrows are like lads, they like punch-ups. But at least when you get that lot in a gang they don't have leaders. They're not pack creatures in the same way as wolves.

After breakfast, I went to fix the puncture on my bike. My breath came out white in the chill air. The sparrows chortled. Suddenly they fell silent. A small brown creature moved in the hedge. Zorro mask was back. No, not a bird – from out of the hedge crept a long, beautifully clean rat. Pink claws gripped a twig, its long dark tail curl-hung after it. Delicately it ate a berry then it returned inside the hedge. The sparrows flew in again, began singing, scarpered when the rat returned. The rat ate, then it crept into the hedge. The sparrows came. They took it in turns.

'Hey!' said Debs, appearing round the corner of the house. 'I knocked.'

I straightened from my bike. 'Didn't hear you.'

'What you doing?'

'Nowt.'

She laughed. 'Learning the language then?'

There was a silence like I was meant to say something so I said, 'How's school?'

'Er…' she said, '… *finished*?'

'Oh yeah,' I said, then added in a lower tone, 'I got suspended.'

'Heard about that.'

I didn't have anything else to say.

'Gonna invite me in then?'

I wiped bike-grime off my hands and led her into the kitchen.

'Bit cold, isn't it?'

'My nan doesn't like to use the heating.'

'Dad's like that.'

'Is he?' I'd thought it was just Nan.

She strolled into the hallway. 'Where *is* Eve?'

'Work,' I said, washing the dirt off my hands, and when I turned, Debs had gone.

I found her in the study, examining a drawing on the wall. She had her beanie on, hands in her jacket pockets high up on her waist so her elbows stuck out at the side. It was sort of tight, that jacket. She seemed to notice me noticing her because when she turned from the picture she caught my eye. For some bit of a second that was too long we kept looking at each other.

'Gonna put the heating on, then?' she said.

She walked up to me, my heart pattered, I got a smell of spearmint and she passed.

I followed.

In the sitting room she crouched to flick through Nan's records, hair falling in her face.

It felt a bit weird standing behind her, so I went to the hearth and started getting a fire ready. Behind me record covers flopped against each other.

'How does this thing work?' she said, sliding a record out of its sleeve and plopping it on the record player.

We knelt side by side, arms touching as she fiddled with switches and dials.

'Here.' I pressed the big button that said *Power* and fired her a sarcastic glance.

She snorted.

A gunshot. We both started. Then a guitar. Someone harangued us with a sneer. Debs clapped her hands.

'This is the best!' she said, jumping up and twirling round before she collapsed into an armchair. I returned to the fire and finished making it, struck a match and put it to newspaper. Flame hissed. Kindling crackled. I sat back on the rug, weight through my palms, heat on my face. Steepling her fingers, Debs peered at me over her hands, evil-genius style. I lay back. The band sounded like they were trying to get somewhere but didn't care too much about it.

Thump thump.

She'd taken off her DMs and curled her feet under her.

When it got to the chorus, I joined in, sneering like the singer.

I let out a howling note that went on for ever and Debs laughed. Her purple-socked feet came out and she prodded me gently.

'Stop it!'

'Nooooh!'

She laughed again but left her feet where they were. I stopped singing and we listened. Some other feeling was in the room now. Flame licked dry wood. Debs slid her feet between the rug and my back. My heart sped up. I kept on watching the fire but all I was aware of now was her. The push of those high wedges under my ribs. My ribs expanding against her, contracting. I hoped she wouldn't feel how fast my heart was beating. She slid one foot out, curled her toes against my ribs.

I put my hand out and held her ankle.

For perhaps a second neither of us moved. Then she snatched both feet away.

'Oh!' she said, standing up and rushing to the record player. She lowered the volume. 'I nearly forgot.' She took a piece of folded paper from her back pocket and held it out.

The blotchy black-and-white flyer showed a wolf. At the top it read, *The Cumbrian Wolf!* and below, *An Evening of Local Stories, The Crown*, and a date in January.

'We have to go,' she said.

The speakers played horrible distorted white noise now, not music.

'Are you all right?' she said.

It stayed in me. It followed me round.

I got up and went over to the record player. There was a pop of static as I lifted off the needle-arm.

'What's wrong?'

The sparrows, busy in the hedge, were sharing berries with the beautifully clean rat. The twigs and branches were dripping. The whole world was in life except me, useless, stopped.

'Luke.'

I faced her.

'We should go,' she said. 'Find out about stuff.'

Her eyes were wide, bright.

I managed a nod and turned to the window.

'I thought you'd be interested,' she said, disappointment in her voice.

I searched the brown mountainside, the black rocks, the snow.

There was a thump and a rumpling sound and I turned

to find her hauling on her DMs, twisting the laces good and tight like she was strangling her ankles.

A car came up the lane.

She stood and put on her beanie. I had the horrible thought that our friendship – if we even had one – was finished. I wanted to say something to stop her, to stop my own brain, but all I could do was watch her getting ready to go.

Nan's little Fiat bumped over the cattle grid.

Debs headed for the door.

'Wait.'

She didn't stop. Before I reached the hall, she met Nan on the front step. I stayed in the sitting room, listening.

'Deborah!'

'Hello, Eve, I'm off as it happens.'

'Oh, what a shame.'

'Bye.'

'Do you not want to stay for a cup of tea?'

I didn't move.

'Oh, stay for a cuppa, Deborah. I haven't seen you in ages.'

Debs must have agreed because Nan said, 'I'll put the kettle on,' and headed for the kitchen and Debs came back into the sitting room and dropped into an armchair without looking at me. I went to help Nan.

'Have you two fallen out?' Nan whispered, preparing tea.

'No.'

Crockery clacked. Milk glugged.

She gave me a squeeze on the arm.

The kettle boiled.

'Right,' she said with a quick smile.

We went back in.

Debs was flicking through Nan's book on the miners' strike.

'So, how's school been, Deborah?'

'Ta,' Debs said, putting the book on the arm of her chair and taking a mug. 'Rubbish, as it happens. How's work? Any good cases?'

'Hard cases,' said Nan.

'Nut cases,' said Debs.

Nan laughed. 'That's about right.'

Debs studied the photo on the back of the book. It showed police on horses charging a line of bare-chested men. I went and stood at the fireplace and pushed at burning logs with the poker.

'Did *you* ever get in trouble with the law, Eve?' Debs asked.

'Once.'

I turned round. Nan looked grey, serious. 'You?' I said, incredulous.

'That doesn't sound like a compliment, Lucas,' Nan said.

'What did you do?' Debs said.

'I was threatened with arrest for driving a pony and trap.'

Debs laughed out loud.

'What were you doing,' I said, 'dangerous driving?'

'No,' Nan said defensively. 'Besides, I wouldn't have done, I had your mother to think of.'

My heart thumped. Why'd she mention Mum? She never mentioned Mum.

'So what happened?' Debs said.

'It was around the time of the Battle of the Beanfield –'

'What's that?' Debs asked.

'When police attacked travellers at Stonehenge.'

'You were attacked by the police?' Debs said, astonished.

'No, but they thought we were part of the Stonehenge group. A friend was crossing the country and she didn't have a car so she went by pony and trap. And she needed someone to go with her so I volunteered. My baby was only a few months old at the time.'

My baby? That was my mum she was talking about. And I couldn't believe she'd taken a baby – my mum – with her anyway. Was she nuts? Was she the worst mother who ever existed?

'In the end, the police had to let us go.'

'Why?' I asked in a sulky voice.

'Probably,' Debs said, 'because they didn't count on

having to deal with a woman who knew how to handle them.'

'Very true, Deborah,' Nan said, still stern but evidently pleased with the praise. 'Although, you need your wits around you with that bunch of thugs.'

Debs snorted a laugh.

'Mum hated you,' I said quietly.

There was a horrible silence in the room. Even Debs, who I'd never seen anything but tough, seemed embarrassed.

'How are your parents, Deborah?' said Nan, after only the tiniest of pauses.

'Oh,' said Debs, surprised for a moment by the change of subject. 'Good. Mum's good. Dad's good. Well … you know what he's like.'

'Still got a bee in his bonnet about the "wolf", has he?'

Debs' manner changed.

'You don't believe in it, Deborah, surely, a girl of your intelligence?'

'Well, in a way I do.'

'There's no wild wolves in England.'

'Well, *he* saw it.' She nodded at me.

Nan peered shrewdly at me, then between me and Debs, which seemed to annoy Debs even more so she said, 'If a thing looks like a wolf, sounds like a wolf, and acts like a wolf, then it's probably a wolf.'

'Unless this young man was mistaken, which he very well could be.'

'It's not just him, is it? It's Dad. Other farmers.'

Nan waved her hand like she was waving away a fly.

Debs flushed.

'Why aren't you at work?' I said crossly.

'It's Christmas,' Nan fired back.

Another long, awkward silence. Debs put down her tea and looked like she was about to leave. But then she said, 'Why haven't you got a Christmas tree?'

Nan was startled. *I* was startled. I also realised suddenly how rubbish and weird Nan was about things – we didn't even have a Christmas tree. I stared into my mug.

'Well,' said Nan, 'we haven't decided if we want one yet.'

'I don't like tea,' I said. 'I don't know why you always make it for me.'

'I'm off,' said Debs, standing up. 'I only popped in to say hello.'

I didn't want her to go.

'I'll go to the storytelling night with you,' I blurted.

Debs stared at me. 'You should get a tree,' she said. 'Some decoration.'

'Okay,' I breathed.

'Right.' But she didn't go, instead she started trying to

get something out of an inside pocket. 'I got you this by the way.' It was a present, covered with Christmas gift wrap and tied by a silver ribbon. She offered it casually like it didn't mean much.

'Thanks,' I said, taking it with a hot hand. She wouldn't meet my eye.

'What did he get you?' said Nan.

Debs shrugged.

'I haven't wrapped it yet,' I lied.

After Debs had gone, Nan said in a voice of deep warning, 'You'd better buy her something.' She took mugs into the kitchen. I followed her and stood in the doorway while she washed up. Finally I asked her:

'What was it like having Mum with you? When you crossed the country on a pony and trap? Why did you take her?'

It was strange saying the name *Mum*. It dropped to the pit of my stomach like a physical object.

'She was a baby. She needed looking after. There wasn't any option. She seemed to enjoy it.'

'Where was her father?'

'Working, I expect.'

'Did you miss her after she left you for good?'

She stilled like she'd been made into stone.

Then, curtly, as if it cost her something to do it, she nodded. She continued to wash up. She looked bowed, sunk under the weight of my question.

'We should get a tree,' I said.

Her back was to me and I couldn't tell what she felt.

She gave another nod, like that cost her something too.

Christmas

On Christmas Eve I spent the morning in Kendal hunting for presents until I had a brain wave and tried the second-hand music shop, which sold new vinyl too, and got the latest twelve inch by The Young Savages; probably Debs already had the song but she wouldn't have the object, and I thought she might like that, even if she couldn't play it. For Nan I bought a box of different kinds of specialist teas. Nan gave me a lift up to Debs' house but they weren't in so I left her wrapped-up gift propped at the door.

I went into the woods and cut holly, too. Dad used to cut holly and mistletoe and bring them home. Home was full of greenery at Christmas. Nan's concession to the festive season was turning on the central heating from four pm.

*

Later that evening, Mitesh phoned to wish me a happy Christmas. Mitesh doesn't celebrate Christmas, though he still likes the stuff that goes with it.

I didn't know what to say. We never spoke that much usually, just played computer games and football and listened to music. Only, now he started to tell me about this new band he was into, The Vanguard. My attention kept getting taken by the sound of the fire in the sitting room where Nan sat reading her new, fat book about the Iraq war. And what Mitesh was saying seemed childish somehow, and I didn't know how I could ever have been interested in any of it.

Mitesh stopped talking. I searched my head for something to talk about. It was suddenly empty.

'How's school?' Mitesh said.

'The best.'

That caused a stormy hiss in the receiver of Mitesh's laughter. He thought I was being sarcastic. I wasn't, I was just lying. So I said, 'Lots of work to do, new books and different syllabus. So it's busy, you know.'

'Made any friends?'

'Oh yeah. Malky, Debs ... Steve, Zed, Alex.'

Silence.

I was about to say I had to help Nan with dinner when he said, 'Your voice has changed.'

'How?'

'You sound northern.'

I didn't know what to say to that except that Mitesh sounded American.

There was a silence then he told me about the mocks

he would be doing after Christmas. He was going to breeze it, he said.

None of what Mitesh was saying was important. None of it. Not in comparison to people dying.

'How's your work going?' he said.

'Exams don't matter,' I said. 'They're meaningless.'

'Well, the mocks matter to *me*,' said Mitesh, hurt-sounding.

There was another quiet.

'Nan wants me to help with dinner. I've got to go, Mitesh.'

'All right, bud.' He sounded like he was weighing something in his mind. He didn't finish weighing it, he just said, 'See ya.'

I went back into the sitting room.

'How's your friend?' said Nan, not looking up from her book.

'All right,' I said.

I stared into the fire. She turned a page. The wind sifted outside, going round the cottage.

'When are we going back to clear my house?'

She looked up from her book.

'Well,' I said, 'we're going to have to clear it, aren't we?'

'We can leave it until half term. Or Easter.'

'Why not do it now while you're off work?'

'I'm not strong enough to do it now.'

She returned to reading.

'What was she like, Mum, when she was a girl?'

She put down her book and took off her reading glasses, considered me without saying anything.

'Like you,' she said.

'Like me how?'

Her gaze stayed on me then moved to the fire, the flames dancing there.

'Like me how?'

'Obstinate. Strong-willed. Dreamy.'

I tried to remember some moment when Mum could have been strong-willed but all that came to mind was her laughing. She liked to have fun. She liked to win when we played football when I was small. Is that what Nan meant?

'You look like her, too,' Nan said.

That stunned me.

'I see her in you,' she said.

I said, 'You remind me of her too.'

Her eyes widened.

'Come to think of it,' I said, 'you're hard-headed and obstinate too.'

She continued to stare, eyes shining. Then she winced.

'What is it, Nan?'

She shook her head.

The fire crackled. We watched it dance.

Strang

After Christmas, the weather turned bad.

We had another day's snow. Granite crags were deep black against it. It filled clefts. The lawn was a white carpet unvisited except by the Zorro-masked sleek brown bird.

They gritted and salted the main road so it was passable, but the radio kept telling stories of spins and crashes. Some idiot who went alone onto the fells got lost and was discovered the next morning, frozen to death.

One day between Christmas and New Year, Nan decided she should deliver items to the food bank in Kendal. It was a smoky blue day. I told her she should wait until a thaw but she said people couldn't wait to eat. She asked me if I wanted to go with her and I said no. Although, I did go out with a spade and chipped and cracked the ice on the lane, shovelling it onto the verge, to make her descent easier. It felt good to do. I enjoyed the sting on my skin and the burn in my lungs of the frozen air. I enjoyed working against the cold that locked the world.

Driving down the frozen lane to the main road was a dangerous business. I stood at the top of the lane and watched her go. The frost on the gate posts stood on end like magnetised metal filings. She edged down the slope. The tiny Fiat billowed white exhaust. She locked brakes at one point and slid then regained control and crawled out of sight.

When she'd gone, I decided to do something useful – make soup. We had plenty of vegetables and I put on that record that Debs had liked and listened to the music drifting through from the sitting room, and whined along where I could to the incomprehensible singer. From time to time I had a sharp fear that Nan was dead. I heard the slam of metal, the crunch. So I sang louder, and chopped and heated and stirred. After half an hour, Nan's car sounded up the lane.

I went to the study to check if she'd need any help manoeuvring through the gate in the ice. The roof of a white car appeared through the trees, then a blue-and-yellow check pattern came into view and a police estate car bumped over the cattle grid and stopped in the turning circle.

All my blood felt as if it had drained out of me.

A policeman got out.

He leaned through the open car door. When he straightened, he fitted a cap to fair hair, slammed the door, and crunched towards the cottage.

Nan was dead.

I went into the kitchen.

The front-door knocker sounded – *Tat-tat-tat*.

Coffins have door-knocker handles at the sides to lift them.

Tat-tat-tat went the iron knocker again, but a micro-second slower than before. It made it sound like a sarcastic comment on the first knock.

I didn't move. The letterbox creaked.

'Hello?' called a ragged, deep voice.

The lid of the saucepan rattled with the pressure of steam.

'Hello?'

The letterbox creaked shut.

Soon the ignition would start and he would go. I waited for the sound of the engine.

A shadow fell and I turned. At the kitchen window, huge, stood the policeman. His shirt was very white and his tie very black.

For a moment we stared at each other. Then he pointed at the back door.

I bring death.

He jabbed his finger.

I crossed the kitchen, opened the door.

'Lucas Pettifer?' he said in a slow voice.

I didn't reply.

'Are you Lucas Pettifer?'

I nodded.

'The grandson of Eve Lansdale?'

'Yes.' It came out as a whisper.

'Can I come in, please?'

I shuffled backwards. He came in, closed the door, and took off his black cap.

'Mind if we sit here?'

His cap went on the table upside down. It had a brown sweatband stained dark in the middle. He sat. I sat.

Big shoulders. Big arms. A line through his fair hair where the sweatband had been pressing.

'Are you aware your grandmother contacted us last week?'

The saucepan lid chattered.

'Friday night before Christmas. Busiest night of the year. And we had to go chasing round for a teenager who's had a row with his gran. Do you know what that is?'

'No,' I said, only it came out as a whisper.

'That's a joke, Lucas.'

I gulped. 'What's happened to Nan?'

'What about *you*, Lucas, more to the point? Do you know what that is?'

'What *what* is?'

'Don't play the muppet with me, son.'

I stared. 'I don't –'

'Shut up!'

I jumped. In a quiet voice I said, 'You weren't clear what you meant when you said "that". I don't know what "that" is. Is my nan all right?'

His colossal frame leaned forward. A vast pair of hands, like an ancient book, opened.

'Wasting police time. That's what I'm talking about.'

Why wouldn't he tell me about Nan?

'I had a word with your school this morning. And you know what?'

'No.'

'You've got a terrible behaviour record.'

'Are they allowed to tell you that?'

The policeman's eyes narrowed.

'Are you ripping it, son?'

A car puttered into the woods.

The policeman kept his eyes on me. I had no idea what he meant. Or why he was torturing me, not telling me what had happened to Nan.

The car juddered over the cattle grid and the policeman's eyes shifted towards the sound. A few seconds later a key sounded in the door.

'Lucas!' Nan shouted.

I jumped up. Nan ran in, her face a mask of terror.

I was flooded by a sense of her physical presence, her short grey hair, her soft skin, her wrinkly *age*. But despite all that age she brimmed with aliveness, with *person*. She was more *person* than anyone I'd ever seen. She gripped me hard. She smelt of soap and soft skin. I rubbed my cheek on her rough wool jacket. Then she stood back and looked into my eyes. 'Are you all right?'

I nodded.

She pushed me away and faced the policeman. It was a thing to see, that. The emotion bled out of her and her body got still like a footballer before a penalty, and she said, crisp, quiet, slow, 'What are you doing?'

'I'm having a word with your grandson about the recent incident that you – '

'What's your name?'

'Strang, madam. Constable Strang. I'm here to have a quiet word with your –'

He stopped mid-flow because Nan had left the room. She returned armed with a notepad and pen. And now she read aloud the numbers on his shoulder and wrote them down.

'Are you aware of the law relating to the interviewing of minors, Constable Strang?' said Nan, finishing her note.

Nan waited for an answer. I waited too. Constable Strang's blond eyelashes fluttered. The tip of his tongue appeared between his lips.

'In what sense …?'

'In the sense that you are not permitted to interview a minor, Constable Strang, without a guardian or another suitable adult present.'

Head tilted, mouth a thin line, Nan waited for a response. Constable Strang moved his lips noiselessly a few times. Then he spoke.

'I was having an informal –'

Nan closed her eyes as if she couldn't bear to look at him a moment longer and raised her palm in a stop-sign. 'Who is your superior?'

'Madam, I'm not going to –'

'Sergeant Thwaite?'

No response.

'Get out,' said Nan.

A moment passed then the policeman picked up his cap from the table and walked straight past Nan, down the hallway, and out. Nan followed him to the door and stood with her arms folded. There wasn't much space for him to manoeuvre his big estate car now that Nan had parked too, so he had to shuttle back and forth and we watched until finally he made it out of the yard, mumbled over the cattle grid, and disappeared.

'Idiot,' Nan hissed, then took a sharp intake of breath and put her hand on her hip.

I was about to give her another hug when she said, 'What's that burning smell?'

She marched past me to the kitchen and I went after her to rescue the soup.

Storytellers

I paced the kitchen waiting for Debs. We were going to the pub for the storyteller evening and her dad was giving us a lift.

'Stop pacing!' Nan called from the study.

The wolf would appear on the road, Debs' dad would veer off, we'd crash.

'You feel nervous,' Nan called. 'That's normal – you like her.'

'What?' I called, stopping.

She didn't reply. I went into the study. Shawl round her shoulders at her bureau, she was lit by a reading lamp in a bright cave of papers.

'No I don't,' I said, and returned to the kitchen where I resumed pacing.

Nan came in.

'What's on your mind?' she said.

'We're going to crash.'

'That's unlikely.'

'But not impossible.'

'No, it's not impossible.'

I felt like saying something back but held it in check.

An engine sounded on the lane. Nan and I exchanged a glance, then a car drove over the cattle grid and I went to the door. The trees rushed in the high wind. The silver estate's headlamps burned furiously.

'Have a good time!'

I slammed the door.

'Hi,' said Debs as I got in.

'Hi,' I said.

Sheridan Benedict said nothing.

We crossed the cattle grid and accelerated down the lane. Debs put her head round the front seat, eyes shining with excitement. 'Good Christmas?'

'Yeah. How about you?'

She made a face and in a sarcastic tone said, 'Brilliant.'

'You two are too young to be going to a pub,' said her dad.

Debs faced front. 'Oh, that's right, like you never stepped inside a pub before you were eighteen, did you?'

We turned onto the main road. Something breathed hot on my cheek and I cried out.

Debs' face reappeared. 'Polka!' she laughed.

The sheepdog stood in the boot, head over the back seat, wet nose at my ear.

'Push her away.'

I didn't have to because Polka vanished. Then she reappeared with her muzzle over my other shoulder, breath hot and stinky, intrigued at where we were going

213

at this time of night. I put my palm out and gently pushed. She didn't move. I pushed harder. She closed her mouth but still didn't move, just stared forward solemnly. I decided that that was better than her panting. At which point she opened her mouth and started panting again. I leaned between the front seats.

'I've been reading the book you got me,' I said.

'Is it good?'

'Yeah. Really good.'

'I thought you'd like it.'

'What's it about?' asked Sheridan Benedict.

'Wolves,' said Debs.

Sheridan Benedict rotated his head and looked at me with the weirdness he was so good at. I sat back hard.

I wondered how long it would take to get there. If we'd get there alive. All I could see was the glowing dashboard and the bonnet, gobbling white lines, and all I could hear was the engine and Polka panting in my ear.

After ten minutes the indicator clicked. We turned and began to head uphill. Sheridan said, 'They won't let you in anyway, you're underage.'

That got no response.

A few minutes more and he indicated again and we slowed towards a stone building. A sign outside. Smoke rising from the chimney.

'I'll pick you up at eleven.'

He stopped. Debs got out but when I opened my door Sheridan grabbed my sleeve. The ceiling bulb lit his discoloured knuckles and a finger-joint wrapped by a dirty plaster. The lenses of his glasses flashed as he lunged. 'You treat her badly, lad, you'll know about it.'

The strap of his seat belt lay twisted across his throat. For a moment I saw Dad – his neck bent – and I whipped my sleeve from his fist and scrambled out, banging my knee on the door.

'Eleven o' –' he called but my door-slam cut off the rest.

I limped across the car park rubbing my knee. Debs bounced on the balls of her feet. 'What did he say?'

I started to mutter something but she said, 'This is exciting!' and I followed her in.

A long bar, brasses gleaming on a hearth before a fire, greeted us. On the walls hung old maps, and drawings of ghylls, waterfalls and peaks. But the place was empty. The only person there was a bored girl behind the bar, leaned over her phone, scrolling.

Perplexed, Debs said, 'Where's the storytellers?'

She lifted her head, condemned us both with an expression of boredom, a level of boredom so extreme I hadn't yet experienced it in my life, and returned to the lit pool of her phone. 'Through back,' she drawled without looking up.

We walked to the only other door and found the back

of the pub different from the front. A passage with a concrete floor and whitewashed stone walls, as cold as a walk-in freezer and brightly lit by a fluorescent tube. Suddenly I didn't want to know any more about the wolf. 'Er … Should we … get a drink or something first?'

Debs headed down the passage and disappeared through the thick curtain at the end and after a moment I followed and once I had fought my way through the heavy fabric I found myself in darkness. The only lights were some blue spots shining on a wide stage and, at the centre of the stage, a microphone stand. A figure loomed from the darkness, leaned close to Debs, and we were led down steps to a near-full row. We pushed along, bumping knees. Unlike the freezing passage, the air in the room was warm, humid, and nearly unbreathable. Twisting to take off my jacket, I met the stare of a bearded man sat behind us. He didn't break eye contact. An elbow from Debs faced me front.

I was immediately confronted by a pair of tremendously thick legs on the stage which belonged a short, stout woman in a tartan skirt who announced in a formal, deep voice, the first storyteller.

My stomach felt tight as a drum.

A man wearing an anorak over a suit stepped to the microphone. He began his story but I was so aware of the room, the pressure of the air, and the concentration of the audience around me, I couldn't take anything in. But gradually, bits of the story filtered through. Something about a woman and a man and their child. But the way he told it, or perhaps it was the story itself, wouldn't let me hold onto it. It was like being back at school, where nothing would go into my head. The man paused. Debs' tension grew. The man went on, only now he kept hesitating. After several hesitations, he fell silent. Debs was shaking, then seemed to gulp something down. The man continued his story but after a few seconds dried up altogether. The only sound was an amplified buzz of silence. The man hummed a high, nervous note. Debs went into a frenzy as if she was desperate for the loo or trying to contain a sneeze. The high hum ended, followed by another long buzzing silence then an involuntary gurgle from the man's throat, at which point Debs exploded with laughter.

She clapped her hands to her mouth and contained the laughter for a few seconds, then in a jagged snort erupted again and her hands flew away and this time she didn't seem able to stop, at least not until the woman with the enormous legs thundered down the aisle and from the end of the row hissed, in what was a surprisingly loud voice: 'I must ask you to leave!'

We stood, bumped knees, then hurried to the steps where I tripped and Debs exploded again. We practically ran out, through the pub, right into the cold night air. Debs couldn't stop laughing. Tears rolled down her face.

Eventually she did stop but then she saw my face and started again.

I kicked at the pub's stone step. I didn't know why she was laughing.

I didn't know why I wasn't.

She laughed herself out.

'It's freezing,' I said to the biting air.

Eyes wide and shining, swaying, a hundred percent alive as if she had just done a sprint, she faced me openly. I don't know why, because I hadn't wanted to know about the wolf, and hadn't wanted to go into the storyteller room, but now that we'd been thrown out, I felt like I'd been robbed of something. Or maybe I just felt cross because Debs could do happiness in a way that I couldn't – so I left her out there in the cold, walked back inside, ordered a soft drink, and sat by the window.

After a few minutes, Debs came in. She bought herself a soft drink and came over.

'God, that was funny,' she said.

I nodded glumly.

'My stomach hurts,' she said. Then, after a shy glance at me, she said, 'I couldn't help it.' She tried suppressing a smile but failed.

I forced a smile back. I wished I'd been able to treat the night like she had. Maybe I would have done a few months earlier.

'What shall we do, then?' said Debs finally.

'Dunno.'

'Don't fancy staying here.'

'Me either.'

She phoned her parents but they didn't answer.

'Can your nan give us a lift home?'

I phoned Nan but she didn't answer.

'We're stuck here till eleven, then,' she said.

I managed not to groan.

*

The storytellers poured in for their half-time break, gathered at the bar. The stout woman with giant calves glared at us.

'Weirdo,' muttered Debs.

'She's probably got stubbly shins,' I said.

Debs laughed.

The woman saw Debs laughing and looked so angry I thought she was going to come over but before she could a bearded man approached us, holding a big glass of beer, the waist of his jeans circling the middle of his belly like it was the circumference of a beach ball. 'You'll have to forgive us,' he said in an American accent. 'We're amateurs.'

Debs fired him a glance. 'Really?' she said, dripping sarcasm.

The man said, 'You like tales, then?'

Debs opened her mouth – to issue another insult probably – so I said, 'We came to hear about the wolf.'

'You kids have an interest in wolves, do you?' the man said, sitting down, at which Debs shot me a glance of alarm. There was an awkward silence, then the man said, 'I met a wolf once.'

'Where, in a zoo?' Debs said.

'No, Siberia.'

Debs and I exchanged a glance.

'I was trekking through a forest,' the man said.

'Is this true?' said Debs.

'Yes.'

He didn't say anything more.

'So, what happened?' Debs said.

'That's it.'

'Good story,' said Debs.

'It wasn't a story,' he smiled. 'Each night they'd gather on a ridge. Watch me. Nothing else. Just watch. And one particular night, one wolf put his head into my tent.'

I stared.

'Sure he did,' said Debs. 'Wasn't your tent zipped up?'

'He kind of wormed his nose through at the bottom then pushed the zipper up.'

'Sure he did,' said Debs.

'There is one story I know about wolves,' the man said, undeterred. 'But this one, I don't know if it's true or not. It's from my part of the world.'

'Met a werewolf, did you?' said Debs.

'Do you want to hear it?' the man said in a jolly tone, seemingly oblivious to Debs' steady stream of insults.

'Yes,' I said.

'This story is about a boy named Sheem.'

'I thought it was about a wolf,' said Debs.

'Shut up, Debs,' I said.

She shot me a glance but kept quiet.

'Go on,' I said, 'we're listening.'

'So, when the story starts Sheem is little. He lived with his parents and sister by the great northern forest. It was a very big forest, very dark. And wolves lived in this forest. Okay so far?' he smiled.

'Yes,' I said, fixing Debs with a stare.

'Sheem wasn't much older than a baby. He was a happy infant, everything delighted him: the forest, the grass, the sky. One day, a bear came out of the forest. He was drawn by the scent of food, and he surprised the family. Sheem's father tried to scare off the bear, which enraged the animal, so much so that he attacked the family. With one blow the bear killed Sheem's father. Sheem's mother scooped up the kids and ran into the forest, pursued by the bear. Now, the bear's a fast animal. He caught the mom and killed her. Like that. With one blow. He would have killed Sheem and his sister, too, but at that very moment, a party of warriors arrived.

They had been hunting in the forest and been alerted by the mother's screams and the cries of the children. The warriors fought the bear. It was a very great bear, and ferocious, and the battle went on for a long time but the warriors were courageous and strong and they defeated the bear. And they rescued Sheem's sister. But of Sheem there was no sign.'

'What happened to him?' I said.

'The warriors searched for hours but in the end when it got too dark to see any more they had to give up their search and return to their village. And they took with them Sheem's sister.'

'What about Sheem?' I said.

'Remember that pack of wolves who lived in the forest?' the bearded man said.

'How could we forget?' said Debs.

'They found Sheem. He had crawled deep into the forest, and they found him.'

'And ate him?' suggested Debs.

'No, they brought him up as one of their own.'

'A wolf-baby,' said Debs.

'Precisely,' the man said. 'A wolf-baby. Then a wolf-boy. Years passed,' the man continued, 'and Sheem's sister grew up. She still lived with the tribe who had rescued her but they were a travelling people and now they lived in another part of the country. One day Sheem's sister was washing clothes at the river. It was early spring, the

222

time of the great thaw, and the river was beginning to break up.'

I remembered the scene in *The Call of the Wild* with the people crossing the frozen river. The ice cracked under their feet and they drowned.

'The ice floes were moving, great chunks of them. Like islands or rafts. And Sheem's sister stood on the river bank taking a pause in her washing, and she saw on one of the ice floes, a boy.

'Sheem's sister couldn't believe it. The boy stared at her. And she stared back. She was so amazed because she recognised him. It was Sheem. Only he'd grown. He was nearly a man now. But he was definitely Sheem – she knew it was him.

'He jumped from his ice floe onto another one. But he didn't move like a human being any more, he moved like a wolf.

'"Sheem!" she called to him. "Sheem!" He didn't say anything but he jumped to another block of ice. It was like he was trying to get to her across the breaking river. Then she noticed a movement on the far bank and saw, gathered on the snow, wolves. And as Sheem jumped from ice floe to ice floe, gradually she understood that he was not working his way towards her but towards the wolves. And he was beginning to change. He was no longer a boy. And he was not a man either. He was becoming a wolf. And when he made that final leap to the far bank, his transformation was complete and when he landed he was pure wolf. "Sheem!" she shouted but the wolf joined the pack and together they moved up the snowy bank and disappeared into the forest.'

'What happened then?' said Debs.

'Nothing,' I said, 'That's the end of the story. She never saw him again.'

The man met my eye, grinned and nodded. 'What do you think?' he said, suddenly cheery and drinking from his glass of beer.

'Yeah, it's all right,' said Debs. Which was high praise, coming from her.

'Thanks,' the bearded man said. 'Like I say, we're amateurs. Ah, they're going back in.'

And with a nod, he downed his beer – about half of the glass – wiped his wet beard, and followed the others back to the storytellers' room.

We sat in silence for several minutes. I gazed out at the black, cold night.

'We could walk home,' Debs suggested.

An icy blast struck the window, shook the frame.

She tried her parents, and I tried Nan, but no one answered.

'I know a shortcut,' said Debs.

Dark

We followed the road for twenty minutes as it wound down the mountain, the wind roaring in our ears, then Debs crossed to some trees. Under them, the darkness was almost total and I stumbled against her.

'Watch it!' she said.

'Are you sure you know the way?'

She went on, along a muddy path. I followed but when she called out for me to get a move on she sounded far ahead. I hurried towards her voice, widening my eyes for more light but there wasn't any. I had to slap my feet on the path to keep upright because I couldn't see where I was stepping.

I bumped into something soft and solid and my jaw clapped shut and I let out a little 'oh!'

From whatever I'd hit came a little grinding sound then a flame from a cigarette lighter showed me it was Debs.

'Watch it!' she said.

'Watch it yourself!'

Her lighter flame died. A cigarette-end glowed. She went on.

I stood watching the tiny orange light.

'People died in the Yukon when they took stupid routes,' I called, keeping my eyes trained on that floating orange dot.

'Well, *you kon* always go another way if you don't like this one,' she punned back.

'Ha. Ha.'

'Better than your jokes, anyway.'

'I don't make jokes.'

'I know.'

We squelched on in silence. I remembered a story Mum had told me about a fairy leading a drunk man out to the marshes to drown him.

That would be just about my luck.

'Hurry up,' Debs called, sounding further away than the cigarette-end suggested.

The wind soughed in the trees. I splattered on, stepped in a deep puddle, and swore.

The cigarette-end moved in an arc to hip height.

'Why'd you have to get us thrown out, anyway?' I said, aiming for the light. 'This is rubbish.'

Silence. The light rose, glowed harder, fell.

'D'you know what you are?' I said, reaching her.

'No. But I bet a thousand quid you're going to tell me.'

'You're a perfect misanthrope.'

'Do you even know what a misanthrope is?'

226

'Yeah,' I said. 'And you are one.'

The cigarette rose, pulsed hard, then relaxed before it flew out sideways.

Darkness. Shoes squelched on.

'Hey!' I strained my eyes for more light.

I ran a few steps, stopped.

'Don't leave me!'

I could hear the wind hissing in the trees.

'Debs! That's not funny.'

The wind gusted in the trees.

'Debs!'

Out of the darkness, faint and far away, Debs called, 'Find your own way home, you *bairn*, if you're fed up spending time with misanthropes!'

'Debs!'

No answer.

'Aw, come ON!'

I broke into a jog, frightened of bumping into her again or falling down a drop. But more frightened of losing her.

Which is when she screamed.

'Debs!'

No response.

'That's not funny!' I shouted.

The wind rushed in the trees.

'Stop messing about!'

I ran forward, blind.

'Debs!'

Nothing.

'Debs!'

Thunder rumbled through the ground. The way the earth vibrated, it was like the fighter-jet was coming towards me. The thunder spread, intensified, and reached up from the ground and into my body and as it filled me a thick-throated snarl ripped the air like a petrol motor bursting into life, then a solid mass bigger than a human flashed through the air towards me. I had no time. It brushed my arm, and was gone.

'Debs!' I bellowed.

No answer.

I ran towards where I'd last heard her. 'Debs!'

My skull clunked something hard: 'Oomf!' I cried.

'Ow!' said Debs.

I sat down hard. My head reeled.

'Debs?'

'Ee-rrrrgh.'

'Debs!'

I clutched her.

She screamed.

'Debs, it's all right. It's me!'

She clutched me.

'My God,' she wailed. 'My God.'

'What happened? Are you okay?'

She smelled of earth; her lips were wet and waxy on my cheek. She gripped me close, moaning into my neck.

Then she pushed me away, struggled to her feet, and splashed away. I slipped on the mud going after her.

'Debs!'

My fingers scuffed her jacket, then something connected with the side of my head and stars exploded in front of my eyes.

'Don't hit me!'

Her breathing cry-juddered. I waited.

Her breath began to even out.

The trees – they sounded like fir trees and pines – sighed breezily.

'What happened, Debs?'

Debs stood absolutely still, then she fled.

I ran after her, caught her up.

'Did you see it?' I asked.

She hurried on.

'What happened?'

She didn't respond. There was just pure concentrated march now, and all of whatever had happened to her in the darkness was going into her march.

After a few minutes we came out from the trees onto tarmac and I could see her outline dimly. Still she marched, then we came to the village and I could see her in the streetlight, a smear of mud on her cheek, her eyes glassy. Something bad had happened.

We neared the point where we would have to go in different directions to get to our homes but I didn't want to leave her. So when we reached the junction I stayed with her. She wheeled on me with an expression I had never seen in her before – real fear.

'What is it?' I said.

She retreated one step from me, and I saw that it was stronger than fear, it was terror.

'Stay away from me!'

Dead leaves pasted her jacket and her clothes were covered with mud. Her eyes had gone big and I realised that this terror was to do with me. She was scared of me.

'But I should make sure you're safe,' I said.

'Stay. *Away.*'

She hurried down the street. I watched her go, walking robotically along the middle of the street, then I started after her.

She heard me and whirled.

'Go away!' she screamed at the top of her voice. 'Go away!'

'Debs, I just want –'

'I saw it. I saw the wolf.'

I stared at her.

'You brought it,' she said. 'You've brought death.'

That rooted me, like I had been turned to iron.

For a moment she swayed like madness had got into her, like she was someone else, not Debs, then she ran down the street.

Skate Shoes

That stupid, horrible room with the coat-stand and plants and the rumbling stomach of a radiator. Ian in his low comfy chair wearing stupid blue skate shoes. Gold wedding ring shining under the electric light. Outside, midwinter dark.

'The first thing to tell you, Lucas,' said Ian softly, 'is that these sessions are confidential.'

I thought about Constable Strang knowing I was in trouble at school. School told him that. Which they weren't allowed to do. This confidentiality thing is just a lie.

'So,' Ian said, 'I won't tell Nan. Or your teachers. It's important you understand that.'

'She *your* nan or something?'

'Sorry?'

'Why'd you call her "Nan"? She's not *your* nan, is she?'

He thought about this a moment, then said, 'Your grandmother.'

The radiator's stomach started making funny noises. The third chair – Nan's chair – had been slid away behind me. I was faintly aware of it, off to my side, behind me.

'So, you decided to come back,' said Ian.

What did he want, a prize for stating the obvious? He sat with his legs splayed too far apart – like he was happy with himself. Arms relaxed. False as those blue skate shoes, kids' shoes on an old man.

The window behind him was dark. I tried staring at that for a bit.

The silence started to get weird.

'I suppose you want to talk about why I got suspended?' I said.

'You can talk about whatever you like.'

That was a surprise.

'What would you like to talk about?'

Computer games. That's what Mitesh and me used to talk about. Or … things. *Stuff.* That's what Debs and me seemed to talk about. I hadn't seen her since the night of the wolf and she hadn't replied to my texts.

'What were you thinking about just then?' Ian said.

'Nothing.'

'You seemed to get sad suddenly.'

I shrugged.

'Why don't we talk about your holidays, if you're not sure what you want to talk about? How have your Christmas holidays been?'

I shrugged. 'All right.'

'They must have been … difficult.'

'Why?'

'It must be the first Christmas without your parents?'

He waited for me to respond.

I shrugged.

'The first on your own,' he confirmed.

'Nan was there.'

'How was that?'

'Fine.'

'Good.'

That got me angry for some reason. As if he'd caught me out. He didn't say anything more. So I didn't say anything. The silence grew solid, like the air was made of a thick, invisible substance.

'Can you open a window?'

'It gets very cold in here.'

The radiator popped a bubble.

He stood suddenly and went behind his chair and opened the window with an unsealing of its rubber edges to a sluice of traffic noise and cold.

He sat down again.

'Is that better?'

I hoped he was getting a draught on his neck.

'Yeah.'

I unclenched fists. I was glad of the winter air. A high-pitched hum sounded from my own ears. My pulse thudded in my skull. I wanted to close my eyes. I stared at the open window.

I glanced at him.

He was waiting.

I felt my breath, which must have been held a bit, go out easier.

Probably I should say something or the silence would just go on. I couldn't think of anything to say. I thought about the night with Debs and how badly that had gone. She hadn't responded to my texts. She didn't want to see me again.

'School starts next week,' I said.

'How do you feel about that?'

'Uh!' I said, sick of the way he kept getting at me.

'Something I said irritated you.'

'No.'

'It's all right if it did.'

It felt like a boxing match and he'd just landed a punch and danced away when I tried to get back at him. I crossed my arms.

'Do you get irritated a lot?'

I shrugged.

'What was it I said that irritated you?'

'Stop asking me these questions. I'm meant to say what I want, you said. But you keep asking me questions. It's not school, is it?'

'No, it's not school.'

Silence. That cold air wasn't dispersing the silence. It was just making the room cold.

'What else irritates you?'

I stared at Ian's stupid bright blue skate shoes, his smug sitting-back-in-the-chair with splayed legs like he thought he was the best. If I'd had my pebble with me I would have hurled it at him. Instead I uncrossed my arms, gripped the wooden chair arms, and said: 'Your stupid skate shoes.'

'My trainers make you angry?'

'You're full of rubbish. You know that?'

'You're angry.'

'How do you know what I am? You're not me, are you?'

'No. I'm not you.'

'And you're not my dad, either. You're just a liar with grey hair who thinks he can wear skate shoes like he was a kid. Well, you're not a kid, are you? You're a man. You're married, aren't you? Have you got a kid?'

He didn't say anything. The silence grew deeper, stronger. The radiator built up a bubble of air, a fart.

He said, 'I think I can help you.'

The radiator began to strain.

In barely a breath, I said, 'You're a liar.'

I hated him. He thought he had it all, didn't he, with his fake happiness, his blue skate shoes, his wife and his child. How did he know what it was like? If I'd had my pebble with me, I would have killed him.

I got up, picked up my jacket from Nan's chair at the back, and went out. The door shut swiftly with its extra-strong closer.

It was a waste of time. Everything was a waste of time.

Grassy Knoll

On Monday, the new school term started. I travelled by bike. I stopped before I reached school, lifted the bike (it was heavy) over a dry-stone wall and locked it to the branch of a tree. Humped my rucksack through field-grass, came into school at the side past the dilapidated hut.

Nobody spoke to me. I bet they were all wondering if I'd savage them with my teeth.

I saw Zed in the hallway. I was sure he clocked me but his glance slid on as if he hadn't registered a thing and he lumbered by, giant and unreadable.

Science was first. Then Geography. Teachers' words skated over my head like vapour trails.

At break I went to find Debs. She wasn't behind the hut. Or on the Grassy Knoll. Or in the library. Or on the playground. She still hadn't answered any of my texts.

After break it was Miss Andrews' English class and Steve Scott was there. He didn't say a word. Didn't even look at me. I was aware of him the whole time.

Miss Andrews let me be silent, didn't fire any questions

at me. We'd nearly finished *The Call of the Wild* and she was summing up themes. I was beginning to think Steve had let our feud go but when Miss Andrews faced the whiteboard to write he turned to me and with his forefinger slid a line across his throat.

I kept my gaze fixed on his stupid sarcastic face and yawned. As Miss Andrews finished writing, he swung front. Her eyes flicked between us, aware something had happened, but not sure what.

*

Lunchtime. Looking for Debs. Keeping alert for Steve and his wolf pack. The head of the pack decides who gets what to eat. So he'd lead any attack. I couldn't find Debs.

I was scared that she didn't want to know me.

She wasn't in the canteen or the library. She wasn't in her form class. She wasn't on the playground or by the dilapidated hut. I walked the long walk to the Grassy Knoll, up the slope to the main road, over the stile and up the narrow path.

There were some couples there, in a group, hunched in the cold, breath white, sat close for warmth on some stones. And on the wriggling roots that ran across the short-grazed turf, stood Debs. With a boy.

I thought about going back to school. The boy noticed me, said something to Debs and she looked.

As I approached, she turned her back on me. She must have made a face to the guy, because he half-smiled. I didn't know his name but he was in her year. Fair-haired.

The couples fell quiet like they knew we'd fallen out and expected drama. I had to go on because to go back would have been too horrible. She was wearing her combat jacket but her hair was different, I didn't know how, and she was saying, 'You'll see.'

'Hey Debs.'

She faced me. 'Oh,' she said, 'I didn't see you there. How can I help?'

How can I help?

'Did you get my texts?' I said.

'I'm sort of busy now.'

The guy sniggered soft. I didn't know what to do.

'So ...?' she said sarcastically, twisting her mouth, with a glance at Fair Hair as if I was ridiculous.

'I want to know...' I said, and wondered what it was I wanted to know, unless it was how I could be this hot when the day was so cold that my breath rose white, then it came to me, '...what happened when you saw the wolf that night?'

'I'm busy,' she said with a bit of hate in her voice and put her back to me. Fair Hair sniggered again.

'Do you actually speak or just make animal noises?' I said to him.

He took a step towards me, chest puffing out, arms gorilla-loose.

'Don't threaten me, you idiot,' I said.

Fair Hair lunged. I danced back. Debs' hand came out across him, fingers spread on his brawny chest.

'He's not worth it, Sam,' she said, like all she ever did was watch terrible daytime TV and repeat the lines.

'Christ, you're an idiot sometimes, Deborah.'

'Get lost, *Lucas*.' She said my name like it tasted revolting.

I turned and walked down the hill. I could hear the couples – chirping birds – laughing and halfway down I gave the whole plastic pack of them the finger.

One of the boys barked like a seal and flapped his hands together at me, and the others howled with laughter.

I didn't listen. Except, I did.

*

When I got home after school, Nan was still at work. Now Nan had internet I went online and checked what Mitesh and everyone else were doing. They had all gone to a party at the weekend.

I made up the fire, laying paper and kindling, and placing small logs, then went out to the shed to fetch a few more logs to dry. The Zorro bird was flickering in and out of his mouse-hole high up on the cottage wall.

Nan came in tired and cold, her face even softer-looking than usual. Her satchel hung heavy with binder files. She dropped it on the floor and rubbed her head and kneaded her stomach.

'Do you want a cup of tea?' I said.

She nodded.

'I made up the fire.'

I went to put on the kettle.

'Did you have a good day?' she asked, peering as if through a fog.

'Go and sit down and I'll bring you a cup of tea.'

I brought her the tea, lit the fire, and sat in the armchair opposite hers and she sat with her mug, staring at the flames.

'What – did – you – do – today?' she asked. She said it like that, machine-weird.

'Are you all right, Nan?'

Slowly, from her fog, she nodded.

'You have to see a doctor if you're not well.'

I wasn't sure she heard me.

'I think I'll go and lie down for a bit before doing tea, Rachel.'

My heart thumped extra hard.

She struggled to stand then stopped, gazing out at the deep dusk.

'What is it?' I said.

'Just the wheatear,' she said. I looked and saw in the dim light the mouse-brown bird flickering from a branch. She went out with her tea, sighed as she put it down on the stair to take off her DMs, then thumped slowly upstairs in her stockinged feet.

Winter

Kendal. Dark. Rush-hour traffic. At the river, school kids. The NHS building where Ian worked. Rooms lit in the darkness. A woman, bundled up, head bowed, slow up the steps with a girl. I watched them go through the glass doors then reappear in the waiting room at the front.

The school kids going by. Yakking. Gone.

Me, late now, invisible in the darkness. The deep winter cold.

*

I knocked on the door.

'Come in!'

I entered.

'Hello, Lucas.'

I sat down.

Silence.

'Do you want to take your jacket off?'

'No.'

The radiator bellyached.

A bit more silence. Then a lot of it.

Before the quiet got too difficult, Ian said, 'How has your week been?'

That surprised me.

'So you're not going to have a go for me being late, then?'

'No. I am interested, though,' he said calmly.

In that case, I thought, I'm not going to tell you.

The quiet went on.

I broke it with, 'How was your week?'

He didn't answer at first. 'Well, the idea is that you talk. This is your time.'

'So, you don't speak.'

'About myself, no. It's meant to be your time.'

More of that quiet.

That radiator really should talk to someone about its indigestion.

'What about last time, then?' I said aggressively.

After a pause, he said, 'What about last time?'

I blushed. 'You know what I'm talking about.'

'Your tantrum, do you mean? Do you want to talk about that?'

'It wasn't a tantrum.'

A quiet again. 'Well, you walking out, then.'

I tried to suppress a little smile of victory but Ian had no expression on his face so the victory felt lost. I glanced around the room: the empty bookshelves, the carpet tiles. Ian wore shoes today. Brown shoes.

His face was tired. His curly grey hair was a darker shade than Nan's.

'What were you thinking of?' he said.

'Nothing.'

He nodded deeply. 'Your face changed.'

I shifted in my chair. His gold ring lay dull on his finger on one of the chair arms. I wondered how long he'd been married.

'D'you have kids?' I said.

He didn't reply for a while. I didn't expect that he would at all, if he's not allowed to talk about himself.

'Yes,' he said. I was surprised he told me.

'Boy or girl?'

'Why do you ask that question in particular?'

One-shouldered shrug. 'D'you see mad people?' I said.

There was a pause.

'Some people have acute psychiatric problems. Some people have mild disorders. Or phobias. But we don't have to pathologise everything, some people are struggling, that's all. They're finding life difficult.'

A longer quiet. The radiator was rolling warm water freely for a bit, like a long sigh.

'What about the people who were waiting earlier on? That girl downstairs.'

'I didn't see you downstairs. Were you waiting outside?'

I blushed, brightly.

He didn't say anything for a moment, then he said,

'I don't know about the people who were waiting before. They're not my clients.'

'Is that what I am, a *client*?'

'Yes.'

For some reason, this answer surprised me too.

I looked to the corner where there was a twin pair of electrical sockets I hadn't noticed before.

'What are you thinking about?'

I couldn't tell him about the plug sockets so I said, 'Nothing.'

I thought about the wolf, waiting on the hillside, watching me here. Waiting to see what I would say.

'Do you want me to talk about the car crash, is that it?' I said.

'Do you want to?'

I put a hand over my mouth.

Time continued.

'Are you in pain?' he asked.

I squeezed my mouth shut with my fist.

'You seem in distress. Can you talk about it?'

He said it so soft and gentle it made me want to puke.

I threw my hand down.

'God, *Ian*, I'm surprised you can *breathe*, you're so fake.'

He didn't seem shocked by my words.

'Not wearing your *skate shoes* today, then, Ian?'

The words didn't seem to do anything to him. I wished

246

I had my pebble with me. I wanted to punch him like I'd punched Steve Scott.

'You can get quite angry.'

The radiator gurgled like it was laughing.

The wolf waited, watching.

'What are you thinking about?'

The wolf. The wolf on the road. Clicking claws.

'What are you thinking about?'

What are you thinking about? What are you thinking about?

A line of bubbles pattered through the radiator.

The silence throbbed, crescendoed, then, as if air could become solid, the silence in the room got flat and dull, and everything drained out of me.

'Nothing,' I said. 'Nothing.'

Photographs

I couldn't remember Mum's face. I tried but I couldn't. With Dad, his head was bowed as if he was working on something, and when I tried to make him look up he wouldn't. Our old house had things in it that *were* clear. The pebbles on the hearth. On the mantelpiece, the china rabbit with the slicked-back ears. The arm of the armchair nearly worn through. In Dad's workshop, his binoculars case hung by a strap on a hook. The blue iron vice on the workshop bench.

Gone midnight, and I still couldn't sleep. I got out of bed and switched on the light. I pulled out the bottom drawer: Mum's board games, a doll. They smelled of old things left in a cupboard too long.

I turned out the light and went back to bed. The dark was a physical thing and I put my hand up as if I could clear it away.

After a time, I got up again and went down to the sitting room and curled in the armchair with a throw wrapped round me and my laptop on the armrest, and went online and saw Mum's and Dad's faces. I touched the screen but all that happened was the surface darkened under my push. Seeing them didn't bring anything back. It was like there was a bit missing in my brain so I couldn't connect the photos to my memory or the presence of the people to their photographs.

A light clicked on upstairs. Slippers slapped down the stairs and Nan came in. I left the picture of Mum and Dad on screen. Her breath smelled slightly sourer than usual.

'Do you want a cup of tea?' she said.

'No,' I said.

The kettle took a long time to boil. She came back with two mugs and handed me one. I didn't have the heart to tell her again. She sat in the other armchair.

She put her mug on the rug with a bump, stood and went out. The study door opened. She came back with an envelope. The envelope. On the front, *Rachel*.

I took it. Photographs spilled out across my lap, washed-out colours. So that's what was in it. Some with faint fingerprints on them like they'd been handled a lot.

The first showed a late summer's day and, unmistakably, Nan when she was younger, with another young woman. They were both grinning, arms round each other's shoulders, Nan with a sling across her chest that held a baby against her.

'That's your mum,' Nan said. 'On the trip across Britain.'

The baby I couldn't see but for a curled fist, her arm raised from the sling as if in a communist's salute. The next picture showed Nan and another woman, in profile, facing each other across a table. They looked mid-talk, good friends, but in the middle of the picture, facing the camera, was a little girl in pig-tails. Her head barely cleared the table and she was propping her head on her hands, mightily bored at the adults' conversation, her eyes half-closed as if she was fighting off sleep. The next photo showed the same girl – Mum – about the same age, with her mouth open wide, standing beside a blue rubber paddling pool in a garden. A green hosepipe dribbled water into the half-deflated pool. The girl was clearly screaming something happily that said, 'Me!' The next picture was in a brown cardboard frame, a school photograph of Mum in a black blazer against a blue background, showing her bright, brown eyes. Then one of a beach. But in this picture was a man. He was shaped like a pear, with a substantial belly flopping over the elasticated band of red swimming-shorts, and he had very thin legs. He had a long droopy moustache, a long oval face, and straggly hair. Smiling shyly but happily. And behind him, in the sea, raising both arms as a wave crashed around her, Mum, when she was a girl. Smash-full of happiness.

'That's your grandfather.'

'When was this?'

'We were still married. Rachel was probably about nine then.'

The next showed that same brown-haired girl in some bar or café, a teenager now, dressed in dungarees and sat beside her mum who held a cigarette, a pile of textbooks on the table beside her. They both faced the camera thinking private thoughts and neither smiled. Next, the same pair on a low orange sofa, Mum thirteen or fourteen in a blue striped T-shirt, arms crossed, head tipped back to rest on the sofa back, scowling down her nose at the camera. Nan sat on the sofa arm, serious and withdrawn. A gap of years to the next one. Mum about seventeen, leaned against her blue bike (*my* blue bike), all happiness gone out of her. Arms crossed, hair neat and short, clothes sombre – a dark Argyle jumper and dark blue jeans. And then her graduation day. The scroll ribboned in her hands, the gown and the mortarboard, her face inexpressive.

For what purpose had any of that been? All that life. And it can't be called back, made back into life.

'I wasn't a very good mother,' Nan said.

There was a quiet.

'She used to come here for weekends when she first started university, but then she stopped coming.'

Nan's gaze was faraway, her head cocked like Mum's.

'You must have got lonely.'

She turned her face away.

The last photo was Mum's wedding day. A crowd of

young people. Men with sleeves rolled up, ties off. Girls with collapsed hair-dos. Shining faces. Breathless. Dad with spiky hair, Mum beside him, beaming into the camera.

'What was Dad like back then?'

'I only met him for the first time on their wedding day.'

That shocked me. I tried to think of something kind to say. The only thing I could think of: 'You would have liked him.'

Nan laughed a cry-laugh.

'Why didn't you and Mum get along?'

'There were times when we did. D'you remember when you visited?'

'Yeah.'

'That was a good time. And she named me your guardian, so that counts for something.' She went quiet. 'She said I hadn't been there for her when she was a child.'

She cocked her head again in that world-gone-away attitude of Mum's, and I thought maybe that's what they had in common – sadness. And neither of them knew how to do anything about it.

'Sorry, Nan,' I said.

Her focus returned.

She winced and put her hand to her stomach.

'Are you all right?'

She shut her eyes and stayed taut.

'Nan?'

She relaxed, opened her eyes.

'Are you all right?'

'What was he like?' Nan said. 'Your father?'

Suddenly I pictured him – walking slowly, quietly. In a wood. Grinning, playing about. Making Mum laugh.

'He was just Dad,' I said.

I put the photos back in the envelope and held it out to her.

She said, 'You keep them.'

'But they're yours.'

'You keep them.'

I held them out further. 'They're yours.'

She wouldn't take them so I put the envelope on my lap again, slid them out. The one of their wedding – Mum and Dad, their friends behind them, crowded and hot like they had all stopped dancing at just that moment.

I slid the others back into the envelope and kept hold of the wedding photo then held the envelope out to Nan again. She took it. Our hands touched. Her skin was super-soft.

Fire

Dusk. January. The dead heart of the year. Skeletal black trees scribbling on the sky. Wearing my jacket, making up a fire. Through the trees at the front was the last faint light in the west. The faint hiss of chopped vegetables hitting a pan, then their juicy, narrow scent.

'How was your day at work?' I said, coming into the kitchen.

'All right,' said Nan, washing up. She wasn't a big one for talking about work. 'How was yours?'

'All right.'

She made room to let me use the sink and stood with her dripping hands held out before her, her head tilted dreamily.

'What are you thinking about?' I said.

'Tired is all.'

She went and sat on the stool by the phone under the stairs and undid her purple DMs, then went upstairs. The bathroom door shut. The boiler fired up as she put on the shower. She'd forgotten her tea. I stirred the vegetables, gazing out the back.

They say, at dusk, you can be standing ten yards from a wolf and be looking right at it and you won't see it.

I put the lid on the pan, opened the back door and in my socks went to the edge of the grass. The white water leapt off the mountain. Water trickled down the drainpipe from the bathroom.

I stared a new darkness into the darkness.

Nothing.

I stepped back into the kitchen. A vehicle came up the lane and I went into the sitting room to see who it was.

It was the black car of Danny Scott.

I stepped out of sight, then hurried to the phone under the stairs. I put a finger on the nine.

The police wouldn't get here in time.

In the kitchen, on the chopping board, lay the vegetable knife.

Then I remembered the night of the knife, and left it where it was and returned to the sitting room.

The car was still there, low, black, purring in the darkness.

The headlamps came on and lit trees. The engine revved. Revved again.

'Who is that?' Nan called, thumping down the stairs in her pink towel-fabric dressing gown, hair wet from her shower. She swept past me.

I bit my lip.

The car sprayed dirt like a bull pawing the ground before it charges.

'Well, he's got a –'

I didn't hear the rest of what she said as the car roared again. She sat on the stool and started putting on her DMs.

'Nan!'

She stepped to the door, a hand rising towards the latch.

'They'll hurt you!' I held her arm.

'Who will?'

There is nothing quite as downright scary as Nan's stare.

In the end I had to bring my eyes to hers. 'Danny and Steve Scott.'

She opened the door and marched out.

I grabbed the cudgel from the stick-bin and hurried after her.

I was slow in my socks but she barely paused for the cattle grid. She knocked on the car window.

The engine fizzed, earth squirted. Nan gave a little cry as the car sprang forward, fishtailing, narrowly missing her legs. Shoeless, I had to cross the cattle grid carefully. The car brake-locked a U-turn at the corner and faced us. Mud sprayed, the engine roared. For a moment Nan's pink dressing gown and DMs were lit up as bright as a summer's day as the car shot towards us. I grabbed Nan and pulled her back. The car flashed past with a chainsaw-rip and a whoosh of dead leaves as Nan fell into me. The gust died, the leaves settled, and we listened to the car descend the lane then turn onto the main road and speed away.

'What is going on, Lucas?'

I didn't answer.

'We can't be threatened like this.'

She started for the house.

'Nan! What are you going to do?' I went after her gingerly over the gravel.

She swept in.

'Please don't!'

When I entered she was vanishing at the top of the stairs.

'Nan!'

Her bedroom door shut.

I went into the sitting room and waited for her to come down.

I paced, then, when she didn't reappear, I knelt at the grate. Struck three matches trying to get the fire lit. The newspaper caught, then the kindling.

I went to shut the back curtains, and stopped. On the lawn stood the wolf.

Its head was dropped between its shoulders, the top of its skull and spine forming a single horizontal line, and it was looking at me. It looked at me the way an animal observes another animal and my heart sped up and I didn't feel any safer for the huge pane of glass between us. There was a stillness in the air and I knew that if I moved something terrible would happen.

Its nostrils dilated and closed. Its eyes on its huge head were surprisingly small, almond-shaped. Amber coloured. It was middle-age grey otherwise, some white on its cheeks, legs too. Then the flame-light flared across the glass between us and I saw the reflection of bookshelves and furniture, the flames in the fire, and myself. I stood alone in the middle of the room, a slight pale person wearing an expression of alarm as if he had just witnessed a terrible accident. All this was flung on the darkness outside, the image conjured by a sheet of newspaper catching light in the grate. Then the newspaper burned through, the fire resumed its low flames, and the reflection on the glass reduced in intensity and once again I saw the garden.

It was empty.

I rushed forward, cupped my hands against the glass and leaned close to block out firelight reflection.

Icy glass on my forehead.

Darkness.

Cold.

Night.

Revenge

'D'you think I'm mad, Malky?'

Malky blew his nose, then gave a half-hearted grunt.

'Thanks a lot, mate.'

We were leaning on the railing of the balcony above the glass-fronted reception, gazing down on the concourse and not taking much notice of the slope up to the car parks or, in the distance through the trees, a bit of the Grassy Knoll.

'Well, you are seeing a psychiatrist.'

'He's a counsellor.'

Malky considered me glumly then returned to leaning over the balcony.

'You do all this made-up stuff, don't you?' I said. 'So what's the difference between what you do and me seeing this wolf?'

Malky leaned further out and thought about this a while. People passed below. He straightened.

'The difference is that I know what I do is fantasy. But you think this wolf is *real*.'

'I *saw* it. Besides, it's in the news. People are talking about it.'

Malky screwed his face up and shut his eyes tight.

'Go on,' I groaned. 'Tell me the truth according to Malky.'

He opened his eyes and his expression cleared, and I thought a chicken-nugget of wisdom was imminent. Then he shook his head like a dog shaking itself after a swim.

'What?' I said.

'Nothing. Thought I was going to sneeze. Anyway, to answer your question – simply because people are talking about something doesn't mean it's true. People talk about aliens but they don't exist, do they?'

'Well, nobody knows if they exist or not, do they?'

He considered me now as if I really was mad, and I blushed. He resumed the balcony-lean. After a while my gaze followed his.

Coming down the road was a police car.

It coasted right down to the entrance, where it stopped.

The door opened and Constable Strang climbed out.

We watched him walk to the main doors. He entered, glanced about, then approached the reception. He exchanged a few words with the receptionist then crossed the concourse. I didn't move. He paused directly below us. I prayed he wouldn't look up. He had taken off his cap and we could see the crown of his head. The headmaster's secretary appeared, greeted him, and the pair passed out of sight.

'I wonder what he wants,' said Malky.

I didn't answer. I had the terrible fear he'd come to take his revenge on me.

*

The bell rang for the end of break and Malky trudged off in his sleeping-bag coat and I headed to Miss Andrews' class, dreading the arrival of Constable Strang.

Miss Andrews wanted us to have a discussion about *The Call of the Wild* now that we'd finished it. Whatever the discussion was about, I couldn't take it in, my mind was on Strang. I didn't even pay attention to Steve Scott. If Strang had come to cause me trouble then Mr Bond would throw me out of school just like he had promised. Children and Young People's Services would come good on their threat and I would be taken away from Nan.

I became aware of a silence, and checked around to see what was going on. Nearly everyone was staring at me.

'Lucas?' said Miss Andrews.

I blinked.

'Just in case you weren't listening, I'll repeat the question – what is the author's view of society?'

Steve twisted in his seat towards me, moving in exaggerated style like he was absolutely fascinated to hear my response.

'Do you think he's saying society is weak? That nature is much stronger?'

Steve was doing his sarky smirk.

'I don't know.'

But Miss Andrews wasn't having it.

'Come on, Lucas. Does he favour society or nature?'

My brain was locked. I turned away and saw the mountain.

He was saying that nature will kill you.

Or society will.

One or the other will kill you.

The door opened. Mr Bond's secretary appeared.

'Sorry to interrupt, Miss Andrews,' she said, 'but the headmaster wants to see a member of your class.'

My mouth went dry.

'Steve Scott?' the secretary said.

Everyone stared at Steve.

Casually, his hair gelled to within a millimetre of perfection, except for those two stupid tufts above his ears, Steve stood, and with a grin swaggered out. When the door shut, the class erupted into a buzz of rumour. Miss Andrews slapped the table.

'Quiet!'

The buzz didn't stop.

'Shut it, you lot!'

*

I was nearly at my next class when Steve appeared, coming towards me, his expression hard as slate. As he approached I began to tremble with the strain of ignoring him. His shoulder brushed mine as he passed. When I arrived at my next class, my heart was going like a pinball bumper when the ball's trapped against it.

I couldn't work out what the expression on Steve's face meant.

But whatever it was, it was bad.

Pup

Sometimes things can go on a long time without you doing anything about them. For instance, a hole in your shoe that you put up with for no reason even though your sock gets wet each time it rains. Or going to school without a raincoat all the way through winter. Or having a wolf in your life.

'You've been quiet for a long time today,' said Ian.

We were sitting in that stupid room in the same stupid chairs, facing each other, him waiting, me biting at a hangnail, the radiator's dodgy stomach gurgling. There was a faint bit of daylight still in the sky, the first time it had been there since I'd been coming to see him.

'Is there anything on your mind?'

I wondered what he'd think if I told him about the wolf. Malky seemed to think I might be mad. Nan didn't believe it existed. Sheridan Benedict did but he wanted it dead. Debs … Debs had seen it, only now that she had she didn't want anything to do with me.

After a good minute, I said, 'Did you see that story about the wolf?'

'Which wolf is that?'

'The one that's been killing animals on the fells.'

He nodded.

I didn't say anything else.

After a while, Ian said, 'Does that story interest you?'

'Not really,' I said.

'No,' Ian confirmed.

'What do you think about it?' I said.

'What do *you* think about it?' he replied.

God, he was hard work. 'No, I asked first. What do you think about it?'

'In what sense?'

'In the sense that – what do you freaking think about it?'

'Do you mean, am I interested in wolves? Or the farmers losing livestock? Or in the call for them to kill whatever is killing their livestock?'

'If it's not a wolf killing ewes then what's doing it?'

'I don't know,' said Ian. 'I didn't think wolves existed in Britain in the wild.'

'It might have escaped from a private zoo. Some people keep them. Or it might've swum here. You get them in Europe.'

'I didn't know wolves can swim.'

'Well, of course they can. Dogs can swim, can't they?'

He nodded. 'You're right.' A long silence. 'D'you like wolves?' he asked.

'No.'

'Do you *dislike* them?'

I could feel my heart beating hard. 'Don't care one way or the other,' I said.

He nodded again, more slowly. 'Do you believe it's a wolf?' he said.

I gave him the shrug.

He didn't respond.

I said, 'No reason why it shouldn't be a wolf.'

'You're right. No reason why it shouldn't be.'

For some reason, that made me happy. For the first time since I'd been in that room with Ian. Like, for the very first time.

'Did you know that wolves have a hormone after a pup is born that makes all the pack care for it? Even the male wolves. The whole pack.'

'No, I didn't know that.'

'And that the pack doesn't have one leader, it has two, the alpha male and the alpha female. Like a family.'

'That's interesting. You know a lot about wolves.'

'Not really.'

'You seem to.'

'Whatever.'

A long silence.

'I was wondering,' said Ian, 'what the pup does if something happens to the alpha male and alpha female? Say, if they get ill, or they die.'

The question made my muscles tense. I crossed my arms.

'How does it cope?'

'Probably the pup's easier for predators to kill,' I said. 'Or it doesn't learn how to hunt properly so it starves to death.'

'Or maybe it grows into a new role. Or other members of the pack take on new roles and look after it.'

'What do you mean?'

'Some other members of the pack become the alpha males and females.'

'Yeah, maybe. But then,' I said, 'I don't really care, because I'm not that interested. And what the wolves are, they are natural predators. And they kill things. So you know, all I hope is, they die. I hope someone hunts them down and they destroy them.'

Ian didn't seem shocked. Or sad. Or bitter and full of hate.

It was disappointing, that.

Bait

Nan driving, head nodding. Tired after work.

I lowered the window.

'Bit nippy,' she said, sitting straighter.

'I'll close it in a minute.'

We drove on.

'Go all right with Ian?'

'Yeah,' I said. 'D'you believe there's a wolf on the fells?'

Oncoming headlamps strobed her face, each car slipping by without catastrophe.

'No,' she said, 'I don't. Can you shut that window now?'

I buzzed it shut.

We rose and fell with the road and followed the gentle curves of the lake. Black tunnels of bare trees. No oncoming cars so Nan switched to full beam. As the road swung away from the lake towards the valley the lights illuminated a black hump on the verge. We passed a lifeless form.

The wolf?

I craned my head round.

'What was it?' said Nan.

Too small for a wolf. Too big for a cat or fox.

'Dunno.'

We drove along in silence.

'Roadkill,' she said.

*

'Can you drop me in the village?' I said as we approached
the turn for the lane.

'Why?'

'I want to get something in the shop.'

'I don't mind taking you.'

'It's all right.'

She didn't pursue it. As we pulled up, she said, 'If you
see the Scott boys, phone me immediately, will you?'

'Nan.'

'Will you?'

I sighed with great patience, which made her smile for
some reason.

I watched her drive away. When she'd gone, I left the
village and walked down the long valley road towards
the lake.

*

I waited until after midnight before getting up. Then I
delved in my rucksack and lifted it out. When I had it
cradled in both arms, I crept downstairs. Without turning

on the light I put it in the sink then I went into the hallway and quietly lifted my jacket off the coat-hook. I slipped each arm into a sleeve then unlocked and opened the back door and returned to the sink and lifted out the heavy mass and stepped outside. It was biting cold. Freezing concrete stung my soles. I crouched at the edge of the lawn. The grass, stiff with frost, made a sound of breaking crystals as I laid the weight onto it. My breath rose white. Holding my hands out to the sides so I wouldn't get any blood on my pyjama bottoms, I went back inside and rinsed my hands. I risked the kitchen light – a few blood drops crossed the lino. I wiped them with a cloth and took the cloth back upstairs. I hid it in my rucksack, slid open the curtains, pulled up the chair, and propped my chin on the windowsill.

*

The alarm clock beeped. I woke in my bed. I didn't remember getting *into* the bed but I suppose I must have. I was meant to have stayed awake and was annoyed with myself for ruining my own plan. I hurried over to the window. I was so sleepy that for a few moments everything was blurred. Then, in the early morning light, I saw – the dead animal, a badger, still lay on the concrete.

The bait hadn't worked.

Silly to think it would, really. If the wolf wanted anything, it wanted living prey. Besides, a wolf is a shy animal. Why would it come down to the valley where it might encounter humans? And why risk something covered in human scent, *my* scent.

Unless, of course, it wanted to find me.

My eyes scanned the fells, watched cloud shadow glide across them. Time to get ready for school. I yawned and went to the bathroom, brushed my teeth, and it was then that it struck me.

I pelted downstairs.

The badger lay on the path but I had put it on the grass.

I crouched beside it. It lay in a pool of dark liquid. Blood? I got down onto all fours and sniffed. Not blood. Urine.

A dog would have eaten it. Only a wild animal wouldn't have. Only a wolf. It had come, investigated, and taken a leak on it. But why?

It was a warning. Or an insult.

A noise made me turn and I saw the bathroom light was on. I hurried into the kitchen, found a carrier bag, ran back out and bagged the animal. Then I ran upstairs, with the bait rustling and thumping against my legs, before Nan appeared.

Valley

Dead leaves rustled underfoot but the trees I lurked under had already begun to bud. I waited for Nan's red Fiat to purr over the cattle grid before I dumped the bait in the woods and sneaked back to the cottage. Changing out of my school uniform, I took the cudgel from the bin by the door, filled a bottle with tap water, and slid the knife into my belt. A soft fuzzy line of shadow crept down the mountain as the sun rose over the edge of the fells and I set out for the shadow-line.

My heart padded my chest, my cudgel tapped the ground.

It wanted something.

A wolf can hear your heartbeat from a mile away. Smell your adrenalin.

I was the prey.

The *tap-tap* of the stick. Wheatears taking flight over the winter grass. This year's bracken shoots, curled like babies' fists, getting ready to open. Water thundering from the little waterfall.

Wolves favour a high ridge. Easy to spot prey either

side. I remembered Sheridan's red pins on the map. On the ridges, above the two valleys.

I reached the ladder over the dry-stone wall and kept going up the path, past the waterfall.

Then beyond where I'd seen the dead ewe. Higher than I'd been before. The village behind me. The Benedict farm. Further along the valley, the lake shining under the low sun. The sky pale, clear.

Ahead, the fell peak. Snow-topped, the crevices on its flanks snow-filled. The place to see and be seen.

It felt as if the mountain's weight pushed against me as I walked upwards. A half hour. An hour. The path thinner. No movement except streaky skylarks darting and zooming, lost when they landed in grass.

I stopped. Before me lay a black length of excrement. Right on the path – deliberate. Wrapped in woolly hair, no dust on it. I crouched, and poked it with my knife. Wolves mark their territory as a guide to other wolves. Their dung is like language. I cut in. A wisp of steam rose. Recent, then. And whatever left it was a predator because inside was part of an undigested rubbery sheep hoof.

This was an invitation, a point on a map.

I continued. Craggy boulders rose to the peak, and I could see it would be a climb not a walk to get there. The shortest route was from a long ridge to my right. I left the path and trod its steep, almost vertical grassy side. Twenty minutes later, puffing, hot, I stood on the ridge-edge.

The other side fell away even more sharply than the way I had come. Straight down and rocky. I walked along the ridge-top. It was like the edge of a razor.

The morning passed. Above me, growing larger as I approached, the fell peak. I thought of Buck hauling a sled up snowy passes in *The Call of the Wild*.

I reached the base of the peak, and climbed. The hand-holds were good. A burst of jet-engine behind me. I glanced over my shoulder and watched a black fighter-jet, its cockpit glinting in the sun, slip out of sight. The ear-splitting roar followed.

My cheeks stung with the sharp air. Giddy on the final blade of rock. My trainers gripped sun-dried slate, slipped on ice. A moment of unsteadiness, then I stood above the world.

Green and granite bodies of mountains. Giants. Down in the valley I had been in their shadow, closed-in. Up here, it was like I could see my way out. And I *could* see my way out. To the west, the sea glittered. South, the faint blue of a bay. East, the mountain range of the Pennines, and north a windfarm in the sea, hazy in the distance.

Now, if it wanted me, it would see me, hear me, smell me.

I stood, my sweat cooling in the cold breeze.

Sound carries much further in the mountains. Perhaps because the air is thinner or because of the silence. And now I heard the chatter of two walkers on the ridge behind me. Half a mile away but they sounded as if they were yards from me. I couldn't make out what they were saying but from the constant chirpy rush it sounded unimportant. Then, as if it might be close, another noise reached me.

A howl.

I couldn't be sure where it came from. Not Nan's valley but perhaps one of the ones ahead. In the wind I tried to work out which one. Several ridges descended from the summit like spokes from the hub of a wheel.

It howled again.

I chose.

The path was worn. My stomach grumbled and I wished I'd brought some food. I cracked the cudgel smartly on the stone.

After half an hour, the ridge declined to a wide grassy plateau. The sun beat hotly. My head began to ache and I finished the water.

Then I had a choice. To the right, where the path led, or to the left into a much shorter valley with a stream and woods. There, a raven turned somersaults above a wood. It fell out of the air as if it had forgotten how to fly, and tumbled into the trees.

That was the way I went.

The descent took much longer than I expected. The grass was slippery and twice my feet slid from under me and I landed on my backside. The cudgel was useful now.

On and on the hill descended until finally I was on the valley floor where the stream ran brownly and clearly and blackly and I got down and cupped my hands and drank the cold tasteless water. After I'd quenched my thirst I sat.

Everything was quiet and still. My eyes began to droop.

The American tribes believe that the wolf can move between this world and the spirit world. That the Milky Way is the Wolf Road down which the first wolf travelled, and that when human beings killed the first wolf that was when death entered the world. Christians believe in the afterlife. I don't believe in anything. I don't know why, I just don't. Would it matter if I believed? My parents would still be dead, wouldn't they?

Spangles of sun fell on the surface of the stream, bubbles caught the light, and further downstream rocks stood out dry-grey.

On one of these rocks stood a small yellow bird. I didn't know what it was. I'd never seen one like it before. Slender and long, it kept leaving its rock as if it was going to escape the stream altogether but then it fluttered, hesitating, before returning to its rock. I watched it do this two or three times, then I realised – it was feeding on insects. And that made me happy and sad, happy because I had worked it out and sad because I knew it was something Dad would have been able to tell me about if he had been alive.

The sadness wouldn't go away. I thought of the trouble I'd be in when I got back to Nan's. The grief I gave her. Literally grief, because I reminded her of her dead daughter. I thought of school, and Debs, and how she had dropped me – as quick as that yellow bird flutters up for insects. And I thought wouldn't it be better to live here, like this, among this green and the water, with the yellow bird. And then, as if to say yes, you're right, pal, you should live here, a stout dark bird zipped out from under the bank and skimmed downstream towards the woods where she landed on the water, half under like a midget duck, then dropped beneath the surface. I waited for her to reappear and while I waited a second bird skimmed out from the bank, then a third, and each of these landed in different places and dipped beneath the water too. Then the first bird resurfaced and shot downstream followed by the other two and the three vanished beneath the canopy of the woods.

I lay back and closed my eyes.

And then I fell asleep.

*

When I woke the sun had fallen below the edge of the fells and I was in shadow. It was cold and my head throbbed with the beginnings of a headache. I filled my bottle from the stream and drank, hoping it would help the throb, then I followed the wide, shallow stream. The

277

yellow bird had gone and any magic in the water's sound over the rocks had gone too. The woods were growing dark as I entered them. Things were hard to distinguish in the departing light. The stream ran around a bend, and on my side the ground rose high so it formed a steep short cliff down to the water. On the other, low bank was a stony beach. I climbed the slope until I came around the bend, where I stopped – on the other bank, on the beach of pale stones, stood the wolf.

When it saw me it shut its mouth and its ears pricked.

My dad once told me about an eagle in South America that is the most dangerous bird on the planet. It lives in jungle treetops. To approach it, you have to wear body armour, including a helmet with a throat guard. When a scientist climbed a tree to film it, the bird watched him carefully. The scientist reached a nearby branch, began to prepare his equipment, and the moment he turned his back, the eagle attacked. Its talons, sharp as skewers, punctured the throat guard, just where it met the shoulder. The talons drew blood but did not pierce the artery in the throat. If they had cut the artery the scientist would have died. The eagle flew away. The target was deliberate, my dad said. The eagle had watched the man carefully until it identified the point of weakness, where the neck guard joined the shoulder armour, and that's where it had made its thrust.

Now, like that man in the jungle, I was being assessed for a point of weakness.

And then the assessment was complete.

The wolf forded the stream in a moment, making huge splashes; it flung aside the distance between us as if that distance was nothing, then slipped out of sight below the steep bank and appeared at the cliff-edge a yard from me. I hadn't even moved. As it sprang I raised the cudgel in both my hands.

I was too late. Its snout, with fur of a honey-bee red that wrinkled as it bared its great teeth at me, crashed through the stick. The wolf collided solidly with me. I was thrown to the ground. When it landed on top of me my lungs emptied of air. It was as heavy as a man. Water dripped on my face. I couldn't breathe. Leaves rustled. The wolf stepped off me and moved away a yard. With its hind legs, it kicked leaves and earth dismissively at me.

Finally air entered my lungs and I gasped. Then pain began. Across my chest first, then across my back. The pain was tremendous. The wolf's stillness was absolute. So was the woods' stillness. I was aware of darkness rising up. I sucked big draughts of air.

The wolf began sniffing the ground. He was a male wolf, I could see. And he had huge feet, each the size of a man's closed fist. His white legs were long, skinny, but hugely powerful at the shoulders. When he turned towards me, I saw the extraordinary width and length of his head. His mouth remained open, and the row of teeth was white in the darkness. He looked like he was smiling. My breath came easier. I was unharmed, I told myself. Winded, but unharmed.

I felt for the knife. I didn't have it any more. The cudgel lay a few yards away. The wolf walked across the leaves softly, stopped to sniff at a fallen trunk.

I had to do something. I tried to get up. Either the wolf didn't hear me or was too interested in the scent he'd found because I got to my feet without him noticing and took an unsteady step towards the cudgel. Another step. I was leaning to pick it up when his weight slammed into my shoulders and I hit the earth face-first, him on top, his heaviness pushing through the small of my back so I was pinned.

I awaited the savage tearing of his teeth.

He stepped off my back.

The smell of wet leaves, mulch, earth, filled my nostrils. Cold, wet leaves pressed my face. Their damp soaked into my clothes. Their cold seeped into my body. These were my last sensations before he attacked and I knew that they were important, and that they ended, and that I didn't want them to end yet. The way they had for Mum and Dad.

Perhaps a minute passed. When, in the silence, I finally rolled my head, the wolf wasn't there. I sat up in the leaves.

The woods were empty.

He had gone.

I scrambled to my feet and ran to the high bank. I slid down, digging my elbows into the earth to slow myself, skidded round, halted at the water's edge. Splashed into the stream – mountain-cold – and stumbled across. Up the stony beach. Into the trees.

I stopped so fast I nearly fell over.

He stood ahead of me. His head hung low between his shoulders.

I took a step back. He took a step forward.

We walked through the woods like this, me backwards, him stalking towards me, mouth shut, stiff-legged. I reached the stony beach, splashed into the stream, lost my footing and fell.

I staggered to my feet, heavy suddenly with water, leaning into a wide, unsteady crouch, supporting myself on one hand on the stream-bed. He entered the stream. My hand was on a rock. Slowly he came forward, head low between his shoulders, eyeing me with amber eyes. My hand underwater-numb. He took another step. He was less than a yard from me. I shifted my weight and lifted the rock. We faced each other. Delicately he extended his head towards me.

I lifted the rock high. He must have known I was going to bring it down on his skull. He didn't take his eyes from me. I drew the rock back. He took one more step so that

281

he was directly below me. I could see his eyelashes and the long, silver whiskers on that massive snout. I would bring the rock right down on his cranium. He *must* have known that. But still he extended his muzzle. Then he took one last step and his front smaller teeth took the fabric of my jeans. Not my skin, just the fabric. I could see his nostrils flare as he breathed. Still I held the rock. Gently, so that the wet denim stretched tight, he tugged.

He released the fabric and moved round me, facing me the whole time, keeping in a crouch until he reached the cliff-side shore where he stood with splayed legs, head low.

My heart pummelled.

He stood more still than any animal I've seen. I could barely see him in the darkness except for the white on his face, his legs. He could have been the woods themselves. Then he swung away and climbed the steep bank, moving steadily then using his powerful hind legs to spring, then sprang again in a long leap up the final vertical.

From high above, his massive skull hung over the edge of the bank, his small eyes on me. They did not leave me. They said nothing.

He moved out of sight.

The water chuckled icy around me.

He wanted something.

I stood with my heart clattering against my ribs. I sniffed a long breath of chill dusk air.

He wanted something.

I waded to the shore. I took a deep breath and climbed the steep bank.

When I reached the top, he was waiting for me. He swung away and walked between the trees.

I followed.

Together but at a distance we moved through the woods. He walked stiffly but at the same time easily. Every so often I had to break into a run to keep up with him and sometimes I could barely see him he moved so fluidly, but then a slip of white leg or white tail-tip caught my eye and I knew where he was again.

Sometimes he would stop and I would stop too, trying to work out what had taken his attention. I could never see what it was. Finally he broke into a bouncy trot and I had to run the whole time. We reached a steep slope at the edge of the woods. He went up. He moved much faster than me and reached the top quickly. I climbed, puffing, and when I crawled onto level ground he was waiting for me again. He walked through the final trees at the edge of the woods. Trembling now with cold, I joined him on a short stretch of grass before a dry-stone wall.

An animal was making a sound. Something stringy was being pulled, like a shoelace through an eyelet. Was there another wolf? A black shape flapped up with an annoyed *caw* and landed on the wall.

A raven.

The wolf moved over to where the raven had been. It was all so quick, and savage, his attack. A sound of wetness mingling with other noises: the grind of an animal's bones, their snap, the difficult rip of flesh, the tearing from sockets of muscles, tendons. Fast and relentless eating. I saw in those moments what the wolf is. It kills. That's all it does. It kills life.

The wolf turned and walked over to me and in the twilight dropped something at my feet. *Thud*. And when I didn't move, he lowered his head and nosed the lump onto my toes. Then he returned to the kill and began tearing again. Eventually he stopped. He seemed tired, weighed down. His head hung over whatever it was – a sheep, a deer? – before he walked to the dry-stone wall. Easily, he lifted his front legs and leaned on the wall and looked over it like a person would. Then, in a spring that took no effort, he bounded over it. For a moment I saw nothing, then a flash of white in the deep dusk, then all I could see was the black fell. The raven flapped up loudly with a *caw* and it was gone too.

The wind blew. I walked over and in the near-dark I saw the white bone and fat of the inside of an animal. The beautiful, untouched head of a deer.

Across the darkness, over a far rise, light spread, then headlamp beams speared the night and a car appeared. It followed a winding road, curved past at a distance, its red brake-lights pulsed at a bend, then it was gone and I was alone on the fell.

I stared into the dark. I was sopping wet from the stream. My throbbing head had become a pounding headache. I shivered.

The wolf didn't reappear. I climbed over the wall and made my way towards the road.

Death

I got back to Nan's late.

I had to walk round the mountain on dark lanes. My clothes were stiff with frost. My legs ached. My vision tunnelled with headache.

I would have got back even later but for a pair of German tourists who braked hard, headlamps blinding, U-turned and drove me the last few miles in the smooth, warm interior of their SUV, playing jazz. 'You lake Ornette Kohlman, huh?' the middle-aged man kept asking me. 'Shush,' his wife said, staring round the passenger seat at me the whole time. 'You lake Ornette Kohlman, huh?'

When I stepped into the cottage Nan said without raising her head from her book, 'You've got some explaining to do.' But when she turned in her armchair and saw me, the book tumbled from her hands and did a little cartwheel towards the fireplace.

'Are you hurt?' She came to me, grasped me, hugged me. I was taller than her, I realised for the first time.

'Is this the Scott boys?'

I stepped past her to the fire.

'Luke?'

The flames licked lazily.

'Lucas, look at me.'

I glanced over my shoulder.

'My God,' she said. 'What happened?'

'I saw the wolf.'

For a second she said nothing. Then she thumped her stomach softly. Her eyes, shining in the firelight, seemed wild and tearful. She stepped to me, clumped the top of my skull with that bony fist and toppled me into her.

'Luke,' she murmured. Then, as if she didn't want me to see her crying, turned and ran upstairs.

Hot water tumbled into the bath. She came down with a towel, fresh clothes.

I took them.

In the bathroom, I peeled off wet things. I couldn't get in for a while, my flesh was that cold. When I could, I sat there a long time, my fingertips wrinkling like an old man's.

Dropping that lump of the deer at my feet. Like I was a wolf. Like in that story of Sheem. Is that what I was? Was I becoming a wolf?

Was I part of death now?

I stood, pale, light-headed, naked. I looked at myself, at my crotch, a few hairs on my chest. Wolfish? I put on fresh, warm things.

Downstairs, Nan was in a ball on the rug in front of the fire.

I couldn't work out why she was on the floor. Was she crying?

'Nan?'

She didn't respond.

I walked to her. 'What is it?'

She didn't answer.

I crouched, placed my palm on her back.

'Call a doctor,' she said.

I froze.

'Call a bloody doctor!'

I dialled 999.

Nan cried out like someone had kicked her.

I gave them our address. I stood in the doorway. Nan gasped quietly, regularly. She rocked back and forth.

I bring death. I am death.

Her cry forced me into action and I raced to her, put my arm round her.

'It's all right,' I said, 'They'll be here soon.'

The hospital was in Kendal. A long way for the ambulance. A long time.

I ran out again, phoned Debs. Her mobile rang but eventually went to voicemail.

I tried again. Again voicemail.

Third time.

'What do *you* want?'

'I have to speak to your dad. Right now.'

Pause.

'Nan's ill.'

I heard rustling.

A quiet.

Sheridan Benedict: 'Hello?'

'Nan's collapsed. I've called an ambulance.'

'Are you at home?'

'Yeah.'

'Stay right there.'

'What are you –?'

The line died.

I got Nan's throw from the armchair and put it round her. I stroked her coarse hair. I told her it was going to be all right. I told her to hold on, the ambulance is coming.

In less than five minutes an engine roared up the lane, bumped over the cattle grid, hissed in the gravel. I opened the door to Sheridan Benedict. 'What happened?' he said, rushing in. 'Eve?' He came over. 'What's happened?'

'It's her stomach.'

'Eve, Dr Cade'll be here in a minute.' He glanced at me. 'What happened?'

'I had a bath. When I came down, she was here.'

Another car zoomed up the lane. Sheridan went to the door. A tall, bald man rushed in. The curtains stirred with the breeze. He asked where it hurt. How long it had hurt. What kind of pain it was.

Nan could barely answer.

'You've called an ambulance?' Dr Cade asked me.

I nodded.

'When?'

'Before I phoned him.'

''bout ten minutes ago,' Sheridan Benedict said. 'Less.'

'You drive,' said Dr Cade to Sheridan.

'What about the ambulance?' I said.

'Forget that. What's your name?'

'Lucas.'

'Right, Lucas, help Sheridan get her into the car.'

We helped her up and outside, she was letting out little cries. It took a while to get her into the back seat. When I went back Dr Cade was finishing a phone call to the hospital.

'What's wrong with her?'

'Come on,' he said, marching out.

'Don't let her die,' I said and when I said it my chest got tight and I thought I was going to cry.

I sat in the front. Sheridan drove, Dr Cade in the back with Nan. We didn't talk except for Dr Cade to soothe Nan.

'Lucas!' Nan called. 'Make sure Lucas is all right!'

'I'm here, Nan,' I said, reaching round the seat.

Her frail hand came up and I held it.

*

People talk about the thread of life. I always used to think that didn't mean anything. That it was one of those phrases they say in films that doesn't mean anything. But life is a thread. It's like that thread the raven was eating, that shoelace of gut or whatever it was, that the raven was pulling out of the body of the deer. A sinew? A piece of intestine? A thread, anyway. Or like veins are threads. Multiple tiny threads. What Nan calls a filigree, a fine network of fabric. Like the faint pattern of rivers on the globe. It flows as if you think it would never stop. But it does, it's cut. And that's the end of a life.

A road's like that, too, that thread that headlamps hold when there's no streetlights and it's night. Then all that holds us to life, to the road, is light and skill and knowledge. The hands of the driver at the wheel. Debs' dad, Sheridan Benedict. He held it in those grim, scarred hands. I held it, bony, warm, in Nan's hand.

He clung to the road. I held her hand. We held the threads.

*

The hospital canteen, shutters closed. One small, ridged brown plastic cup before him, one before me.

I didn't touch mine. He'd got me tea.

Sheridan took a call from his wife and got up and paced. Nan was in surgery. Dr Cade was long gone.

Sheridan ended the call and returned to the table,

sipped his tea, made a face. He turned his whole body sideways so he was sat over the side of the plastic chair.

'How long d'you think we'll have to wait?' he asked, leaning forward, forearms on thighs, hands grasped. Head up. Sort of like he was sitting on a toilet.

Why did he think I would know? He got up again, checked the different options on the drinks machine. Returned to the table.

'D'you know how much it cost me to park here?'

Had the wolf brought this illness to Nan? Had I?

'Twenty pound. That's preying on people in life-and-death situations, that is. Profiteering. Do you know who gets that money?'

Perhaps I should leave now. Get as far away from this place as possible. As far from Nan as possible. Maybe then, she'd live.

'It isn't the bloody NHS, I can tell you that much. Enough to *make* you ill.'

He was unshaven, hair wilder than usual. He needed something to distract him.

'Is this where Debs was born?' I said.

He stared at me, lenses flashing under the fluorescent lights.

'Are you aware *at all* of what happened tonight?'

'I was trying to take your mind off things, you're a bit wired-up.'

He stared at me with such a mix of disbelief and rage

292

I thought for a moment he was going to punch me in the face. Then he let out a heavy sigh, as if something had deflated him.

We were quiet. Someone came up the corridor. We both waited to see who. A medic appeared, continued down the corridor, disappeared.

'Yes. She was born here. My wife was very sick.'

He took off his glasses and rubbed each lens with the corner of his shirt.

'They thought she was going to die.' He looked around the canteen like he'd heard a noise, then he frowned at me. Without his glasses he was blinky and vulnerable-looking. He put them back on. 'She bloated.'

I nodded.

'She was big as an airship. The bloody Hindenburg.'

I nodded.

'The doctors said I should prepare myself for the worst. And I went home with Deborah, and I thought, how on earth am I going to look after a *baby*? And I didn't *know* how to look after a baby.'

He stared into the middle distance.

'But your wife didn't die,' I said.

He gazed at me fiercely.

'Aye,' he said.

The hot drinks machine hummed thoughtfully.

Sheridan Benedict said, 'Your grandmother's not dead either.'

'No,' I agreed.

But I wasn't convinced.

*

The doctor appeared.

He had a round, healthily glowing face.

Sheridan and I stood.

I knew what the doctor was going to say before he said it, as if I'd been struck with the truth, and I knew what the American tribes mean when they say that the wolf brings death from the spirit world.

'Your grandmother's going to be all right,' the doctor said.

For a moment this didn't register. Then my eyes got stingy and my chest felt tight.

'The surgery went well. She's resting now. In ITU.'

I swallowed the sobs.

'Can I see her?' I managed to say.

'She's sedated.'

'What's wrong with her?' I said.

'Did you know she had a stomach ulcer?'

'No.'

'Has anything been worrying her lately?'

I stared but didn't answer.

'Her ulcer burst. Lucky we saw her quickly. Any longer and … she'll be here for a few days. But as long as there's no complications, then …' He didn't finish his sentence, smiled instead.

'She'll get better?' I said.

'Well, let's say the signs are hopeful,' the doctor smiled.

'You don't want to commit yourself, then,' Sheridan Benedict said sourly.

The doctor smiled. 'You can never say, Mr …'

'Mr Benedict. Dr…?'

'Mr Partigan,' the doctor smiled.

I thought Sheridan was going to punch him.

'So the lad can't see his grandmother, then?'

'He can at the end of the day.' He glanced between us. 'Go home. You've done what you can. You got her here quickly. That was the most important thing.'

Sheridan Benedict nearly said something to the doctor, then he put his hand on my shoulder, and we left.

*

All the cars in the hospital car park were doing good impressions of igloos. Sheridan turned the fan up high on his car and scraped ice.

Town was empty. The wolf seemed about as real as a dream. The car heater got to me and I fell asleep lolling my head against the passenger window.

'Hey, wolf boy!'

I jolted awake. Dawn on the fells.

'Eve Lansdale's a good woman. She does a lot for people. She's done a lot for you.'

The diesel roared powerfully. Sheridan had to raise his voice to make himself heard.

'So think about what you're doing.'

I stared out the passenger window at the gold and red-tipped mountains.

'D'you hear what I said?'

'I saw the wolf yesterday,' I said.

Grudgingly, trying to keep mad eagerness out of his voice, he said, 'Where?'

'In a little valley over the mountain. A wood by a stream.'

He kept looking across at me.

Has anything been worrying her lately? Yes, I should have said to the doctor. Yes, yes, yes.

'What was it like?' Sheridan Benedict asked.

He kept his glances coming.

'It's my fault.'

'What is?'

'Nan getting sick like this.'

He kept driving. The dry sound of the diesel engine.

'I missed school to hunt the wolf. He killed a deer. I didn't get back until late. Nan was worried where I was. That's why she got ill.'

Sheridan fixed his gaze ahead.

We entered the valley. When we reached the lane, he

roared up it, and in the yard he braked hard. For a few seconds he stared ahead. I started to get out.

'Listen,' he said, turning to me. 'You think the world is one thing.' I didn't know exactly what he meant. 'But it's not,' he went on. 'It's something else. It's dangerous.'

I sort of understood what he meant. At least, I think I did.

'Your grandmother almost died last night.'

I looked away, to the woods.

'Leave it alone,' he said. 'Leave this wolf to people who know what to do with it.'

I got out.

The cottage was empty and cold. I thought about putting on the heating but went and poured myself a glass of water. He was right. I had to stay away from the wolf. For Nan's sake.

Trying

Cloud the colour of slate. Slate the colour of cloud. The fells showing the cloud-line, a flat base slicing off the peaks. Jets screaming down the valley, stupidly low. Pilots visible in the cockpits. The big boom of their fat engines coming after. *The British state practising for murder.* I missed Nan. The cottage silent. Sheridan Benedict right. The cloud deepening to coal-smoke. Then the rain. Crackling on the windows. Pelting the walls. Lashing the bare, budding trees. The wolf's coat keeping off the rain.

When I walked down to catch the bus to the hospital, I met a car coming the other way, its wipers going tick-tock fast.

I made way. The estate stopped and the window buzzed down and there was Debs' mum and, beyond her, Debs.

'We were coming to see you,' said her mum.

'I'm on my way out.'

Debs remained facing ahead. I could only see her chin, mouth, and the bottom of her nose.

'Are you going to see your grandmother?' said Debs' mum.

I nodded.

'We can give you a lift, if you like,' she said.

I looked down the lane. It was raining hard.

'Nah. Cheers, though.'

Debs leaned across.

She met my gaze, and held it. 'Get in.'

I got in.

*

Nan was woozy, drifting close to sleep. I held her hand. I promised her I'd stop my obsession with the wolf, and that I wouldn't give her any more trouble. I told her that I loved her. Then the doctor said I had to go. Nan gave my hand a frail squeeze. Hardly there. The metal stand of blood bags, liquid bags, all tubed-up. What had I caused here?

*

I did what I promised. I biked in early, went to the staff room and knocked on the blue door and asked for Miss Andrews. She wasn't in so I had to wait, and she rocked up at a run, late, but listened while I told her why I'd been off – that Nan had been ill. I said I wanted to work hard. That I wouldn't cause any trouble. She said she'd give me the support I needed.

I visited Nan each afternoon. I kept the house

super-clean. I ate with Debs' family. And Nan came out of hospital after three days.

I was at school when she was discharged. I wanted to be home to welcome her but decided I had better go to school otherwise it would just cause trouble. So I stuck it through the whole day, trying to concentrate, and when I got home, I found Nan in front of the cold hearth, the throw over her knees, asleep. The cottage, as usual, was cold, but I didn't want to put the heating on because it would only annoy her, so I started the fire that I'd made up the night before, and heated the meal for that night – lamb stew that Debs' mum had brought round. When I went to check on the fire, I found Nan awake.

I made her a cup of tea then I did my homework in the kitchen. We had dinner in the sitting room in front of the fire with the TV on. When the local news gave an update on the wolf attacks, I immediately switched channel. Nan didn't say anything about that. She didn't say much at all. I washed up, fed the fire, finished my homework, brought her a cup of tea and her book, then sat with her again but she'd fallen asleep. When I told her I was going to bed, I asked if she wanted anything, and she wanted me to make her a hot-water bottle and help her up the stairs. Nan had never asked for my help before and it frightened me that she asked now. It took her a while getting up the stairs. She had to pause twice to get her strength back. And she really did need my help, she leaned her whole weight on me.

I realised now that I had to work hard because Nan was relying on me. If she didn't recover and couldn't go back to work, then she would need someone to help: to buy her shopping; to pay bills. She didn't have anyone else – there was only me. So I had to get my exams so I could get a job so that I could help.

The wolf didn't go away, of course, he was only pushed from the front of my mind to somewhere else. Up on the fells, where he belonged, I hoped.

Then we had bad weather and spring seemed to recede – days of snow when the world seemed like someone was shaking a vast box of feathers above the valley. I couldn't cycle to school so I started taking the bus again, sitting on the top floor to avoid the Stazaks. They didn't follow me – Malky told me that the reason for Constable Strang's visit to school had been to warn off Steve Scott. Apparently Nan had complained to the police after Danny Scott's black-car visit to the cottage. Steve and his mates still shouted things but I ignored them. I held it all beyond me like I had a force-field, like in those games Mitesh and me used to play a million years ago, back when we were kids. I wasn't a kid any more, I was like an old man, and I sat there with a faint smile on my face like Yoda and I found the Stazaks idiotic even when, in the flow into school once, one of them shoved me in the small of my back so

I went flying into the person in front of me and crashed down onto my knees.

One evening, Debs visited with her mum. Nan was glad of the company. I suppose if you're an old person, it's not much fun being stuck in a cottage with a fifteen-year old. Debs' mum sat in the armchair and I went to make them tea.

Debs came in while I was getting out mugs. I didn't say anything to her, just popped in the tea bags, took out the milk, found sugar. I folded my arms waiting for the kettle to boil, leaned against the worktop.

'All right?' she said.

'All right?' I said. After a pause, I said, 'Still talking to me, then?'

She flushed, fired me a bit of hate, seemed on the verge of storming out, then shoved her hands in her combat jacket's side pockets and twisted her mouth around like she was thinking about saying something. On the other hand, she might just have been cleaning her gums with the inside of her lips.

'And how's the boyfriend doing, all right, is he?' I said.

'Watch it, Lucas,' she said, dropping her tone. 'He *is* my boyfriend as it happens, but he's nothing to do with this.'

I turned my back on her and made the tea. She was still there when I turned with the two mugs.

'I want to be your friend,' she said.

If I'd have been drinking tea, which I wouldn't have been because I don't drink tea, I'd have snorted it out my nose in surprise.

I said, 'Why'd you not talk to me?'

She let out a breath. 'I got freaked out,' she said.

'About what?'

'Seeing the wolf.'

'You were horrible to me: not returning my calls, and you blanked me on the Grassy Knoll.'

She flushed again.

'Apologise for how you treated me, and I'll think about being friends again.'

She did the gum-cleaning thing with the inside of her lips.

'Whatever,' I said, walking past her with the tea.

'Luke.'

I stopped.

'I'm sorry,' she said.

I could feel the heat of her. No bubblegum or cigarette smell, just the warm scent of her skin. The fineness of her hair. It was as well I was holding the mugs because it was like she was exerting some physical pull on me.

'All right,' I said.

After Debs and her mum had gone, Nan sat quiet in front of the fire. 'So you and Debs made it up, then?'

'Don't know what you're talking about.'

Her best attempt at a laugh in weeks – a sort of coughy breath.

'You're blushing!' she crowed.

I got up and stabbed the fire a bit with the poker.

'Getting a bit warm in here, is it?'

I couldn't help but grin. I returned to the armchair, and sat back.

'She's got a boyfriend,' I said.

'Boyfriends can come and go quickly when you're that age.'

The wood popped and sparks skied up the chimney.

It held our attention for a while.

'I'm glad you're applying yourself again at school,' she said.

She was still gazing at the fire.

After a while she put her head back on the armchair and said, 'I messed up with your mother. I can't mess up with you as well.'

She closed her eyes. She was breathing more and more deeply and I could see her chest rising and falling, and she must have fallen asleep. I wondered whether to wake her or let her sleep. Then she said, 'Your mother would be proud of you.'

I glowered at the fire and wished she hadn't said that. And suddenly I hated this place, I hated being here. The valley, the fells, strangers' land that was nothing to do with me.

I wondered if I would ever call a place home again.

Nan sat with her eyes closed, her eyelids strangely papery and lighter than the rest of her face. Her jaw was dropped slightly, and the two vertical lines from the corners of her mouth to her chin made her face seem a lot like Mum's face. She twitched, and the fingers on her hand sprang in the air like a skylark startled from the grass, then dropped back.

Snap

One chill March day, when frost had stiffened the grass and glazed the granite on the fells and I was getting ready for school, I heard a car on the lane. Nan had already left for work – she had started back at her office doing shorter days – and immediately I thought of Danny and Steve Scott.

I rushed downstairs, saw nothing from the study window so put on my shoes and jacket and stepped out.

The deep chill hit me. No sign of a vehicle so I went to the gateposts. Up the lane was a white van. Two men stood at the open rear doors. I crossed the cattle grid. The men, in dark outdoors gear, were removing small rucksacks, and both had long black leather bags, which they shouldered. The van doors slammed. One of the men turned, saw me, then the pair started up the track with those odd, long bags.

Just before they disappeared round the bend, I called out. They stopped.

'What you doing here?' I said.

'What's it to you?' said one of the men.

'I live here. What's in them bags?'

'Fishing rods,' the man said. The other laughed.

'You got a licence for them, then?'

'Piss *off*,' said the man, and walked uphill. The other threw me a wave and followed his mate. I remembered the farmers on television with similar bags: scabbards.

'They're guns!' I shouted. 'I'm going to phone the police.'

They both stopped and turned and, in a low voice, the first man said, 'We *are* the police.'

The pair walked on, towards the fells.

While I was getting ready for school, I thought about those two men going steadily uphill with those dark long bags, moving onto the fells, lying down in the grass. And the wolf, flowing over the land. A gunshot a mile away and he's dead.

*

Debs came to find me at lunchtime. I was in the library, trying to read for English but worrying about those two policemen. I hoped it would snow or that they'd get lost in fog. I hoped the wolf would smell them and keep well away.

I told Debs about them.

'That's Dad,' she said.

'How'd you mean?'

'He's kept on at the police. They've been out a couple of times, hunting the wolf. He showed them his map and

307

everything. They've been round the woods on the other side of the mountain and are trying this side now.'

I stared. Those woods were where I'd told him I'd seen the wolf.

'What is it? You look like you've seen a ghost.'

'Nothing.'

Everything was my fault: Mum and Dad; Nan nearly dying; now the wolf.

A jet roared down the valley. We waited for it, then it slid past, sharp-winged, the helmeted pilot visible in the glass bulb of the cockpit. The big roar followed.

It was always there, death, seeking things out.

I was finished with doing its work.

*

In the afternoon I had my meeting with Ian. To get there in time, I left at the start of the lunch break and cycled uphill to the station but I thought I shouldn't really be going. What I thought was, I should be with the wolf. Even if he had brought death to my family. Because he was still a living creature, wasn't he? And each time I thought this, I immediately changed my mind, because I had to do right by Nan.

As I cycled uphill stood on the pedals, slowly bobbing up and down with each revolution, I was wondering what I should do for the best when I heard the familiar snarl of an engine behind me and Danny Scott's black car swept past. I stared it out of sight and once it had gone felt a surge of relief.

It returned on the other side of the road, slowed as it passed, then there was that familiar chainsaw rip as it accelerated past me.

I kept going, wobbling uphill from side to side.

The chainsaw rip came from behind, and he came past again. Perhaps a foot away. Worse, he braked a few yards ahead so I had to slow right down to avoid hitting him, then I had to stop.

I stood with one foot on the tarmac, the other on the pedal. For a few seconds, nothing happened while music twanged through the car's bodywork. Then the passenger window buzzed down and Steve Scott's head appeared.

'All right, mate,' he grinned. 'Out for a ride?'

The engine roared, there was a burst of laughter, and Danny accelerated to the brow of the hill and disappeared over it.

I stood waiting.

They didn't come back.

I figured I was going to be late for Ian if I waited any longer.

I pedalled on.

The hill goes up in several stages, arriving at a summit where it flattens out before going around another bend then making a further climb, each time leading away from the lake before it arrives at the shops and the train station. On one of these false summits, I found Danny Scott's black car. It was on the other side of the road, facing me.

All I could hear was my uphill gasp, the creak of the chain.

A reflection of trees slid up the car bonnet and across the black windscreen as the black car moved off. It came missile-straight for me, accelerating. I dived off my bike just before it hit.

A loud, clear snap then a metallic clatter was followed by a squeal of tyres.

I lay face-down among tiny blue-and-yellow flowers, and when I rolled over there was a puff of tyre smoke rising and the scent of burned rubber. Danny's car was halfway down the hill, dropping through the gears.

My bike's front wheel was folded like a piece of paper.

I dropped the bike in the flowers and marched, not towards the station but downhill. I felt a black narrowing of my mind.

*

I walked past reception, under the balcony, and down the wide corridor. On the playground, I took a straight line through the various groups, their calls and shouts echoing off the school buildings with airy glee. Out beyond all that.

They say that the wolf likes to play. That its play only

seems violent to us – bashing a fellow wolf to the ground, clamping its jaws round a muzzle or throat – but with us humans, it's the other way round, isn't it? What we call play is really something violent.

Banter is bullying. Games are murderous.

Steve Scott, black hair perfect but for his stupid tufts, was back from his lunchtime ride in his brother's car and in the Cage.

The Cage door honked as I opened it.

Their eyes were on the game. The scuff of soles, a shout of 'Pass!' Steve Scott less than ten yards from the Cage door. He was side-on to me, arms out, head lowered, anticipating some movement in the match.

He sensed me when I was about one yard from him.

He looked across his shoulder. I was still travelling. Then my fist was. He didn't have time to work out what I was going to do so the last image I have of him is that expression of surprise. It's funny. It's sort of without any personality in it. It's like it's just the animal part of him. The physical thought before any decision or emotion gets in there. My fist connected with his cheek. His cheek made a sound like a cricket ball being hit by a bat. Because he was stood side-on to me, he stumbled sideways. He tried to keep his balance but his legs tangled and he toppled. He had no chance to break his fall. I suppose he was lucky he was standing sideways. If he'd been facing me, he'd have fallen straight back and banged his skull on the ground. He probably would have died. I would have killed him. As it was, he hit the ground first with his shoulder.

I was already walking away.

I didn't say anything. I just walked out.

The boy who was near me – who I didn't know – didn't try to stop me.

The door honked its appreciation and I slammed it shut after me.

No one tried to stop me until I was in the main building, when I heard running. I was nearly at Reception.

'Oi! Death Boy!'

It was Alex and a whole gang of the football players.

And just then, ahead of me through the double doors, walked Zed.

Zed's gaze lit on me, slid to Alex and the others behind me.

'Get him, Zed!'

Zed's gaze returned to me. Our eyes met. He winked and kept walking. We passed. I didn't understand. He just kept going. He didn't try to stop me. Then I was through the double doors, across the reception, and outside. I ran uphill towards the main road.

For some reason, they didn't come out immediately. The only explanation I have for that is that Zed did something to stop them. I don't know why he did something but he must have done.

A bus was pulling in. The indicator blinked slowly and an old lady in a purple overcoat got off then turned to lift a tartan bag-trolley off the bus. I helped her, and got on.

The doors sighed shut and we pulled away.

Good Luck

During the short train journey to Kendal across the open, rolling land at the edge of the fells, and late for Ian, I thought of the wolf, hidden during winter in impassable weather, now exposed. And I thought of those two police snipers, hunting him.

And I thought, that was where I should be.

*

Ian was wearing his blue skate shoes.

'I shouldn't be here,' I said after the longest of silences.

Following one of his extensive pauses, Ian said, 'Where should you be?'

'On the fells.'

'Why?'

'Because people are trying to kill the wolf.'

'How do you feel about that?'

I sighed as if he was a little kid who has done something idiotic for the millionth time.

Ian tried to break the Olympic record for longest silence.

World record.

Finally he said: 'What *would* you like to talk about?'

I gazed around the room – the empty bookshelves, the carpet tiles, the pushed-back chair where Nan had sat when we first came. The one thing I was glad of was that the heating wasn't on and that stupid radiator wasn't sending a fart through its pipes.

Ian sat with his legs a little apart wearing canvas grey trousers, a bright blue lumberjack shirt with the cuffs too tight and also too long. Gold wedding band. And those blue skate shoes. It was a shame he couldn't speak to me about what was going on in his life the way that I had spoken to him about mine.

'Ian,' I said. 'Don't take this the wrong way, but those skate shoes are not a good look for you.'

Then I stood.

His eyes widened with surprise, the first surprise I'd ever seen in him, but I didn't feel any satisfaction in penetrating the calm. He was thinking about saying something, I could tell, only he wasn't sure what to say. Which made me warm to him.

'Good luck with things, Ian.'

'Wait, I don't think you should –'

'Thanks for trying to help me.' I stuck out my hand.

A pause, then he stood and took it.

'Listen,' he said, 'I'll be here next week. At the same time, all right?'

I gave him a sympathetic grin, and left.

Hunt

Mid-afternoon. The skylarks springing from my feet. High in the air and invisible, singing their tiny hearts out. Shaggy-dog sheep that some reckless farmer had pastured, staring at me like they'd never seen a human before. A sleek creature, a ferret or stoat, on its hind legs for a look-out, dropping to all fours and slinking through the grass and vanishing into a dry-stone wall.

Far below, the white van visible at the edge of the woods.

If the policemen were any good, they'd be hidden somewhere.

It took several hours to get up properly onto the fell tops, following the paths. The wind blew. The scars from where water had fallen valleywards were like creases on a craggy face. Granite showed like bony outcrops on a body.

The gruff sound of an engine reached me. A red quad bike bumped up the path from the valley, the rider jiggling around on top like a puppet.

It took him a while to reach me.

From his back, strapped to him, rose a long black scabbard. I knew what that was.

Sheridan Benedict stopped his quad bike and dismounted.

'I thought I told you to stay off the fells,' he said, but he didn't have the rage he always seemed to have in him. He studied me, his eyes tired under the lenses. 'Your nan is just out of hospital.'

His voice didn't have the usual edge in it when he spoke next. 'You'll regret this. If something happens to her now, you'll regret it the whole of your life.'

I opened my mouth to say something in reply, I didn't know what, but he turned his back on me and mounted his quad bike. Revved it hard and went on, bumping up the rocky track.

'Don't you bloody kill it!' I shouted.

I could see him for a long time after, going over steeply sloping grass, the quad bike holding to the land the way a spider clings to a near-vertical. I headed in the direction he had gone, although now I could no longer see him.

*

It was about five o'clock and I had walked all day and seen nothing and the sun was low through a white haze and the sea glittered beyond the distant mountains. Windfarm rotors turned on the coast, and I saw fell-walkers on other ridges getting down before night came. But I had to keep going.

A gunshot.

I stopped and listened.

Nothing. No bits of conversation of walkers. No tweetling skylarks. Just the wind.

I walked fast, scanning the land.

Another shot.

I ran.

*

Over the rushing wind came my gasps, the beat of my blood. Somewhere, perhaps in one of the narrow ghylls off the tops, the wolf might lie, wounded, dying. Dead.

Dusk spread from the east. My shadow lay long and faint across the grass.

I was near the edge of the fells where they descended to the rolling hills that spread to Kendal when a helicopter rose ahead of me, its red and green lights blinking in the gloom. A searchlight swept across the land. I stumbled towards it.

About a half mile distant it hunted, its searchlight moving like a long finger. The helicopter veered below the fell edge and its buzz ceased. I came to a road. I paused to take my bearings and catch my breath. My heart was fluttering like a bird. The light was draining. In ten minutes, I wouldn't be able to find my way.

To my left, light glowed from a crag, then twin beams flashed over the brow of the fell and a car appeared. It swept its way along the road towards me. I watched it come. Its headlamps swung round the final bend and it blinded me.

I must have been standing upwind of it because it was only when it had rounded the corner that I heard its engine – the rip of a chainsaw.

I leaped onto the high, bouncy heather, and ran.

I ran for nearly ten seconds before a weight hit me in the small of my back.

I was pulled over by Steve Scott. Another figure appeared over his shoulder. His brother.

I couldn't breathe. My heart clappered but there was no air.

They were dragging me across the heather, back to the road.

Tiny breaths that wouldn't go all the way down. Pain throbbed across my back.

Onto tarmac. Them round me. Flashes of jeans, trainers.

''e's dying.'

'Panic attack, I reckon.'

Pulled onto my feet. Swaying unsteadily, my jacket in bunched fists.

Air!

Air.

I gulped it down.

Three of them – Steve, his brother Danny, and Alex.

Steve's cheek had a big red mark where I'd hit him earlier.

The wind blew.

'In the car,' said Steve.

Danny laughed. I tried to thrash my way out of his grip but felt a swift pain in my side and my arms flew to my body for protection. A palm in the small of my back ran me forward, another ducked my head, and a shove flung me headlong across the rear seat-well. Someone bundled in after me. Car doors slammed. We sprang forward.

*

I was on the floor in the back, laid across the shaft that ran down the middle of the car.

Where were we going?

Alex on the back seat. I scrambled up beside him.

A heavy blow on my chest. A fist swam out. Alex loomed after.

Steve's face appeared around the seat, a long paleness.

'All right, mate?' I couldn't see the smile, but I could hear it.

It hurt to breathe and I didn't answer.

Alex said, 'We are going to kill –'

'Shut up,' said Steve. 'We're hunting the wolf.'

I didn't say anything.

'Here,' said Danny from the driver's seat, slapping his brother's arm. 'Keep an eye out, would you?'

Steve's face vanished.

For a while we drove in silence, the engine deep, going too fast for the corners. Steve was leaned forward, searching the near-dark sky.

'Still can't see it.'

Into my ear, Alex whispered, 'We're going to murder you.'

The radio flared with static, then a voice like a mini-cab dispatcher said something muffled.

'That's south,' said Danny.

We braked and accelerated, braked and accelerated as we came down from the fells. I didn't move. If I tried to get out of the car at this speed, I'd die. Minutes passed. We swung onto a bigger road and now Danny gunned the engine. I felt myself pressed back into the seat.

Steve's face reappeared.

'You doing all right there, mate?'

'Yeah thanks, mate,' I said.

'Shut up,' said Alex, and elbowed my chest.

I cried out with the pain.

Steve said, 'We're tuned to the cops.'

Steve stayed with his face swung round the seat, even though he wasn't saying anything.

'The cops shot the wolf,' he said.

The radio voice said something that they could only hear in the front, and Steve swung away to listen. A light glowed in the darkness – phonelight.

'That's near Cartmel.'

We rose and fell with the terrain. Each time the car rose over a bump, my guts lifted like I was in an elevator.

After a particularly sudden drop, Steve chuckled.

Alex sucked air between teeth and Steve must have heard him because his face reappeared and he said, 'What's the matter, Alex, you scared or something?'

'No.'

'How 'bout you?' Steve said.

I met his gaze.

The car turned sharply, Steve's eyes widened in fear, and I grinned.

He grinned back.

We slowed slightly, went through several bends, reached a straight, and again I was pushed back into my seat.

Danny braked hard and we were thrown sideways as we swung onto another road. Gravel scraped under the tyres and for a moment we had no traction. Fear opened inside me, then treads gripped tarmac.

We raced down a narrow lane between hedges. If something came the other way, we'd hit it.

I hunted out a seat belt.

'Can you slow down a bit, mate?' said Alex.

'You messed your underpants?' shouted Danny, and accelerated.

Steve laughed.

Hanging from the roof handle, pressed against the door, Alex said nothing.

I clicked home the seat belt and leaned forward between the seats.

'This as fast as you can go?'

The brothers said nothing.

I sat back and laughed.

The car sped up.

'Jesus, Danny,' said Alex, pleading.

The voice on the radio said, 'It's moving towards the Head.'

'D'you know where he means?'

The police dispatcher said something I couldn't make out.

In silence we sped down a straight road then Danny slowed a fraction as we entered a village. A white figure appeared in front of us. A girl in chef whites holding a deep container.

We veered.

A parked car filled my vision, Alex screamed, the chef threw her container, water leaped, we clipped the parked car's wing mirror, shot past the chef, zoomed out of the village. For a few seconds there was silence and we all seemed stunned at the narrow escape. Then Danny banged out a machine-gun laugh.

Steve swung round. 'How you doing, Luke?'

'You're getting a bruise there, Steve,' I said.

''kin 'ell, bro,' said Danny. 'You going to let him speak to you like that?'

'Oh, he'll have it, all right,' said Steve to his brother, his eyes still on me.

Danny said, 'Let's see how he likes this.'

We accelerated again. On the gently glowing dashboard, the needle rose above the speedometer's mid-point.

The police voice said, 'Confirmation – it's moving towards the headland.'

'Go faster,' I said.

'The little –' said Danny, finishing his sentence with a burst of acceleration. The speedometer needle tapped seventy.

The grey wolf ran.

Mum and Dad gone forever.

I died back then, in the car crash. I am dead.

Or not. I am alive now. The pulse ticks in my wrist, beats on the left side of my tongue, courses in my brain like white water hurdling the mountain rocks. The grey form rushes beyond the hedges.

All these possibilities. Balanced. Neither side winning.

I leaned forward between the seats.

'Go faster for the bend.'

Fear isn't a thing you can hear. But I heard their fear, Danny's and Steve's.

'Go faster,' I said.

Danny slowed for a bend, and I laughed.

We rounded the bend.

He didn't slow enough.

A wolf stood in the middle of the road.

Steve screamed good and proper. We tipped in a jolting rumble that widened into roar. I hit the back of the passenger seat, the side window. A tearing of earth, hurled –

Upside down.

Stop.

All windows whitened.

Everything quiet. No one moved. The engine stopped, clicking with heat. Above it I could hear a drone, a buzz.

I pressed the seat belt button, kicked my way out the smash-white window which fell out with a few stamps, slid out.

I came down the bank, and stood.

The wolf sat in the centre of the road, his head dropped low.

'Hello,' I said.

Someone beat at a window. The drone of the police helicopter grew louder.

The wolf didn't take his eyes off me.

I walked towards him. I walked funny, slapping the tarmac with my soles. I could taste blood on my tongue.

The wolf flowed across the road. He slipped into the hedge.

I slapped after him. My hip felt odd.

There was a narrow gap beneath the hedge. I got down on all fours. I glanced over my shoulder.

The car was on its roof. Danny was hoisting himself out. Steve was already out, on his knees, vomiting. Alex was crawling from the rear window. The helicopter roared near. Its searchlight blazed on the scene, turned it to daylight.

I faced the darkness.

I slithered after the wolf.

Headland

I followed the wolf across the broken land. He did not flow now, he plodded. But he was still faster than me and I stumbled on the furrows and by the time he reached the far hedge where he stopped to look over his shoulder I was only halfway across. He dropped into a ditch.

I broke into a run but my legs wouldn't do what I wanted them to and I lost my balance and fell. The helicopter roared lower. Its searchlight held steady above the spot where Danny Scott's car had crashed. Then the long finger of light slid out over the field, sweeping in wide arcs, and I got up and ran again. The shoots of grass went daylit and I was in the beam, then it moved beyond me. The grind of rotors filled the air, the searchlight fixed on something in the next field, and the helicopter flew on.

I reached the hedge. There was another gap beneath it. I went under, my jacket caught, and it ripped when I tugged.

The land beyond was completely flat except, half a mile away, against the dark sky a hill rose like a black wedge that had been plonked on the fields. The helicopter was moving steadily towards it. To my left I caught sight of the headlamps of several cars, and flashing blue police lights. They were moving along a road that ran parallel to me, also towards the hill.

I reached it after several minutes. Four vehicles were pulled up, two police cars, a beaten-up Land Rover, and a white van. A policeman stood with his back to me. His attention was on woods on the hill's far edge that ran from the fields to the summit. It was over the woods that the helicopter hung, spearing its beam down among the trees. The policeman shifted and I saw it was Constable Strang. With the roar of the rotors he didn't hear me as I slid between the two police cars and onto the hill. Then, bent double, I ran across the slope towards the trees.

Out of the darkness two figures appeared so close it took me by surprise.

Glasses, stubble.

'What the –?' said Sheridan Benedict, startled.

I tried to side-step him but a weighty palm struck my shoulder, then my sleeve was snatched. I tried to wriggle off my jacket. The fabric went slack and I thought I'd got away but a tug of my sleeve jerked me back. I was reeled in and no matter how hard I fought, the jacket would not come off. A huge hand grabbed my collar.

'Stop dancing about!'

A stony fist blossomed between us and probably

would have connected with my face except two small pale hands prevented it.

Debs. She put herself between her dad and me. For about ten seconds there was a complicated wrangle over my torn sleeve until, out of breath, we were separated, both my shirt collar and Debs' forearm in those dry-stone-wall-lifting, sheep-wrestling fists.

'Cut it out the pair of you or I'll clout you into next Tuesday.'

'Get lost!'

A gunshot cracked, audible above the roaring helicopter.

Several torch beams jagged through the woods.

Sheridan let out a neighing scream and I turned to see Debs holding his hand to her teeth, lips drawn back, mouth bloody.

She dropped his hand and ran.

For a second Sheridan and I gazed at the pale palm held out before him, a row of bloody teeth marks printed in it, then I ripped out of his loosened grip and pelted after Debs.

We reached the woods, hurtled through the undergrowth. Far behind, weakly, he called: 'Stop! Stop!' We kept going.

'They've got guns!' Sheridan shouted. But we did not stop.

No sign now of the torches. The helicopter rose, its

light swinging. We crouched on a carpet of ankle-high ivy beneath the trees.

'What are you doing here?' said Debs.

'What are *you* doing here?'

'Trying to save the wolf. Dad wants to kill it.'

'And you want to kill your dad?'

She frowned, not understanding.

I pointed at her mouth.

'Hilarious,' she said humourlessly, wiping blood from her lips with the back of her hand. 'So,' she said, 'wolf-expert, what are we going to do?'

Down the slope lay a giant toppled tree. Above was the roar of the helicopter in the darkness. How could I find the wolf?

'Listen,' said Debs, standing up, 'I'm not waiting around for you to come up with a brilliant idea while the police –'

'Be quiet!' I said, grabbing her arm and pulling her down. 'I'm thinking.'

We stayed silent, crouched on the ivy.

It would smell me, probably hear me. But I had to let it know that I wanted, I needed, to find it. I stood. Then I tipped back my head and howled.

'Shh!'

'Ow, Ow-ooooh!'

'For God's sake, will you shut up!'

'Ow-ow, Ow-OOOOOH!'

She took hold of my arm and shook me. 'The police will hear you, you idiot!'

'So will he.'

Her fingers were still on my arm, and suddenly they tightened. Her eyes were wide, her body rigid. She was staring over my shoulder.

I looked.

And there, coming over the dark land, was the wolf.

He came weak. There was something tired-looking in his face, sick.

He stopped about four yards away. He opened his long mouth so he seemed to be smiling, and his long tongue lolled out at the side. His coat seemed darker than usual.

I took a step forward.

'Don't!' Debs hissed, still holding my arm.

I detached her fingers, fixed my eyes on his. Tried to ignore his teeth. And took another step towards him.

He didn't move.

His coat was matted dark round his neck.

Killer of flocks. Killer of deer. Killer of Mum and Dad.

I lifted my hand, slowly.

'Don't!' hissed Debs.

The wolf clapped shut his mouth. Not smiling now.

My hand hovered between us. His nostrils dilated and closed as he sniffed the air.

I leaned forward, moving my hand slowly alongside his huge face. I moved my fingers to the great ruff of matted coarse fur where the dark colour seemed. I touched the soft fur.

His head whipped round and his jaws clamped on my wrist. Great teeth that broke bones.

Trying to keep fear out of my voice, I said, 'I won't hurt you.'

A wolf can smell fear-chemicals.

For a moment he didn't move. Then his jaw opened. Slowly, I removed my forearm. I stepped back.

Bumped into Debs.

She bunched my jacket so I could feel her fists in my back.

'You all right?' she whispered.

When I raised my arm, Debs gasped. My hand was black with blood.

'It's his.'

The wolf was staring beyond us as if we were not there. Then he sank down, front legs first, then hind. He lay like a king. Then he lowered that mighty head on his giant feet.

'Have you got any water?' I said.

'No.'

'How far's the sea?'

'There's streams down the slope. Marsh and river on all sides – we're trapped.'

'Seriously?'

'Yes.'

I started down the slope.

'Where are you going?' she cried hoarsely.

'To get water.'

She waved her arms about. 'Don't leave me with it.'

'He won't hurt you.'

Down past the toppled trunk to a barbed-wire fence which I climbed, ripping my jacket some more on its barbs.

The marsh lay wide, vast, still. Along the shore, miles in the distance, twinkled houselights. Beyond the marsh the other way was a great bay and, minuscule beyond that, southwards, the lights of a town. I splashed down onto the mud and knelt at a channel. I tore the sleeve right off my jacket and soaked it. I cupped the soaking fabric in both hands and made my way back uphill.

When I got there, Debs was stood in exactly the same spot, in exactly the same attitude. The wolf appeared to be asleep.

'What took you so long?' she whispered.

'Stopped to admire the scenery.'

'Have a nice time?' she sarked.

I knelt and said to the wolf, 'I'm not going to hurt you.'

The wolf opened his eyes but did not turn his head.

I leaned to place the soaking material on his neck.

'Don't!' Debs hissed.

The wolf rolled onto his side. I hesitated, then I leaned again and touched the cold material to his neck and felt a quiver run through him. The eye that I could see stared. Not at me, but at nothing. I wiped away clotted blood and dirt. I washed as best I could. Then I took my jacket off and tore out the lining, the cleanest part and, hesitating a moment, finally summoned the courage to clamp it over his neck wound.

I felt him flinch, his skull jerked off the earth, and I froze. He settled.

'He probably needs to drink,' I said.

Debs said nothing.

I became aware of my own thirst.

'If we don't get him off this headland, they'll kill him,' said Debs.

The wolf breathed roughly and deeply; my hand rose and fell on the powerful neck.

With difficulty, I tied the fabric around his throat. Then sat beside him.

We stayed a long time like that.

The helicopter prowled the woods, its searchlight beam piercing. When it approached our part of the woods we moved down the slope to the toppled tree. We found a hollow where we could hide beneath the trunk, and there we waited. The wolf rose and plodded over to us where, with a groan, he flopped down.

We waited, listening to the helicopter buzz above the woods, watching the searchlight.

For several hours we stayed like that, huddled in the

darkness, leaning on the bank of the hollow, half laid down, half sat up, hidden in our shelter by the toppled trunk, the wolf asleep, his chest rising and falling, his breath noisy, his massive white feet twitching, letting out little dream-whinnies of fear.

'What are we going to do?' Debs asked.

'Can we cross the marsh?'

'No.'

We were quiet.

'How about we wait until it gets lighter, and see if we can sneak past them.'

Silence.

'Okay,' she said finally.

Quiet.

She shuddered.

'You cold?'

'No,' she said, as if the word was a punch she was throwing at me.

I couldn't see her eyes properly but they were open and she was facing me.

We were quiet a long time.

'Where would you go,' she said suddenly, 'if you could go anywhere?'

I thought for a while. 'Right beyond everything. Beyond all the human beings. Into the wild. What about you?'

'I'd travel. I'd see cities and mountains and rivers and

oceans and forests and highways and deserts and I'd do what I want and say what I want.'

I gave a little grunt.

'What?'

'Bet you would, that's all.'

She seemed to relax. I thought I could see her eyes shining. She seemed, too, to get very still.

I touched her clenched fists. They were cold. I cupped them.

We stayed like that a long time.

She rested her head against mine. I could feel her breath on my face. I began to feel drowsy.

'You asleep?' I murmured.

She was pressed against me and I could hear her heartbeat. I listened to the wind sifting through the trees.

'We'll get to those places,' I whispered.

Debs didn't say anything and my words sounded stupid to me suddenly.

I felt her ribs expand and contract as she breathed. The night was cold. The helicopter roared.

*

I woke to the sound of a bee.

Sunlight. Weak mist. The sound of flowing water. Lying back in a sea of green. Further off, bluebells.

The bee, big as a thumb-joint, steered by buzzily.

On my chest, her head pillowed, lay Debs. Her arms tucked against her for warmth. My arm round her. Through the trees down the slope, the sound of water. The woods going crazy with birdsong. For a while I watched a tiny bird with a down-curved bill, moving up and down a trunk more like a squirrel than a bird. I couldn't work out if it was flying or scampering.

The helicopter had gone.

The wolf was alive, his fur rising and falling. Now, in daylight, I could see him properly, the mixed colouring: white, grey, and on the muzzle black and bee-orange and pine-brown. The fur coarse but not stiff. The bulk of his chest and shoulders and at the neck blood-matted.

A twig snapped.

Gently, I rolled my head to the side. About forty yards away, stepping through a carpet of bluebells, was a policeman. One of the policemen from the van. He held a rifle, butt to shoulder, barrel pointed at the ground. To his side, at a distance, another policeman with a gun. They were walking through the woods. They hadn't seen us.

The wolf slept.

I watched the policemen pass out of sight.

I shook Debs awake.

'Groff,' she murmured, trying to snuggle down into her jacket.

'Debs,' I breathed, 'it's the police.'

She stiffened into wakefulness.

I pointed towards the marsh. We rolled onto our fronts and crawled down the slope.

The wolf stirred. Then he struggled to his feet, and followed.

A bird from the marsh cried. We reached the barbed wire. Beyond that was the marsh. The air was bright with sunlit haze. The mist hung as low as the treetops – that must have been why the helicopter had gone.

Before us, the channels flowed. We moved along the marsh-edge, then followed the slope that climbed to the headland. Not speaking, not hurrying. The wolf followed. And then we were out of the woods and on the headland properly in the mist. It was like we were on a little island in the clouds.

From somewhere nearby came a bleating of lambs.

A shout, a glance back, and dark shapes emerged from white air.

We ran.

We were fast but the wolf would not run. He stepped solemnly on his delicate, huge feet. We neared the top of the headland. Still they came. Three. Four shapes. Five.

The summit.

There was one way down by a path to a tapering tip of rock, the marsh-channels on either side meeting at the end where they flowed out, into the whiteness, towards the sea.

'Stop!' shouted a male voice.

The black shapes spread out like a nightmare spiderweb.

We ran down the path towards the sea-channels. We reached the slender finger of rock. The water was deep and fast. There was nowhere left to run. The wolf followed. The dark shapes came down. I stepped in front of the wolf.

From the mist, policemen emerged. Two of the policemen had rifles.

'Move away!' one shouted in a hard bellowing voice.

The marsh bird let out a *peep-peep*. Sheridan Benedict appeared, running behind the policemen, his coat rising behind him on the breeze, the thump of his boot-soles like hoofbeats through the earth. He passed them, thudding towards us. I balled my hands to fists, ready to fight him. 'Stop!' a policeman shouted. Sheridan didn't touch me but ran right past. I heard a scream then he was holding Debs, walking backwards and away from me while she flailed.

The policemen moved forward as Sheridan and Debs moved back. It was like a choreographed dance, their approach. It was like, I realised, what wolves do to their prey when the pack gathers for the final savagery on the wounded animal.

I did not move because that shows weakness – gives the signal to the predator to kill.

I faced them out.

The marsh bird *peep-peeped*, the lambs bleated.

The sunlight shone everywhere, diffused in mist-haze.

The wolf was close against my side. I felt his bulk, I put my hand on his neck and felt the wetness. Saw dark spots on the grass round the policemen's black boots – wolf blood.

What had we done? Killing and more killing.

'Move away, lad,' said one policeman.

'Shoot it,' another said.

'No!' screamed Debs.

The ones with rifles became like statues, cheeks pillowed on black gunmetal. The British state, as Nan would say, practising for murder.

'Step away!' shouted Sheridan Benedict.

An unarmed policeman took a step towards me. His eyes stayed on me. He held out a big roughened palm.

Like Dad's.

'Come on, Lucas,' he said.

How did he know my name?

'What other choice is there?' he said.

I didn't move.

What other choice is there?

That was the question, wasn't it?

I nodded. Then I said, 'Let me hug him first.'

'Don't. It's wild.'

I crouched. One gun clicked. The other gun clicked. I put both my arms underneath the belly and ribs of the wolf and he let me and he was cradled under my forearms.

'Step away, now,' said the policeman, like he was afraid.

I whispered into the wolf's ear. Then I pushed off the balls of my feet as hard as I could.

It wasn't so much a jump as a fall. The wolf, as he fell through the air towards the water, flipped the way a fish flips when it's caught. Then we both hit the channel with a splash.

Ice-cold water vanished the breath out of me. I surfaced gasping. The wolf surfaced. Head held high, he swam. I flung an arm, spread myself, put myself between him and the guns, struggling against the dead-weight of sopping clothes.

'Don't!' shouted Debs to the policemen.

'Wait!' shouted a policeman.

We half swam, half flowed with the current. We went very slowly. So slowly the policemen could step from rock to rock and keep abreast of us.

'Shoot it!' screamed Sheridan Benedict.

It was hard to keep my head above the water my clothes were so heavy, and it was hard to swim. I kept on the headland side of the wolf so the police wouldn't shoot. And the wolf seemed to understand what I intended, because he kept pace with me, keeping me between himself and the police.

'Go, Luke!' screamed Debs.

I laughed. I actually laughed.

We moved beyond the fingertip of rock where all the channels joined.

The policemen said nothing. There was only the sound of the water flowing between the banks, and my splashing limbs. Then, when I turned over on my back, all I could see through the haze were the dim shapes of the policemen, then, for a moment, a clearer and slighter shape that I knew to be Debs, standing right at the tip of the land, and I gave a howl and Debs howled back. And then we were in the mist.

I could see the banks of the channel. A few more yards and the mist deepened and the banks were hidden. The wolf moved with me.

It was hard now to know how fast we were going because I had nothing to measure the current's speed against. The mist thinned and thickened but did not clear.

I wondered how far it was to the sea. Or if this already *was* the sea, but when I tasted the water, it was not salty like seawater.

Then I saw, off to my left, two figures at the level of the bank. The shapes did not grow clear, only seemed to keep pace with me for a few moments. Then they were gone.

A chunk of something scraped my leg and butted my

back. A small chunk of ice, was it? Several of them, now, as if I was moving among ice floes.

The stream – or was it a river? – had a bend. It must have. How else could the two figures have loomed from the mist directly ahead in the way they did? I wondered if this was another error. A fault in my brain. A madness. Because ahead of me on the bank stood Mum and Dad.

And while the mist did not clear fully, it thinned a little and I could see them. They didn't come down the bank. Or even call out to me.

I dipped below the water. Saltwater. Cold. I surfaced. Numbness crept inwards. The ice flowed past. Mum came down the bank to the little beach, where relaxed waves unfolded themselves.

'Mum!' I shouted.

I could feel nothing now of my own flesh.

The crinkles round Dad's eyes from weather. Mum's broad face.

Brown, cold darkness as I sank. I surfaced.

'Dad!' My voice was weak, breathy.

He didn't move. She didn't move.

It was getting harder to keep afloat.

Sand-murk, gulp of water.

'Mu-! Da -!'

I rose. They were beckoning me.

Behind me, the dull marsh. Beyond that, police, school. Mr Bond. Ian. Social workers.

Malky, Miss Andrews, Sheridan Benedict.

Debs. Nan.

Love – that difficult country, always at your back.

I looked at Mum and Dad. They did not move.

I turned and, against the current, I swam towards the marsh.

I heard nothing from Mum or Dad. I swam hard.

The current was strong. I kicked, I crawled, I screamed out loud against the brown salty river and my muscles ached with each impossible stroke as the river flowed. My foot grazed mud, slipped off. And now I ran my legs furiously against the current and reached with both hands as far as I could, trod mud, my foot sucked in, then another step and I stood on, in, mud and, leaving the sucking, drawing power of the river itself, shoulders above the water, I climbed, like climbing with a rucksack full of rocks, climbed up, each push painful, then I staggered onto the muddy bank by the tiny heather flowers and strange lettuce-like marsh-plants and fell down with a bump.

I rolled over.

The far beach and bank were empty.

But still there, mid-river, was the wolf, nose lifted above the water.

It was like he was waiting for me.

I took a breath to call to him but didn't because he turned away and the mist closed in, and as I watched he

344

seemed to be carried out along the channel. Then the mist enveloped him.

I hoped he would be safe. I hoped that he would live. The world needs wolves.

The mist rolled. It drifted. I was aware of my long-drawn breaths.

Water lapped against my numb, useless legs. I dragged myself further up the mud, onto the heather fully, where I lay, regaining my strength. Mist drifted above me, wet, thick, cold.

I struggled to my feet.

I stood with the wind on my skin. I began to shiver. I couldn't stop shivering. I set out across the heather. I kept thinking of Debs' laughter and Nan's quiet, and even though my body was heavier than it had ever been, I felt empty. Lighter. I was glad of the wind shaking the heather, sifting over my skin and over the mud caking on my skin, and of the sound of the water flowing between the banks. And when the breeze dropped, I heard from a far field the faint bleating of lambs, and somewhere in the mist the wooden-whistle *peep-peep* of the marsh bird, then blown from somewhere across the marsh, the murmur of voices.

Acknowledgements

It turns out that although writing is a solitary business, it relies on other people – readers, editors, friends. So, Alex Ivey, Armando Celayo, Birgit Larsson, Ellie Wasserberg, Gordon Collins, Tom Benn and Vicky Rangeley-Wilson all read and commented on sections of the novel and helped me improve them; Ellie and Vicky read the whole thing and showed me how to make it a better book. Central to bringing the manuscript to a finished state was Cherise Saywell, who read two drafts and showed me where development was needed; her thoughts and friendship have been vital. Jo Guthrie and Wiebke Behrens helped with research. Arts Council England backed me with a grant. Andrew Cowan gave generous attention as a reader and supporter. Charles Walker had faith in my writing and got this story out there, and Mikka Haugaard had the belief in the novel to publish it. Many other people helped along the way, in many tiny ways and big ways, more than I can mention here, but in particular my dad, who has never stopped believing in me.

About the Author

Richard Lambert was born in London. He has had many different jobs including teaching medieval history. For the last ten years he has lived in Norfolk where he works for the NHS and writes stories and poems. One of his stories was shortlisted for the Sunday Times Short Story Award and another won the Fish Short Story Prize, and his poems have been in the Times Literary Supplement, The Spectator, and The Forward Prize Anthology. His second poetry collection, The Nameless Places, was published in 2017 and many of the poems in it are a response to the landscape around the River Waveney, on the Suffolk-Norfolk border. The collection was shortlisted for the East Anglian Book Awards.